LUKE MONROE NOVELS
STEVE ALLEN

What readers are saying

FORCED REACTION

When Luke won the United States National Lottery, it was the luckiest day of his life, but he soon realized that fellow winners were dying off in a series of unrelated accidents. When he finds himself targeted for extermination, he uncovers a trail of corruption that leads all the way to the White House.

Readers' Favorite ® FIVE STARS

★★★★★

"Forced Reaction reads like an action adventure movie. It is a maze of action, with surprising unknown factors waiting around the bend." — *Cheryl E. Rodriguez*

INTO THE MINDFIELD

"I just finished reading this book. It's now on the list of my top three favorites of all time. I highly recommend it!"
— *Gail Becker*

Readers' Favorite ® FIVE STARS

★★★★★

"There's more than enough action and intrigue in this book to keep the pages turning fast and furious."
— *Ica Iova*

INTO THE MINDFIELD

INTO THE MINDFIELD

A LUKE MONROE NOVEL

By

STEVE ALLEN

Kevin,
Stay out of The
Mindfield!

INTO THE MINDFIELD

Genres; Fiction, Suspense, Psychological, Thriller, Technology, Mystery, Romance, Racing.

This book is dedicated to my nine year old granddaughter, Adriana. Your never-ending zest for life and insatiable thirst for knowledge is more than merely inspiring. You've shown me that no matter what age we are, we should always maintain a fascination for all things possible… and an imagination for all things not. In your own words, I say to you….

"The future _is_ now."

PROLOGUE

"The brain," began Dr. Reginald Ackerman. "The human brain to be more specific. What do we actually know about it? Not as much as some would lead you to believe."

Dr. Ackerman was a tall, gray-haired man, sporting a neatly trimmed beard of matching color. He wore a pair of reading glasses that sat well below the bridge of his nose, giving him an intellectual nuance that suited a man with his distinguished title. His attire was crisp and well-fitting, as you would expect to see on most any keynote speaker. He stood tall and straight, emitting an air of confidence and authority.

He was the Director of the Walton Center for Brain Research in Liverpool, England. Ranked among the top neurologists in the world, Dr. Ackerman received numerous awards for the advancements that he and his team had made through their work in neuroscience. This year he was the recipient of the Nobel Prize in physiology and was speaking to a crowd of doctors, students, scientists, researchers and surgeons on the topic of advanced brain research.

"Over the years we've mapped virtually every area of the brain. We now know which portion of the brain triggers physical activity and activates motor skills. We know where imagination originates and where sight and sound is processed. We also know the portion of the brain that drives emotional responses to pain, pressure, and temperature sensitivity. We know how the brain plans and analyzes to form judgments, resulting in our unique ability to make informed decisions. We understand how the process of thought enables a person to find the right verb or noun. We also know that the brain, in all of its magnificence, has a massive ability to retain and store short and long term memory."

The audience appeared to be riveted to his every word. This was the field that they had chosen to study and build their careers upon and they found it to be a most fascinating topic. To the majority of the population, this discussion would be a far better sleeping aid than a first-rate educational experience.

"Yes, the brain. It's an impressive machine. One that can shut down at night and repair itself while keeping you entertained during the REM dream state. Then it reboots again, directing the user through yet another busy day of activity and thought. Over the past several years we've studied the brain's ability to communicate with every part of the human anatomy. We've studied the neurons and pathways, as well as their behavioral patterns, to gain a better understanding of the entire central nervous system. Even though we've conducted a massive amount of research, we believe that we're still in the early stages of understanding this complex machine, and have only achieved an understanding of about forty percent of its overall capabilities."

"Recently, I've been involved in a series of experiments on the glial cells. As you know, these cells reside in what's commonly called 'gray matter'. Until now it was believed that these cells merely provided protection in the form of padding for the more active neurons. We now believe that they also possess the ability to transmit information from one part of the brain to another. The issues we've experienced in proving this theory were limited, in part, by our technical inability to measure them. If we were to prove that these cells did in fact aid the cognitive functions of the brain, we'd need to come up with a more comprehensive integrated solution."

He paused and took a sip of the water that had been strategically placed on the podium before the event. Clearing his throat, he continued. "Almost two years ago I partnered with the staff and students at the Cornell Medical College and SIA Medical Technologies, a private research firm. Together we embarked on a journey to design a model for a device that would measure the brain activity associated with those areas previously considered to be inactive. The results of which, could change the very essence of what we thought we knew to be true."

INTO THE MINDFIELD

CHAPTER 1

One explosion led to another, then another, rapidly firing in in sequence over twenty-five thousand times per minute. Each explosion drove the piston deep into the cylinder inside the massive engine, applying torque to the crankshaft while steadily grinding out a monstrous roar. The speedometer pegged one hundred and forty miles per hour as he applied the brakes and downshifted, slowing the Hennessy Venom F5 to just sixty miles per hour in less than two and a half seconds. Luke knew that in order to maintain control of a machine named after the most destructive natural force known to man, his work would be cut out for him. He felt that with practice he could command this *tornado* along a chosen path of destruction. He slid the mechanical beast around the hairpin turn, returning to the accelerator at the apex.

As requested, without hesitation, the machine shot off like a rocket. A rocket that could be driven on the road, one that could steer and stop upon demand. Its 1,400 horsepower engine was twice as powerful as an Indy car, which boasted a mere 700 horsepower. But, even an Indy car had the capability to propel itself to over two hundred and thirty miles per hour. This car was much more than that, *this* was a new generation of supercar.

Luke was breaking it in. He had shelled out the one and a half million dollars required, and was now putting it to the test. Built in Texas, the manufacturer proclaimed it to be the world's fastest production car. It was capable of running over two hundred and eighty-seven miles per hour. The manufacturer claimed that it would be a variation of this car that would ultimately break the three hundred mile per hour barrier. Of course, that would be on a long stretch of straight road, inside a restricted area, one that's made exclusively for speed. That's not what Luke had available to him today. Today it was a series of twists, switchbacks and turns, one hundred and fifty six in all. It was a course that was almost twelve and a half miles long…. *all uphill*.

It was the Pikes Peak International Hill Climb in Colorado Springs, which rose to an altitude of 14,115 feet to the finish line above. Luke was hoping to complete his run within the top ten in his class, and was well on his way.

He now had the time and resources available to pursue his passion of racing since he'd won the United States National Lottery a few years earlier. Now, as the Chairman of the Lottery Oversight Committee in Washington, he pretended it was a burden for him and that he *begrudgingly* had to report to work four weeks out of the year, two weeks in January and two in July. He was a classic car connoisseur and had only recently begun investing in racecars.

"How you doing, buddy?" asked Raj. He was linked to the radio affixed inside of Luke's helmet.

"It's incredible," Luke replied, "I've never experienced this much power in an automobile. The acceleration *literally* takes my breath away."

"I'm here with Sam," Raj said. "We're watching the course ahead of you and it looks like you'll catch up with the Lamborghini soon."

Raj and Sam were standing in the roadway at the finish line near the summit. They were watching Luke on a credit card sized computer that Sam had previously invented. Even though it was hand held, it projected an image that was over twenty inches diagonal. A small arm snapped into place which housed a vertical laser creating a wall of light that the device projected onto. This created an image that was high quality, yet remained opaque.

"If you get stuck behind him, it could slow you down," Raj said. "You should see him any second now."

Entering the fourth leg of the course, he saw the tail end of the orange colored Lamborghini Aventador. "There he is," Luke announced. The Aventador, with all of its sharp lines, had the appearance of a stealth fighter winding its way through the mountain road at high speed in search of its next target. Luke knew that *his* next target was to be… the Aventador. The narrow winding road didn't lend itself to passing freely. Adding to the danger, this road, one of the highest in the continental United States, didn't even have guardrails. He had to find a strategy and knew that it would be in the next series of switchbacks in an area known as the *Devils Playground*. This could give him the advantage he needed.

Accelerating, he met up with the Aventador just as it was slowing for a hairpin turn winding to the left. Although it was quick, Luke noticed that its driver had a tendency to ride high in the curves. He hoped that he'd repeat the same pattern in the next turn, which arrived only seconds later. The taillights on the Aventador illuminated as the brakes were applied, and it once again rode high into the sharp curve to the right. This gave Luke the advantage he was looking for. Upon reaching the apex, he accelerated while steering the F5 tight on the inside. The surge of acceleration applied all fourteen hundred horses to the drive train. As expected, the rocket-like launch catapulted him ahead of the Aventador. Now there was no roadblock, nothing to slow him down. His next target would be the finish line.

Sam turned off the tiny computer and shoved it into his shirt pocket. He and Raj were still standing in the middle of the roadway just under the checkered-flag banner at the finish line.

"You got this," Raj said, "bring it home."

Maneuvering through one last hairpin known as the *Olympic*, he set his sights on the final few hundred yards. Sam and Raj saw the nose of the F5 as it came into view. It was traveling as fast as Luke's driving ability permitted. As it came closer, Raj and Sam remained in the middle of the road, their feet planted firmly on the asphalt. The Aventador then came into view and was respectfully trying to keep pace with Luke.

Luke was nearing the finish line. Raj and Sam remained in place, as if they were playing some twisted game of *chicken*. The outcome of such a game would not bode well for either of them.

Five hundred feet, four hundred, two hundred, Raj showed signs that he was about to bolt, but Sam held firm. One hundred feet, fifty feet, twenty feet and then Luke zipped across the finish line followed by the Aventador moments later.

As the cars passed where Raj and Sam stood, they drove what seemed to be right through them. There was no impact, they were like ghosts in the road.

"Excellent!" Sam proclaimed, "What a rush."

"I don't care how many times we do this, I still tend to lose my nerve," Raj said.

It turned out that they weren't at Pikes Peak at all. While Luke was actually finishing the race high atop the mountain road, Raj and Sam were safe and sound at Luke's house playing with another one of Sam's inventions. He called the new technology 3D+6. Built in the '*white room*' at Luke's Evergreen, Colorado mansion, he created an environment where it was like standing inside of a room-sized computer display. Factually, you were. The room was covered with an electrically conductive polymer known as OLED that transmitted images on all four walls, the ceiling and the floor. With a combination of 3D cameras strategically placed, and with the semi-authorized use of government spy satellites, he was able to produce a four dimensional simulation so real, it was just like being there.

Luke slid the F5 to a stop, unstrapped his safety harness and climbed out. As soon as he had removed his helmet, he was embraced by the lovely Holly Vaughn, his fiancé. Eagerly, she planted a big kiss on his lips and said with excitement, "You did it! You did it!"

"Did what?" He asked with a puzzled look on his face.

"You broke the record," she said while giving him another kiss. "Nine minutes and fifty-three seconds."

No one had ever completed the course in under ten minutes using a production vehicle.

Marilyn Jones, Holly's best friend, came running with a bottle of Champaign in hand. The cork was out, and what hadn't shaken out from her short sprint across the parking area, she poured over him and Holly. A cameraman was at the ready and captured the moment, which was now frozen in time for all the world to see.

"Congratulations," she said, joining the celebration.

A crowd, eager to join in, formed around them. They patted Luke on the back and shook his hand. A news crew made their way through the crowd for the first of many interviews to come. The headline would read: *"Luke Monroe Sets New Pikes Peak Record."*

Since Holly had moved to the Denver area, she and Marilyn had become best friends. Marilyn, helping her become familiar with the local area, had taken Holly under her wing. They regularly planned shopping excursions together, and just did the kind of things best friends do.

People thought it was strange that Luke didn't feel awkward that his fiancé and *ex-wife* were so close. He was perfectly comfortable with it. After all, he had fallen in love with both of them for some of the same reasons. Why shouldn't they end up being the closest of friends?

He actually had a little fun with it too. Whenever they were out in public, he would introduce them as his wife and his girlfriend, to see if it would stir up some kind of reaction. It always did!

INTO THE MINDFIELD

CHAPTER 2

A piping hot cup of coffee sat to the right of his keyboard in a white ceramic mug, with an image of a four leaf clover pasted across the front. It was still early and Luke was in the process of updating his calendar when the phone rang.

"This is Luke," he answered, while perched at his desk mining through the long list of tasks to be completed by the end of the week.

"Luc-ass," a familiar voice said on the other end. Luke's formal name, as written on his birth certificate, was Lucas. He could only think of one man, a man from his past long ago, who frequently called him by that name.

"Double G?" Luke replied, surprised to hear the voice of an old friend. "It's been a long time. I don't believe we've talked since college. That's been what, twenty years? My God, has it actually been that long?"

Luke first met George Graf, aka *Double G*, at Carnegie Mellon University, where they both attended. Luke had focused his studies in technology and business, while George pursued his doctorate in neuroscience. They belonged to the same fraternity and regularly participated in its many sponsored events. Luke, who possessed a dry, intellectual wit, found that George was much the same. His subtle sense of humor went unnoticed by many, but

Luke got it. He considered George to be one of the funniest people he knew. He had the ability, armed with only a simple glance, to crack him up uncontrollably. He was one of the smartest too, but that was years ago. They were still young men. A lot of water had passed under the bridge since then.

"So, what have you been doing with yourself all of these years?" Luke asked.

"You're not going to believe it," George replied. "I'm working for Sam."

"Sam Jenkins?" Luke asked, taken by surprise.

Sam had been one of Luke's closest friends for more years than he cared to admit. After college, they moved to Denver where they had shared an apartment together. They both wound up working at the same place TCC, an international telecommunications company. Luke was a project manager, and Sam a PC and network technician, who later advanced to the role of supervisor within the IT department.

As George continued to follow his own career path in the field of medical technology, he eventually drifted away and lost contact with the other two.

"I've been here a couple of months now." George explained. "After the divorce, it seemed like a change in environment was needed. So I hit the reset button, you know, to get a fresh start. I performed an online search and found Sam. I thought I'd reach out to him just to say hello. I had no idea about all the businesses he's started, and the huge success he has become. Once I explained to him what I'd been doing over the past few years, he made a couple of calls, and hired me the next day."

"How do you like it so far?" asked Luke.

"I love it," George exclaimed, "I'm glad to be working with Sam again. It feels like old times. Even though he owns this big technology company now, he acts exactly the same. It's taken me a bit to get used to the geography. The middle of Wyoming feels quite different than what I had been used to back east, or in the Pacific Northwest, where I've spent the last ten years. I'm used to lots of trees and greenery. The work is extremely interesting though and the town has started to grow on me. The people who live here are great. They make me feel welcome and treat me as if I've lived here my entire life. So what are you doing these days?"

"Well, I retired from TCC a few years ago." Luke said.

"Retired?" George interrupted. "You can't be much past forty. How was it that *you* were able to retire?"

"It was pure luck, I swear. The odds are against it, but I was lucky enough to win the United States National Lottery."

"The lottery! No shit?" George was shocked. He had seen Sam practically every day for the past two months, and he'd never mentioned it. "We need to get together sometime and you can tell me all about it. I assume you're still living in Denver? At least that's the area code I dialed."

"Yeah," Luke replied, "I've been here a long time. I can't see myself actually living anywhere else now, although I do plan to build a second house back in Ohio on my parent's farm. I live just outside of Denver, in Evergreen. It's up in the mountains and we love it."

"We?" George asked. "I assumed you'd still be single. Don't know why. It's just how I pictured you."

"Technically, I *am* single," Luke said. "But not for long. I'm engaged to be married in the spring. I was married once before, but it turned out that I was more married to my work than to her, she just couldn't take it any longer. We're still friends. Turns out that my fiancé Holly, and my ex-wife Marilyn, hit it off well and are now best friends."

"Whoa, that sounds awkward." George couldn't quite get his mind around that concept, since he had just come out of a less than amicable relationship and had been feeling a bit lonely since.

"I agree, we *should* get together to talk about all the trouble we stayed out of when we were younger." Luke suggested.

"Stayed out of?" George replied with enthusiasm. "As I recall, it was somewhat the opposite of that. Between your schemes and Sam's experiments, I felt that I was *always* in trouble. You guys could talk me into almost anything. I'd love to get together with you, it will be fun to reminisce. What's your schedule like? I assume that you have a lot of free time now that you're *retired*. I could drive down to see you. I expect it's only about five hours or so from Green River to Denver."

"Actually," Luke said. "I'm busier now than I've ever been. I think I can save us both some time. I returned to flight school and earned my pilot's license... for the second time. I have a plane here at the house and Sam's got an airport at SIA. I can fly up in a little over an hour."

"That would be awesome," George said. "I'm excited about having the three of us back together again. Oh, by the way, did you know that Sam calls that airport an *intergalactic space port*? Leave it to Sam. All this time I assumed we were the weird ones."

"Believe it or not," Luke explained. "The city of Green River named it that long before Sam ever came to town."

"That is bizarre," George replied. "Hey!" he said changing the subject. "Do you remember that '71 Mustang you owned when we were in college?"

"Oh yeah," Luke said. "The *Stang*! I could never forget it. That was my first car. Wow! That brings back a lot of great memories."

Luke's mind began flashing images of the old Mustang. He'd driven it for almost eight years. It had gotten him through both high school and college. He recalled the first date he ever had, it was in that car. He remembered how cramped the back seat was and that it wasn't exactly the best place for a make-out session. "Hell, at that age," he chuckled to himself, "any place was a good place for a make-out session."

"Well, listen to this," George said lowering his voice as if he were sharing a secret. "I know where it is. I ran across it a few months ago. Not one that merely looks like it, but the actual car. I remembered that you sold it to Buzz McCoy, then he sold it to his cousin Tom. I saw Tom in an electronics store when I traveled back to Pittsburgh to visit my family. I couldn't believe that he still owned it. It's been in his barn for the past fifteen years. He sent me a picture. It's covered in all kinds of filth, but it looks to be all intact."

"Seriously?" Luke began to show signs of excitement. "Do you think he'd sell it? It would be so cool to get my first car back. I'd do a complete *nut and bolt* restoration, bringing it back to a like new condition. What do you think?"

"I'll make the call," George said. "It's not doing him any good just sitting in that barn."

"If you can pull this off, buddy, I'll owe you big." Luke pulled up the calendar on his pocket computer. "Let's talk more about it next weekend. I'm open and will come up on Saturday. Then you can meet Holly."

"Which one is she?"

"My fiancé, future wife, intended, bride-to-be, significant other, love of my life, soul mate...."

George interrupted, "The better half, old ball and chain, stick-in-the-mud, old lady, fatal attraction."

Luke realized that George still had his twisted sense of humor. "You've still got it, I see. I'll see you Saturday, around noon."

"You bet," George said, "I can't wait!" He hung up the phone, eager to see his old friend again.

Luke's thoughts drifted back to his time in college. At one point, he had dated George's sister, Aubrey. They'd double-date and occasionally would stay up past sunrise. As he reflected back in time, he smiled at the fond memories. They truly were good times.

Luke was staring off into space, recounting a vast number of memories from long, long ago, when Holly passed by the open office door, "Good morning, you handsome man."

He snapped out of his trance, smiled, and countered with, "Morning."

"What are you thinking about?" she asked.

"Oh, I just got a call from an old college buddy. I haven't heard from him in years. I was just thinking about some of the things we used to do. Along with Sam, we were like the three musketeers, inseparable. It seemed like one of us were always coming up with some big idea that would change the world forever. He works for Sam now."

"That certainly sounds like you and Sam," Holly paused for a couple of seconds trying to remember, "Oh, is this the guy you told me about who builds test equipment for brain research? Double P, or something?"

"Actually it was Double G, which stands for George Graf," Luke explained. "We all had nicknames back then. Of course you know that Sam was, *Sam I Am*."

"What was yours?" she asked with raised eyebrows.

"Well... George called me Luc-ass at a fraternity party once... unfortunately it stuck." He looked at Holly with sad eyes, indicating a need for her sympathy.

She jumped onto the desk directly in front of him, grabbed his face with both hands and planted the most incredible lip-lock Luke had ever experienced. Not that he didn't always enjoy her kisses, in fact he could hardly wait for the next one. This one however, took him by surprise. He stared into her beautiful green eyes. The room faded away, she was all he could see. The only object in the room was the object of his affection and she felt the same. He slid his chair closer to the desk and wrapped his arms around her waist, while moving in for another kiss.

At that exact moment, Raj walked into the room and announced that a special delivery had arrived. Once he saw the interaction between Luke and Holly, he raised his hand covering his eyes. Struggling for something to say and coming up blank, he blurted out the first thing that popped into his mind, "Get a room you guys."

Raj was a former coworker who was still employed at TCC. He was living in the apartment above the garage where Luke stored his automobile collection. They'd spent countless hours together tinkering on restoration projects, going to races, shows and auctions.

Quickly slipping out of the room, into the hall, Raj stood with his back against the wall and looked up to the ceiling, "This delivery guy needs your signature. He says it's an envelope from Washington, D.C."

"Duty calls," Luke said with a sigh as he stood and headed toward the door. Raj and Holly navigated to the kitchen for a fresh cup of coffee. He signed for the envelope and returned to his office. It was a letter from Washington. In fact it was from the White House. He received similar packages every six months that contained reports associated with the United States National Lottery. Luke had previously uncovered corruption within the lottery program and had been asked by the President to chair the lottery oversight committee.

This required him to review these reports and give a speech in Washington every six months to address the state of the program.

The reports contained three parts. The first was a letter from the President's office indicating that these items had been thoroughly reviewed by her and the six members of the oversight committee. The second was a letter from the Chairman of the Federal Reserve certifying that the financial statements had been validated using a multi-step process and were deemed to be accurate. The final part was a report from the director of the FBI, whose ongoing investigation concluded that there were no signs of conspiracy or illegal activity in association with the lottery during the past six months.

Holly and Raj returned to Luke's office each carrying a steaming hot cup of coffee. Raj slipped ahead of her and grabbed some coasters from the credenza behind Luke's chair and placed them on the desk. With a heavy sigh, Luke slid his ever growing lengthy *to-do* list over to the side of his desk.

"What's wrong?" Holly asked, "Bad news from Washington?"

"No, no, nothing like that," he replied, "I just have too many things to keep up with right now."

The list was long and continued to grow month after month. In addition to the oversight committee, Luke managed the household activities, including the expenses and the coordination of ongoing services such as the landscapers, pool maintenance, and security. He also scheduled himself into automotive events across the country and co-managed a charitable foundation that he and Holly had created.

Home security had once been managed by his close friend Sam, but he'd since moved out of the area. After Luke won the lottery, he had given several of his closest friends a quarter of a million dollars each, to be used for a specific purpose. For Sam, he had created a technology lab above the newly built garage he'd erected for his classic cars. Sam was a brilliant man, but due to cash flow limitations he could never utilize his intellectual gift through practical applications. Up until this point he was just an amateur inventor. You might have called him a technology tinkerer, for lack of a better term.

Sam didn't squander this gift however. He submitted several of his inventions to companies across the country who were in a position to sell internationally through their marketing and distribution channels. As the proceeds came in, Sam reinvested his earnings and was soon manufacturing his own products.

Unfortunately, he eventually outgrew the space above Luke's garage and set out to find a facility of his own. A property became available at a fraction of its appraised value. This property had once been used by the Federal Reserve Bank as the location for their primary shredding operations. It had even been equipped with its own airport. The building was practically new. It had only been in operation for a period of five months before it was shut down due to a scandal that caused the incarceration of the Chairman of the Federal Reserve, as well as the resignation of the President of the United States. It seemed that the FED had been motivated to dump the building and put all this bad news behind them. It became an excellent opportunity for Sam. As they'd soon discover, the hardest thing for Luke and Sam would be adjusting to the location. It was in Green River, Wyoming.

Luke had decided to retrofit the old technology lab into an apartment. His friend Raj had been appointed to oversee the project and once it was completed, Luke gave it to him to use as his primary residence, at no charge. After all, Raj was a close personal friend and was always hanging around Luke's house anyhow.

"I know how I can help," Holly said. "Let's make a list of your priorities."

Luke chuckled at her eagerness. Having been a project manager for years, he thought how incredibly cute she was as she tried to help him get organized. Of course, he thought everything she did was incredibly cute.

She picked up a pen and a small paper tablet. "Where do you want to start? What's the most important thing you need to do?"

"The wedding," Luke stated without hesitation.

"Wedding?" Holly asked, pretending to be unaware of such an event.

"Yes." He replied. "Didn't I tell you I was marrying the most beautiful woman in the world?" They leaned toward one another for a kiss.

Raj stuck his finger in his mouth pretending to gag, while rolling his eyes up toward the ceiling. He began to tap the face of his watch as if to indicate that he didn't have time for this nonsense.

After the kiss, Holly opened her eyes and smiled, "Alright, you've convinced me. The wedding it is!"

CHAPTER 3

It was Saturday at 8:00 am, and Luke was preparing his aircraft for departure, starting with his preflight checklist.

He'd erected a hangar, approximately one hundred yards out, adjacent to the house. When he originally started the project, he quickly learned that this would not necessarily be an easy task. Upon submitting his request to the city planners, he was told that landing an aircraft in a residential zone was forbidden.

As an experienced project manager, he'd trained himself to automatically transition into a troubleshooting mode. He began by attending zoning and council meetings to gain a better understanding of the nuances associated with this zoning rule. His research brought him to one conclusion. It merely came down to noise pollution. He asked the city planners to validate his assumption by requesting their tentative approval. The approval would be based upon one contingency. If he could show that his aircraft produced no more noise in his neighborhood than that of a passing car, he would be given permission. They remained skeptical, but the council agreed.

No problem, he thought. But it *was* a problem.... a big problem! It seemed that nothing currently on the market would meet this requirement. He spoke with several aircraft engineers who said it couldn't be done. Even if you could quiet an engine down, you'd still be faced with *some* engine noise along with the turbulent rush of wind created from the displacement of the air during takeoff and again when landing.

Luke discussed the problem with Willis Redman, a fellow lottery winner. He was a young man who had recently received a degree in engineering and an advanced degree in aviation design. Even though he'd also been a lottery winner, enjoying an income of five million dollars per year, he remained diligent in his quest to complete his education. This said a lot about the nature of his character. He was only twenty-four years old but remained wise beyond his years. Luke understood that this was a result of maturity and accepting personal responsibility for what one says or does.

He chuckled as he recalled once telling Sam that he was *wise beyond his ears*. When Sam objected, Luke further explained each step of his self-proclaimed *wisdom* theory.

Wise beyond your YEARS: When you're mature enough to have achieved, through a lifetime of experience, an understanding of how to use your acquired knowledge to provide sound advice to others in an enlightened and comprehensive manner.

Wise beyond your EARS: You have reached a level of maturity when you realize that it's not possible to learn anything if *you* do all of the talking. You watch, *listen*, and take in information around you, which ultimately builds your intuition.

Wise beyond your REARS: You love to tell everybody what you know in a *noble* attempt to help, but you're really just blowing it out your ass.

Luke flew to California for a brainstorming session with Willis. Together they came up with a design for a completely new type of aircraft, a residential friendly transporter they called the "SkyKar".

It was a sleek, low-slung, canopy-styled design. Like most aircraft, it was built using ultra lightweight materials such as carbon fiber and magnesium. They knew that the key to its success would be in its propulsion system. It was a hybrid petrol-electric configuration. It didn't actually look like a helicopter... it didn't look like an airplane either. There were two engines mounted in the center of the fixed wings, with a more traditional engine located behind the pilot's seat. It appeared, to the uninformed, that the builders were confused, not quite sure what they were building. Engines were affixed to a tilting rotor assembly on each wing consisting of two layers of blades that would turn in opposing directions. Two other much larger assemblies, were mounted to either side of the main engine. The purpose of this design was to provide more downforce focused in a narrower pattern than those seen on traditional helicopters. This permitted greater stability and lift. A smaller rotor was affixed to the tail. This gave the pilot the ability to hover, move the craft from side to side and even backward if he so desired.

The wing mounted engines were electric but exceeded the necessary torque to weight ratio required to lift the craft into a vertical climb. The main engine was a Continental IO-550-C twin piston configuration.

They met their first targeted goal during test flights less than a year later. The SkyKar was able to lift off in a vertical direction using only the electric motors. This produced zero engine noise. All that could be heard was the rush of the wind through the blades of the propellers. An onboard gyro and computer system was designed and built by Sam at SIA Technologies. It provided the required stabilization, both during the transition from electric to fuel engines and while in flight. Once the SkyKar reached an altitude of fifteen hundred feet, the tilting rotor assemblies would move to a forty five degree angle providing it with forward motion. When the craft was out of the residential zone, the gas powered engine would start and shift the output to the rotor assemblies. The wing rotor assembly would continue to tilt to a full ninety degree angle, at which time a series of clutches would transition the power away from the electric motors.

At this point the SkyKar would make its transition from a helicopter to an airplane. It was an airplane producing over 300 horsepower and was capable of cruising at over two hundred knots per hour. Upon its return, the reverse procedure would be followed, once again landing the aircraft back to its point of origin in virtual silence.

There was also a lot of FAA paperwork required consisting of test results and documented proof that it was equipped with backup control systems. Eventually they were approved to fly it as an experimental aircraft.

The City of Evergreen approved it unanimously. To unveil it, Luke invited the entire planning committee out for a round of golf. Much to everyone's surprise, he made his entrance to the outing by landing the SkyKar on the front lawn of the clubhouse.

~

As they prepared for their trip to Green River, Holly packed a small cooler with cold drinks and placed a couple of healthy snacks into her purse. She was ready to go.

With a hand operated dolly, Luke pulled the SkyKar out of the hangar and into the courtyard. He opened the deeply tinted canopy. Inside, there were four seats. Luke grabbed the cooler and placed it on the floor behind the pilot's seat. He closed the hangar door, then in a gentlemanly fashion, assisted Holly as she climbed in. She stepped over the pilot's seat and positioned herself into the right side of the cabin. Luke followed, settling into his seat. They each fastened their safety harnesses. Luke performed a final check on the instruments, which had a futuristic appearance, even though they had been built with components currently available.

The inside of the canopy was covered with the same flexible, electrically conductive polymer, known as OLED, that Sam frequently used on several of his inventions. This permitted the canopy to also act as a display. It was semi-opaque and non-obstructive. Among the features included was an inflight traffic recognition system, co-invented by Sam and Willis. This system would detect any objects in the sky, day or night, and highlight them onto the canopy display. This included aircraft, weather balloons and even birds. A center armrest, when lowered, contained a joystick that Luke used to control the direction of the craft. Pull back and you increased altitude. Push forward and you decreased. Tilt it to the right and you turn to the right or left to go left. For such a complex machine, it was very easy to control. Willis made sure that with each electronic control, there was a mechanical backup. It was designed to have a cable that could manually move each of the control surfaces, even if the SkyKar lost all power.

Luke turned a locking knob exposing a red cover with a warning symbol printed on it. He lifted the cover revealing a toggle switch, which he flipped to the ON position. The joystick controller was equipped with a rotating grip that could be turned to increase engine speed. It worked much like a motorcycle throttle. As he rotated the grip, the rotor blades began to turn. The further he rotated, the faster they turned. After a few seconds, they were in the air. They climbed to fifteen hundred feet in near silence. Luke grabbed a second controller located to his left side that had been affixed to his armrest. When he pushed it forward, the tilting rotor assembly moved into position, transitioning the craft into a forward motion. Once they passed 170, he flipped a second switch which powered up the continental aircraft engine, and away they flew.

With a cruise speed of over two hundred knots and a total distance of two hundred and sixty-six miles to cover, Luke figured that they would be on the ground in Green River within an hour and a half.

~

Just as expected, Luke and Holly arrived in Green River at four minutes before noon. Sam ran out to greet them as they exited the SkyKar. He shook Luke's hand and gave Holly a welcoming hug.

"I just spoke to George," Sam said, "he should be here any minute." While waiting, they discussed how pleasant their ride was and commented on the nice weather. Sam tried to refrain but couldn't help himself. He began asking Luke about how the electronic gear was performing in the SkyKar and if any adjustments needed to be made. He was constantly tossing around ideas for new modifications that could be added. His head was always full of ideas and there were times when he just needed to let them out. As they talked, Holly was rubbing the bug specks off of the nose of the SkyKar. She was particularly proud of it as well. This was the first time she had ever participated in the creation of a new invention, although she suspected it wouldn't be the last.

A car pulled into the entrance, it was unbelievable, but Luke recognized it immediately. He turned to Sam, "Is that...?"

"The very same," Sam said.

They were referring to the 1956 Chevrolet Bel Air. It was the same car George had owned in college. It was the high end model offered by Chevrolet that year. This one was two tone, white on blue. That color combination was believed by many to be the most attractive of any of the colors offered that year. Of course that sparked a lot of debate among Chevy owners. The paint was perfect. It was like looking into a mirror. The chrome flashed sparks of light as the sun reflected off of the many angles of the bumpers and trim pieces. The distinctive low rumbling growl could be heard as the V-8 powered machine came closer.

George pulled the car up to within a few feet from where they were standing, placed it in park and climbed out.

"Luc-ass!"

"Double G," Luke volleyed back.

George ran up to Luke and embraced him with a big bear hug. "I can't believe it," he said. "Here we all are, the old gang back together again."

"Plus one," Luke said as he pointed toward Holly.

"Whoa, had I seen her first," George proclaimed, "I would have said forget about you guys." He gave her a big giant hug, just like the one he gave Luke. "If you ever get tired of him… you come and see me." He followed with a wink.

Holly felt that he was coming on a bit strong since this was the first time they had actually met. The guys didn't think anything about it, that's just how George was.

George focused his attention back to Luke and Sam. "So you two guys have been together all these years?"

"We sure have," replied Luke. "I moved out here after college and picked up a job working at a ski lodge for the season. When an opportunity to work at TCC materialized, I was in. Shortly after that, I was able to recommend Sam, and he was hired as well."

"That's how it worked," Sam said. "This guy has been taking care of me my entire life. If it weren't for him, I wouldn't be where I am today. He gave me the opportunity to become self-employed. His encouragement and sound business advice enabled me to grow into what is now known as SIA Technologies. I owe him everything."

"Nonsense," Luke said. "*You* made SIA Technologies work. It was your ideas and late hours that made you a success. I merely poked you with a stick from time to time."

"I wonder how many people know what SIA really stands for." George commented.

"I think it's cute," Holly chimed in.

"I thought *Sam I Am* Technologies was creative," Sam said.

"You would," Luke chuckled.

"Say, why don't we continue this discussion over lunch?" Sam suggested.

"I'll drive," Luke said as he held out his open hand, expecting George to pass him the keys.

George looked at Holly, shaking his head with a smile, "Just like little children." He dropped the keys into Luke's open palm and walked around to the opposite side, opening the passenger door. Sam tilted the front seat forward and slid into the back. Luke escorted Holly to the driver's side holding her hand as she did the same. He jumped into the driver's seat and inserted the key into the ignition. With his left foot he depressed the clutch, then turned the key. With a deep rumble, the engine came to life. Adjusting the mirrors, he familiarized himself with the car all over again, just as he had done twenty years earlier. He peered in the rearview mirror and saw Holly grin, knowing that Luke was in his element. Being around old cars was his favorite thing, driving them.... even better.

"I know it's been a long time, but this looks nicer than I remember it," Luke said.

"It is," George explained. "I had it restored a few years ago after the engine blew. I upgraded a few things in the process. The old cloth seats were replaced with leather. The chassis and suspension were modernized, but the biggest improvement was the addition of the ZR1 Corvette engine. It's got everything I ever wanted, and it's one of the few things I came away with after the divorce."

"I certainly approve," Luke said, scanning the interior. "It appears to have been done right." He couldn't resist spinning the tires as he pulled onto route 530 heading toward town.

CHAPTER 4

They settled into their seats for lunch. The restaurant was a throwback to a 1950's style diner, constructed with mass amounts of stainless steel. The floor was done in a black and white checkerboard pattern. It reminded Luke of a checkered flag. The booths and chairs were covered with a red vinyl material filled with silver metallic sparkles. Old time napkin dispensers, salt and pepper shakers and condiment bottles were neatly placed in the same configuration on each table. It felt like old times. Just as if they had picked up where they left off twenty years earlier. They reminisced about the characters they knew in school, and dove into the details surrounding some of their many adventures.

"Do you remember that time we went to Vegas?" Sam asked. "We spent the entire weekend there, and never took the time to gamble in any of the casinos. How can that even happen?" They all laughed.

A perky young girl appeared from the back. She cheerfully distributed their drinks and promptly took their food order.

"Oh! Oh!" George said to Holly, while stirring with excitement. "I have to tell you about Luke's first date with my sister."

"Ugh," Luke moaned, as he leaned forward and covered his face with both hands. "Does she really need to hear this?"

"Why yes…. yes she does," George replied, "This was a key milestone in your development toward becoming a man."

Intrigued, Holly leaned in closer to the table. She wanted to ensure that she heard every word. "Do tell."

"It was like this," George began, "Luke had it bad for my sister Aubrey, but didn't have the nerve to ask her out. He was kind of nerdy back then."

"Still is," Sam chimed in, while smacking Luke on the shoulder. Luke rolled up his fist and shook it at Sam muttering like one of the *three stooges*, "A wise guy huh? Why I oughta…."

Sam chuckled and smacked him again.

"So I had to set it up," George continued, "We arranged for Luke to pick her up at her apartment on Saturday evening at 6 o'clock, take her to dinner, then follow with a movie. Seems easy enough, right? Well it was about twenty minutes before six and I got a call. It was Luke. He was in a panic. He couldn't get his old Mustang started and didn't have time to figure out the problem. He asked if he could borrow my car. He was desperate. Mind you, my car didn't look quite like it does today. The seats were torn and it was rusted, with dents all over it. The most important thing for Luke at this time was that it ran and it could get him where he needed to go. Of course I had to mess with him a bit. I told him it was in the shop."

Luke pointed at George, "I still owe you for that one, too!" insinuating that after he took care of Sam, he would be next on the list.

"I made him squirm for a while, then finally gave in and told him that there was nothing wrong with the car and he was free to drive it. I had to go over to his apartment to pick him up, then drive back to my place. He now only had five minutes to get to Aubrey's, which was almost four blocks away. Everything was set.... so I thought. What I didn't know was that Luke had never driven a car with a manual transmission before. Sure, he could run a tractor out on his parent's farm, but this was a lot different. He jerked away from the curb, hit the brakes and stalled the car. He started it again, this time, with a lot more care, ultimately achieving success. I assumed everything would be fine as he drove down the street and out of sight."

"In Luke's defense," Sam pointed out, "I drove that clunker before, myself. It was not exactly the easiest car to drive."

"The next day I stopped by to talk to Aubrey." George continued, "You know, see how things went, big brother kind of stuff. I was not at all prepared for what happened next." He looked at Luke with one raised eyebrow in an accusatory manner.

"What?" Holly asked, "What happened?"

"Well," George replied, "Aubrey opened the door and she looked like she had been in an all-night street fight. She had two black eyes, a scratch on her left cheek and a bandage over her nose. She was a sorry sight to see."

Luke let out a moan and buried his head inside his crossed arms on the table.

"It appeared, that *Mr. Cool* over here, messed up in a big way." George said, "My first instinct was to defend my sister's honor. I didn't know what had happened, but my immediate reaction was to think the worst. She got me to calm down so that I could hear her out. It seems that the date was going well. At dinner they talked about all kinds of things and were warming up to one another. At the theater, he took her hand and held it all evening. She was getting all *fluttery*, thinking he was pretty sweet. After the movie, they got back into the car, but this time she slid over next to him. Now keep in mind that my old Chevy only had bucket seats. I had placed a small wooden box between them where I kept my cassette tapes. So when she slid over, she was actually sitting between the seats, on that box. Luke started the car and put it into gear. With his focus on Aubrey and not on driving, he popped the clutch out too fast and the car shot forward with such a lurch, that Aubrey flew into the back seat. As she was falling back, her foot kicked the shifter and jammed it into reverse. This caused the car to lock the rear wheels and sent her flying forward. This time, she landed face first into the windshield. She caught the rearview mirror first, breaking her nose."

"Oh my God," Holly said. "What did you do?"

"I took her to the hospital," Luke replied, "I didn't know what else to do."

"She told me that he cried more than she did," George laughed.

"That's not true," Luke said. Then after a slight pause, "well.... maybe a little bit."

"Aw," Holly said, "I think that is so sweet."

"That's when I started calling him Luc-ass," George said, nodding his head, indicating that this was unmitigated proof, "you must all agree with me."

"Can we change the subject now?" Luke asked.

Providing Luke with some welcome relief, the food arrived and they all dug in.

"Sam, I hear you've been quite busy lately," Luke pried.

"I sure have," Sam replied. "It's been tough to keep up with everything. I now have the company organized into separate divisions, and am in the process of forming corporations for each one. The attorneys tell me it's a good idea because it isolates my liability within each one. Now, instead of one, I have several companies, SIA Technology Research, SIA Medical Technologies, SIA Aviation Technologies and SIA Computer Technologies. My newest one is SIA Venture Capital."

"Venture Capital," Luke noted. "It's great to see you get that up and running."

"Now I'll be able to invest with other inventors and *their* dreams," Sam said with pride, "not just my own anymore." It had become a form of validation for Sam.

Up until this point, he had viewed himself as a creative guy, but he remembered how hard it had been to get a break. Now *he* was the one who could help others get started, just as Luke had once helped him.

"To the most successful man I know," George said while raising his glass. "You've done very well for yourself my friend."

"The secret to my success," Sam responded, "is that I'm just too dumb to know that I *can't* do it."

Everyone at the table knew that it was just his modesty speaking. Sam was a true genius. He'd been tested in college, where he had been involved in several studies focused on individuals having an advanced IQ. They placed him in various situations and documented his responses to each one. Ultimately, he had creatively solved his problems with solutions that most people tested with average IQ could not even begin to devise. This way of thinking later led him to the creation of one invention after another. He was still in his prime and held thirty two patents to date.

"What's Sam got *you* working on, George?" Holly asked.

"I'm working on the ANT project," George replied.

"ANT?" Inquisitively, Holly tilted her head to one side indicating the need for more information.

"It's the Ackerman Nano Transmitter," George explained. "Think of it as a micro sized robot that could be inserted into the human body and accomplish all kinds of tasks, anywhere from medical research, all the way to performing minor surgeries."

"It sounds a little like something right out of a science fiction story," Holly said, but quickly recanted. "Not that what you do is fiction. I don't mean it sounds like a story, or... maybe it could be a story, wait... this isn't coming out right. I don't want to offend you. I'm going to stop talking now."

"No offense taken," George said. "This is a topic that most people don't know much about. The fact is, there's an entire industry focused on nano technology research. It's come a long way over the past several years. We think we're on the leading edge of it. I'll bet we see a new discovery in this field, of some type, almost weekly."

"Careful George," Sam teased, "she could be a spy."

Pretending to be shocked, George straightened up in his seat offering an expression of surprise. This was a real problem in the high tech world, but he hadn't considered that she might be anything other than sincere.

After a few seconds of silence, Luke laughed, "She's okay George.... I've had her tested."

Holly responded with a poke to his chest ordering him, "You be nice."

"So these nano things," Holly asked. "What do they do exactly?"

"Each design has a specific purpose. For instance, one might measure the enzymes in a particular gland, while another collects data from brain cells and transmits it to a receiver. They are far too small to program a bunch of features into them like you would a computer," George continued. "If you build them to perform a specific task however, the capabilities are endless. This is where a partnership with Sam has worked out tremendously. I have a background in neuroscience. He has a background in computers and electronics. We both understand each other's field of expertise to some degree, but when we are together, we are unstoppable." Sam 'fist bumped' him from across the table in agreement.

"I had been negotiating a project with a neurologist in London," Sam said, "to come up with a model for a device that could more precisely measure and transmit brainwave data for his research. He had grants from both the United Kingdom and the United States, so funding wasn't an issue. He was looking for the most qualified technology company who could build the device. It appeared that I was losing that bid to a company in Boston, until George called, that was."

"It turns out," George said, "that I had worked with this guy before on a project that was key in helping him win the Nobel Prize."

"Once I was able to bring George into the project," Sam explained, "the deal was done."

"It worked out for all of us," said George.

"This all sounds very exciting," Holly said. She raised her glass of diet cola and said, "I wish you all the luck in the world."

Changing the topic, Luke turned his attention to George, "Did you ever get ahold of Tom.... about the Mustang?"

"I did indeed," George replied. "He said it's all yours for fifteen grand, if you want it."

"Done," Luke said. "I can't believe you actually found that car."

He turned to Holly and said with excitement, "I'm getting my *first* car back."

He was beaming, like he had just nailed his first performance in his second grade play. It was that boy-like quality that she loved about Luke the most. She couldn't resist, leaned in, and gave him a kiss on the cheek. He smiled, looked into her eyes and grabbed her hand. How could he have been so lucky to have won over such a perfect woman?

To celebrate their reunion, they ordered a round of hot fudge sundaes for dessert, paid the bill, and walked into the bright sunlight. They boarded the '56 Chevy and headed back down route 530 to SIA.

Holly made an observation, "It appears that you have *now* mastered the use of a clutch."

"Now," Luke demanded, "it's *your* turn to be nice!"

She reached up from the back seat and rubbed Luke's neck and shoulders while whispering in his ear, "When we get home, I promise I'll be *real* nice!" He could see her wink at him through the mirror.

Back at SIA, Sam conducted a tour of the new medical research wing. This was the department that George was in charge of. The work was performed in a *cleanroom* environment. A technological cleanroom was somewhat different than a medical cleanroom, it was more focused on the prevention of sensitive information leaking out of the facility.

Individuals entering the cleanroom were required to empty their pockets, remove their shoes, belts, watches and jewelry. Anyone with electronic aids, such as hearing aids or pacemakers were not permitted inside. This was to prevent any device from entering the room that could have been modified as a recorder or transmitter. Persons who wore glasses were required to have an approved copy with the same prescription waiting for them inside. They were also required to go through a daily scan and pat-down.

The network inside the cleanroom was isolated to the computers and devices located in that room only. Electronic access of any type from the outside was strictly forbidden.

"It takes several minutes a day to process each person in or out of this room," Sam said. "A breach in security could cost our client billions of dollars in future revenue. Of course, that is assuming our research uncovers the breakthrough in science that we expect."

"We could completely change the world as it's known today." George said, "Imagine a world where you could actually direct the brain to heal itself."

"That *would* be amazing," Holly replied with fascination.

"This, right here, what you see in this room, my work," George said, "could actually be the beginning of that reality." He was clearly passionate about his work and you could see Sam, standing there with his arms crossed, proud and downright satisfied with his decision to hire him.

INTO THE MINDFIELD

CHAPTER 5

Holly stood in the doorway of Luke's office. She was an undeniable vision of beauty. He remembered when they first met, and how he'd acted like a complete fool when in her presence. He chuckled as he recalled learning about her military background and how, by being a martial arts expert, she could kick his butt nine ways 'til Sunday. He'd always believed that she was so far out of his league that he would never have a chance. But here she was now, and she was to be his future wife.

Luke never understood how it was possible for her to remain so striking at any time of the day. In the morning or the evening, indoors or out, it was a natural beauty that seemed to be reserved for only a few women in the world. Luke felt like the luckiest man on earth.

Holly felt the same about him. She was drawn in by his innocent boyish qualities and good looks. She was proud of him and his accomplishments and often thought to herself in disbelief, *I'm with him.* She felt that *he* was out of her league and that *she* was the luckiest woman on the planet.

She slowly walked over to Luke and climbed onto his lap whispering, "So, Mr. Monroe, wanna fool around before my fiancé gets back?" She kissed him on his forehead, then on the tip of his nose, then on the mouth while simultaneously unbuttoning his shirt. "I'm not afraid of that guy," he replied, as he slowly slipped his hand under her blouse.

Raj walked into the room and announced that a delivery truck was here. He quickly looked to the floor and shielded his eyes. "Oh, God," he said. "Are you guys at it again?"

Luke tilted his head to the right brushing a few locks of Holly's auburn hair from his face. "What is it, Raj?"

"I think you'll want to see this," he replied. "It's the Mustang!"

Luke looked at Holly with excitement. She was excited too. She knew how much this meant to him. They quickly pulled themselves together and followed Raj outside to the courtyard.

There it was, perched high on the back of a transport truck. It was just as Luke had remembered it. Perhaps a bit more worn for the wear. Time had taken its toll, but to Luke, it was still a thing of beauty. He looked past the faded paint and grime. He didn't see the dents or the cracked and faded glass. He didn't notice the rust on the rims or bumpers, or even the worn and rotted tires. What he saw was his past, his first car. One that had escorted him through life from the age of sixteen all the way to the age of twenty-four. Wherever Luke went, so went this car. A tear welled up in his eye. Thinking it was silly, he turned so no one could see. Quickly he regained his composure and said to the driver, "Well let's get it down from there and take a closer look."

The truck was equipped with a hydraulic roll off bed that made loading and unloading fast and efficient. The operator engaged the power take off (PTO) inside the cab, which routed the hydraulics to the controls at the rear of the truck. He then walked to the right side of the truck where there were four levers protruding out of the control box. He grabbed the first one and moved it to the right. The bed remained flat but it slid toward the rear by about four feet. He stopped and moved to the second lever. This caused the bed to tilt, carefully placing it onto the concrete drive. The operator then walked around the car and removed the ratcheting nylon straps from all four corners of the Mustang and returned to the control panel. He selected the third lever. This powered a winch that slowly unrolled a cable allowing the car to gently roll off the bed onto the driveway below.

"There it is," the driver said, "it's all yours now."

Luke signed the necessary paperwork. The driver neatly rolled up the nylon straps and placed the bed into its normal position. He shook Luke's hand, climbed into the cab and drove away.

Raj had already opened the doors and hood to begin the inspection. "I've not seen many of these," he commented.

"There's several out there," Luke said. "It's hard to find one that still has all of its original parts. This one does. It's a 1971 Mustang Mach 1 with its original 351 Cleveland engine. One thing that makes it rare is the vacuum actuated Ram Air system." He inspected under the hood. "It appears to be all here."

Holly was looking at the interior. The dash was cracked and the seats were tattered and torn. It had a foul odor like a dog had been living in it. "It doesn't look too good in here." She shouted out to Luke.

He walked around to where she was standing and whispered, "It's perfect! All of these things can be fixed." He gently pushed her backwards against the car with his arms around her waist. She wrapped her arms around his neck and once again, they kissed.

Raj, suspecting that they were going to be tied up for a while, announced that he would move the Mustang into the garage.

CHAPTER 6

"The partnership between Cornell University and SIA Medical Technologies produced a process that used nanobot technology as the key medium to collect and transmit data originating from the glial cells of the brain," Dr. Ackerman explained. "This video will help explain the process."

He signaled to the audio/visual technician to start the simulation. The lights dimmed in the auditorium. Then, just like the opening credits of a movie, a title screen appeared, displaying Dr. Ackerman's name followed by Cornell Medical College, and finally SIA Medical Technologies. Below these names a tagline read, "The Future is NOW."

An image of an odd looking device appeared. It looked sort of like a capsule-shaped pill, but it was much smaller. Perched on the tip of a man's finger it appeared to be no larger than a millimeter in length. As the image was enlarged, you could see that one end consisted of four protrusions resembling small pins, yet each thinner than a strand of hair. The opposite end had only a single protrusion, a bit larger in diameter than the first set. It was wound into a coil resembling a stretched out spring.

The narrator began, "Welcome to a new age of medical technology. SIA Medical Technologies is proud to present the next evolution in advanced research with the ANT."

The acronym cleverly transitioned into its true title.

Ackerman **N**ano **T**ransmitter

"What exactly is the ANT?" The narrator continued. "ANT is a device that can be inserted into the human body to collect and transmit information to a nearby receiver. It will provide supporting data for leading edge research that had previously been unavailable. Its proprietary software collects and interprets data, displaying it in virtually any format. The user may choose between multiple views, statistical, graphical or visual. It is believed that this device will someday be able to provide complete and comprehensive diagnoses of a wide range of conditions, while interfacing with the brain to direct itself to repair the defect, whatever the defect is, wherever it may appear in the body. This will practically eliminate the need for non-injury related intrusive surgeries."

"The first step is to insert the device into the body. There are two standard methods for performing this task. The first method is to inject it directly into the blood stream."

The simulation then showed an image of a man being injected with a saline solution via a syringe into his neck. The nano-device exited the syringe and entered his bloodstream.

"This method does provide some mild discomfort for the patient." The simulation continued, showing the image of a man squeezing a couple drops of liquid into his nose.

"The second method is the more desired, only leaving the patient with a sensation resembling a sinus headache for a few hours."

The animation continued, depicting an image of the ANT entering the body through the nasal membranes. The small protrusion with the coiled spring began to spin. The narrator explained this as the method used to propel the device to its desired location.

Once the proper location was identified, the image showed the four small protrusions attaching themselves to the glial cells within the brain matter. It then showed a simulated signal leaving the device, transmitting out of the body to a receiver positioned on a nearby desk. This triggered a simulated data stream to appear and scroll on the screen of the computer sitting next to it. The narrator wrapped up his description of the device and its possible uses.

After the simulation completed, Dr. Ackerman returned to the podium, "The data collected during our research while using this device showed varied, yet unexpected results. We had data, but it was becoming very clear that we either didn't know how to interpret it, or the activity from one person's brain compared to another was so vastly different that we were unable to correlate a clear pattern."

"In order to conduct our first experiment, we needed to create the overall test criteria. Under no circumstances could we risk outside stimulus of any kind to enter our environment. We set strict rules surrounding personnel access into the testing room and tighter rules associated with the ANT equipment. Actually, I was to be the only authorized user of the system.... period. Beyond those authorized to gain access, it was to be tightly secured, locked down if you will. In addition to myself, staff was only permitted into the room for the purpose of conducting the question and answer portion of the experiment, and of course the test subject himself. We had speculated on how the results would appear, but this was uncharted territory and we had no way to know for sure until the experiment was well under way. The lighting in the room had been controlled, not too dim, or not too bright, in order to prevent over, or under stimulation to the test subject. To obtain optimum data collection, it was a *must* that he remain comfortable during these sessions. To avoid external distractions, the room was soundproofed. A sound deadening mix was blown into the wall cavities, as well as the walls themselves padded in a foam rubber material. No electronic devices of any kind were permitted into the room, no phones, watches, tablet computers... nothing, not even a flashlight. We wanted the environment to remain as pure as possible."

"Next, we created the criteria for the selection of the test subject. This would also turn out to be a difficult task. Not only in creating the requirements, but in actually finding a subject that would measure up. The specimen was required to be in good physical condition, have a higher than average IQ, and maintain a healthy lifestyle. There could be no family history of mental illness or addiction. The subject could have no history of any major traumatic event. Believe you me, this was much more difficult to find than anyone could have ever imagined. Even the location was kept a secret. The test subject would arrive at my office an hour before the experiment was scheduled and I would personally apply a blindfold and escort him to the chosen location."

INTO THE MINDFIELD

CHAPTER 7

It was getting late, seven o'clock and George was still in the SIA cleanroom. He rubbed his tired, bloodshot eyes after another long day of staring at microscopic devices and software code. He found his work to be particularly fascinating, but it *was* hard on the eyes. It was tiring work, not in the sense that he was physically exhausted at the end of a day, but rather mentally drained. He tried to keep up with an exercise regime outside of work, but because of the late hours he found that difficult to maintain. As a matter of fact, he often found himself working 'til eight, nine or sometimes ten o'clock in the evening, before packing up to head home. He felt the ongoing pressure of deadlines. Adding to this stress, was his own personal need for perfection. This was the first major contract he had been assigned in his new role. He would need to be especially attentive to detail and to meticulously oversee every step of the project. He was not about to disappoint Sam.

This day in particular, wasn't turning out to be one of his best. He had been in the research business long enough to know that each day was filled with numerous ups and downs, especially when the project was nearing completion. Only then would he be able to see the results from the months of hard work, he and his team had produced. This day was to be more exciting for them than most because, it was this day that the first experiment would be conducted on a human subject.

George, with Sam's help, had modeled the software to capture data coming directly from the subjects' brain through the nanobot transmitter that had been designed by his team. He'd been informed only a couple of hours earlier that he would not be permitted to witness, or even attend the experiment in person. This was a huge disappointment for the entire team. In the past, lab-work conducted by him or his team usually resulted in someone from the team being present for the purpose of data analysis, or to make adjustments and corrections to the equipment being used. It had been decided that due to the sensitive nature of the experiment, it needed to be conducted in a totally controlled environment. Only essential personnel would be present during its execution. Those deemed to be essential included only the neurologist, Dr. Ackerman and his research assistant. George was invited to stand-by in a facility that was located a few doors away in case something went wrong with the equipment.

He knew that the results derived from this experiment would drive the next steps in their research by clarifying the many unanswered questions that remained. He didn't want to wait for this data, he wanted answers immediately. He deserved them. After all, it had been *his* hard work that had gotten them to this point. The more he thought it over, the more he began to feel not just slighted, but actually insulted. He felt that he deserved better treatment than this. Without him, this experiment could never even take place.

He began to think of alternate ideas to move his research along at a faster pace. *What if I were to conduct the same experiment as well?* He thought. *Then I could continue to develop my work with no one being the wiser. There isn't any medical procedure that's required. I know every step. I should, I invented it. I would need a volunteer. Who would be a good.... and willing candidate?*

He thought about each member on his team and one-by-one eliminated them all from the running. He thought about his friends and acquaintances, nothing. Then, eureka! It came to him. *Why not me? I could do this on myself. I'm certain it's safe. I'm only collecting data, that's it.* The more he mulled it over, the more convinced he became that this was the most logical choice.

Now, how do I do it? He asked himself. *I would need three components. The ANT device, the ANT receiver and the software that drives the ANT program.*

All of these items were locked in the cleanroom. Security was high. Nothing entered or came out without going through the screening process.

Ironic, George thought, *I was the guy who insisted on this level of security.* It was now working against him. He knew the security process well. He had helped write it. George knew all the protocols the guards were required to follow and how they were implemented. He slowly devised a plan. *Simple,* he mused, *I'll wait for the guard to take a break. He's been drinking coffee all evening and should be ready for a restroom break anytime.*

Protocol dictated that when a guard left his station for any reason, he would flip a switch, which in turn would activate a motion sensor that would scan the area just outside of the cleanroom door. Personnel had been instructed not to exit the room unless the guard was present. The entire end wall of the cleanroom was made of glass, so you'd clearly see anyone in the area. A phone was mounted on the wall near the door opening and could be used to call a restricted list of numbers, including a wireless phone that had been issued to the guard on duty.

Timing, George thought, *It's all about the timing.* He decided to wait until the guard took leave.

Stephen was the guard on duty that evening. He raised his head and scanned the cleanroom. George was the only person remaining inside, everyone else had gone home for the evening. He knew that George was the head of research and there was no reason to be suspicious of him. He grabbed a magazine from his desk and left the room.

George, witnessing Stephen's departure, looked at his watch and counted down two minutes. He knew that would give Stephen enough time to walk the length of the two corridors that led to the restroom.

Stephen took his time, it was good to stretch his legs for a bit. He strolled the distance of the corridor and entered the door labeled 'Men'. He walked into the stall, closing and latching the door behind him. He dropped his trousers, sat down and opened the magazine.

Two minutes had passed. George dashed out of the cleanroom door and headed straight for his locker. The alarm sounded. George opened the locker and quickly rummaged through his possessions selecting a portable flash drive to take back into the room with him. He dashed back inside and picked up the handset of the phone, located just inside the door. He called the number listed for the guard on duty.

Stephen heard the alarm and immediately pulled himself together. He dropped the magazine on the floor and pulled up his trousers. Just then his phone rang. He answered, "Stephen."

"This is George. I'm afraid I didn't see you leave the room," he said. "I accidentally stepped out and triggered the alarm. Thought you should know, everything's just fine in here."

Stephen accepted the explanation and told George how to reset the alarm and turn off the motion sensors. George followed the steps as instructed, chuckling to himself that this would be easier than expected.

Stephen dropped his trousers again and retrieved the magazine. *False alarm,* he thought.

Now it was about timing. George assumed that he only had a maximum of four or five minutes to complete his mission. He immediately rushed over to the server that stored the ANT program. *This,* he thought, *will take the most time. I need to start it first.*

He inserted the flash drive into the designated slot on the server, located the appropriate files and selected *copy.* He then created a new folder on the flash drive, opened it, and selected *paste.* The file transfer began. He knew that he would be cutting it close. Files of this size, he knew from past experience, would take a few minutes to load. A few minutes was all he had.

He rushed over to a workbench covered with electronic test gear and components. He selected a handful of parts including a circuit board chocked full of wires and connectors. These were the specialty components, parts made exclusively for the ANT receiver. *Everything else,* George rationalized, *I can get at the local electronics store.* He found a small sheet of bubble wrap and quickly rolled the parts up inside, immediately stuffing them into a small plastic container. He circled back to the server to see how the file transfer was progressing. The display showed that it was still running, but was only forty percent complete. George checked the time. Over two minutes had passed. He knew that Stephen would return soon. Beads of sweat formed at his temples. He was moving quickly, but knew that he needed to maintain a steady consistent pace if he were to successfully accomplish this task within the window of time that was available.

The next stop was at a different workstation. There was a workbench here as well. Mounted on the top and in the center of the bench was a robotic arm. To the right was a rack that stood about eighteen inches high and about the same in width. There were slots within the rack consisting of, what appeared to be, well over a hundred miniature sized doors. George entered a few commands into the keyboard which caused the arm to move. It selected one of the positions. The tiny door opened. The tip of the robot's arm was actually a six inch rod, with what looked like a miniature three pronged claw on the end. The rod was inserted slowly through the opened door. After a few seconds it reversed its direction and exited the opening. The claw held something that was smaller than a grain of rice. The robotic arm rotated its tip toward a small pallet on the table and released the item into a plastic container the size of a small pill box.

Looking at his watch again, George knew he was running out of time. Four minutes had passed and Stephen could be back any second. He rushed back to the server, which now displayed eighty-seven percent. "This is taking longer than I thought," George muttered to himself. There wasn't much he could do at this point other than to wait it out. He watched as the indicator slowly moved ahead. Ninety two percent, ninety four percent. It seemed to be taking forever even though it had only been a few seconds.

George reflected back to something his grandmother used to say, "A watched pot never boils." That was her way of telling him to be patient. It didn't work for him then, and it certainly wasn't working for him now.

Stephen washed his hands and wiped them dry. He stepped out of the restroom and began his walk back up the corridor to return to the lab.

Ninety-eight percent.... ninety-nine.... one hundred. George quickly selected *eject* and removed the device. He grabbed the container from the workbench and bolted through the cleanroom door. He ran to the locker and quickly stuffed the ANT parts inside.

Stephen neared the door to the lab. He whistled while he walked. George could hear him just outside, as he approached the lab door. In one final sprint, George rushed from the locker area through the glass door and slipped back into the cleanroom.

INTO THE MINDFIELD

The lab door opened and Stephen stepped in, walked over to his desk and looked into the restricted area. He immediately noticed that George was covered in sweat. He pressed the intercom button and asked, "Are you feeling okay? You don't look so good."

"I might be coming down with something," George replied, "I think I'll clean up, head home, and get some rest."

He started to make his final walk around the lab, just as he had done every other night. His heart sank when he saw *it*. It was the ANT nano transmitter still resting inside the pill box on top of the robot bench.

Oh no, George thought, *I had the perfect plan. How could I have missed this?* He immediately began to think over his options. *Obviously, I can't just walk out of here with it in my pocket. I can't expect Stephen to take a break anytime soon. Even if he did, I couldn't trigger the alarm a second time without raising suspicion.*

That left him with only one possibility, to administer the device into his body while he was still in the lab.

There were two recommended methods to insert the device. The first was to inject it into the bloodstream. George wasn't mentally equipped to do that on himself. He had always been a bit squeamish around needles. He was fine using them on someone else, but for some reason he just couldn't self-administer.

The second method was to insert the device through the nasal cavity. This would be the way he would choose. He scanned the room for something he might be able to use as a straw. There was nothing obvious available in his line of sight so he decided to make his own. He peeled off a piece of paper from a sticky pad sitting on his desk and rolled it into a small tube. He knelt within a few inches of the pill box, inserted the makeshift straw up his nose and sniffed. The nano device disappeared.

Success, George thought, *as long as I didn't inhale it into my lungs or worse, swallow it. Stomach acid would destroy it in minutes.*

George continued with his final inspection of the lab. His right eye began to twitch. He felt the sensation of a sneeze coming on, but resisted the urge. A sneeze could blow the device out of his sinus cavity, which would end his attempt to continue with the experiment. He pinched his nose with his fingers and began to breathe through his mouth. After a few seconds, the urge subsided. The twitch in his eye was still there, but was becoming less frequent. George resumed his cleanup activities. He wiped down the robot and workbench areas. He cleaned the top of his desk as well as the keyboards using a cloth that had been dampened with rubbing alcohol.

As he wiped off the desk he noticed a drop of blood on his shirt. When he looked down, another drop fell onto his desk. He had a nose bleed. As the nanobot burrowed its way through the sinus cavity near the ethmoid bone, he knew bleeding could occur. At that moment he felt the sensation of a needle being shoved into his brain. Although he had never had one, George guessed this must be how a flash migraine would feel, similar to ones he'd read about. He closed his eyes tightly and sat down at the desk, while clenching a tissue to hold back the nosebleed.

Stephen once again saw that George was not doing well. He broke protocol again and entered the cleanroom to offer assistance.

"Do you need an ambulance?" Stephen asked.

"No," George said, "This happens all the time." But in truth, it didn't. This was the first nose bleed he'd had in years.

Five minutes later, the headache subsided and the bleeding stopped. Stephen helped him back to his feet.

"Much better," George said, "All I need is a nice quiet evening of rest at home."

In reality, that's not at all what he was planning to do.

CHAPTER 8

Throughout their lives, people are faced with a lot of options. All of these options are analyzed, sorted and then reanalyzed from differing points of view before a decision is made.

For example, some people may find that something as simple as buying a car for everyday use, is a dull and mundane experience. They just want to find something they like, satisfy themselves that they are paying a fair price, and get it over with.

For an automobile aficionado, however, it's much more complicated. Not at all a laborious task, it becomes a labor of love. They must decide on a type of automobile to buy. Perhaps a car, truck, SUV, or specialty vehicle. If they go with a car, what body style should they choose? Maybe a convertible, two-seater sports car or a four door sedan? They will buy magazines with every make and model listed to study the specifications of each. How much horsepower do they put out? What are the fuel economy ratings? How fast can they go from zero to sixty and on the opposing end, how many feet does it take to stop from that speed? They study the body design, stance, and poise. They look at it from the perspective of a collector making a selection to purchase a rare piece of artwork. Once a decision is made, only then will they start to consider model and color. They'll focus on the many selections from the long list of options available. They know, down to the penny what the cost should be, but are willing to pay just a bit extra to get exactly what they want. What has taken the first person only a day to do, this guy requires an average of three months to achieve.

Enter the collector: The collector operates on an even higher plane. They have to define not just the car, but they must define themselves before collecting even the first piece. Who they are should be represented in what they choose to collect. For instance, a farmer may choose to collect antique tractors. Collectors need to choose a category, of which there are many. Should he collect antique cars and trucks from the onset of the horseless carriage industry? Or perhaps choose classics built from the nineteen twenties, through the thirties. These were known as the *rich man's car*. The ones that movie stars were frequently seen in. Maybe hot rods, chopped and lowered, or custom built. Vintage race cars might be another man's poison. Then there are muscle cars, sports cars, and tuners.

Luke was a man who had always loved the automobile, and throughout his adult life had completed several restoration projects. He had bought a few, and sold a few, but had never had the financial freedom to openly choose what he wanted without some restrictions. Winning the lottery had changed all of that. The problem for Luke now was his unwavering love for all automobiles.

Collectors need to decide what to add to their collection. Will they only seek out unrestored originals or will they only be interested in vehicles that have undergone a complete nut and bolt rotisserie restoration, with the underside looking as new as the top?

Luke made his decision. He chose not to decide. Instead, he would collect those things that he merely just.... well, *liked*. Cars that he enjoyed looking at and driving. He had previously collected muscle cars, classic cars, trucks and even a couple of limousines.

Today, he was looking at a different kind of car, one that he had never considered before, but had recently been studying. Today he was looking at a vintage race car. A Porsche 917 Laser to be more precise. Built in 1970, it was low and sleek. It had a closed canopy design with the body beginning low to the ground in the front, transforming to a huge wing at the rear. It was equipped with driving lights and headlights, as well as a windshield wiper for racing in almost any weather condition, day or night.

Luke approached it with caution, not quite sure it was safe to touch. It was as if he were stalking a wild beast not knowing if it would reach out to bite him.

"Well, there she is," stated a tall thin aging man. "Carl Mason here. I'm the one you spoke with on the phone." He held out his hand and Luke responded with a firm shake. Standing next to Luke was Holly, who offered her hand to Carl as well.

"I drove her in the Le Mans racing series back in the day. She's still quite capable. I won a few races with her. She could have won more. The truth is, I just wasn't that good. I can say that now, but I was too cocky back then, wasn't willing to let anyone in on my secret. When my wife and

I decided to retire, I knew it was time to let her go." He turned away and remained silent for several seconds, stretched his neck and turned back toward Luke. "You want to drive her?"

"You bet I do," Luke said with excitement. This was all new to him, he had never driven an actual Le Mans Series race car before. He was actually feeling giddy.

They were meeting at a county airfield near Denton, Texas. It was used mostly for private aircraft. There were no signs of commercial traffic. Behind Carl, off in the distance, appeared to be an ultralight flying club preparing for an outing.

"I'll check with the man in the tower," Carl said, holding up a two way radio, tuned to the tower's frequency. He handed Luke a helmet which was gray, adorned with blue and red stripes, matching the paint scheme on the car. It even had the number five on the side of it. Luke chuckled. How appropriate, it was the number five that had been pulled the night he won the lottery, multiplying his total winnings by five times the original amount, which now earned him five million dollars a year, tax free, for the rest of his life.

Walking to the car, Carl opened the door. It was hinged at the fender and roof causing it to open toward the front of the car. He explained all of the controls to him once Luke was inside. Holly stood nervously beside Carl as Luke secured his helmet. She was experiencing a wide range of mixed emotions. On one hand, she adored Luke and wanted him to be happy and was willing to support him with anything he truly wanted to do. On the other hand, she instinctively wanted to steer him away from danger. She couldn't bear the thought of him getting hurt.

Carl could see that she was getting worried and proceeded to explain all the safety features that had been built into the car. The more he explained, the more she began to relax. That was, until Luke started the engine.

Luke quickly read through the start-up procedure printed on a laminated card that hung under the dash. He grabbed the shifter and placed it into neutral. With the ignition switch in the *off* position, He turned the key to crank the engine for a period of fifteen seconds, paused and repeated the process three times. The purpose of this technique was to build up the oil pressure inside the engine. Once the pressure registered on the gauge, Luke pulled the ignition switch to the *on* position. He pulled the second switch out to engage the fuel pumps. A mild whirring sound could be heard as the fuel filled the lines. With his left hand on the key and his right on the fuel enrichment lever and throttle, he rotated it to the right. The engine turned over for a few seconds, then came to life. It let out a roar like a lion posturing to protect his turf.

Fear shot through Holly, as she was not prepared for the abruptness of the start, and the speed at which the RPM's rose and settled back to an idle. She held her hands up to her face. She tried to think about how Luke must have felt at that moment, and blew him a kiss before backing away from the car.

Once the engine indicator lit, telling Luke that it was up to temperature, he depressed the clutch and placed the car into first gear.

Using the two-way radio, Carl called the tower. The controller replied that there was no air traffic in the vicinity, giving them a *go* for one lap the full length of the runway. He gave Luke a nod and a thumbs-up indicating that he was good to go. Luke accelerated with his right foot, while lifting off of the clutch. The car shot forward snapping Luke's head into the rear of the seat. Sure it was powerful, but a little lackluster, Luke thought. He had felt that kind of power from his muscle cars at home. In a matter of three seconds, the gauge read 8,500 RPM. Luke shifted into second. Then it happened, the rush that he was looking for. The boost of adrenaline that was due to a surge of power so great, he felt like he was on a spaceship that had just jettisoned its main fuel tanks, while firing up the stage two rockets. Not only was the car designed for speed, it was also designed to corner on racetracks with twists and turns in all directions. When Luke slowed the beast down to around eighty miles per hour, he tested its handling by weaving the car from right to left. After he had reached a speed of almost two hundred miles per hour, eighty seemed like a crawl to him.

He drove the car back to its starting point and followed the shutdown procedure listed on the reverse side of the laminated sheet attached to the dash. The door opened. Luke removed his seat belt harness and helmet. He stood with the helmet in one hand, raised both hands into the air and let out a wolf howl until his lungs had completely emptied, thus indicating his overall approval of the experience. He climbed up and out of the car, ran over to Holly and gave her a huge hug, lifting her into the air.

"It was incredible," He said, as his inner little boy began to show. "It was nothing like I had ever experienced before. I've been around cars all my life, but that.... that...." It was all he could get out while shaking the helmet toward the car which was now as subtle and tame as a kitten. A kitten that Luke now knew could very quickly turn into a ferocious lion.

Carl smiled, partly because Luke had obviously enjoyed it so much, but mainly because he knew that he had just made the sale.

"There's a diner a couple of miles from here," Carl said. "We could do the paperwork there over lunch."

"Perfect," Luke said. "We'll meet you there." Luke headed toward the SUV they had rented earlier that day from the Airport, so they could spend the night and do some sightseeing in the area.

Holly shook her finger at Luke, "No, no, no," she said. "This time, *I'm* driving!"

Luke smiled and tossed her the keys.

INTO THE MINDFIELD

CHAPTER 9

He pulled the hammer back on his pistol. "Last warning," Luke said. "Drop the money and step aside."

"You got it all wrong," the man replied. "You need to drop *your* gun and walk away."

It was a standoff, an *old west* standoff. Luke stood in the middle of a dusty street with Raj by his side. Buildings lined the street consisting of businesses including a barber shop, dry goods, and of course a saloon. At one end of the street stood a church. It appeared to be the only painted structure in the entire town. Luke was dressed in authentic western garb representing the period accurately, from his white cowboy hat, all the way down to the spurs on his boots. His vest was adorned with the badge of Deputy Sheriff. Raj wore a black derby, but unfortunately he resembled an Amish-Indian man, more than that of a lawman. However, he also wore the badge of Deputy.

"No deal, Tucker," Luke said. Jim Tucker was a notorious outlaw who moved from town to town robbing banks and homes, taking liberties with the ladies, and killing anyone who stood in his way.

"I'm givin' you one chance to walk out of here," Tucker replied. "I guess I'm feelin' generous today. If you choose to do anything other than that, you choose to die."

"I don't think so, Tucker," Luke said defiantly. "We have the law on our side. Besides, there's two of us and only one of you. You've robbed the bank and killed the Sheriff. I can't let you get away with that. It ends here."

"Uh, dude..." Raj said, while poking Luke with his elbow. Luke turned and saw that six men had stepped out of the surveyor's office and were now beginning to surround them. Each had their gun drawn, aimed directly at them. They closed in, one step at a time.

A couple of the townspeople were seen peeking out of second story windows. One man flashed a rifle for Luke to see and gave him a nod indicating that he had his back. *One man with a rifle,* Luke thought, *wasn't enough to cover the odds he now faced.*

The six gunmen each stepped closer. A decision had to be made. Luke raised his pistol and aimed it directly at Tucker. "I may not be able to take out all of these men before they get me," Luke said, "but I think I can at least get one." Following his lead, Raj cocked his gun and did the same. The man at the window called out, so they could see that his rifle was pointed at Tucker as well. Following suit, another man appeared on the roof of the saddle repair shop. At this point several of the townspeople slowly exited their businesses, all armed. They began to surround the six gunmen. Raj then stepped behind Luke, back-to-back, pivoting from side to side, attempting to provide cover.

Luke remained steady as a rock. "It's up to you, Tucker," he said. "Do you choose to die today?"

A breeze picked up causing a tumbleweed to roll into Tucker from behind. He quickly spun around and fired his gun, but no one was there, only that lone tumbleweed. A mere tumbleweed, apparently acting in a valiant attempt to defuse the situation.

Now it seemed as if the *entire* town was watching.

"A real tough guy, eh," Luke asked, "We'll be sure to notify that weed's next of kin." He followed with a chuckle. The spectators saw the humor as well and began to laugh at Tucker. Jim Tucker had the reputation of being the *baddest* ass in the west. Now he just looked like a *dumb* ass. As his rage boiled over, he blamed Luke for his current predicament. He repositioned himself and raised his gun. A decision had been made, but not a good one. Certainly not one based on logic.

Luke, and a minimum of three other townspeople fired. Before Tucker could get a shot off, he fell. The remaining gunmen raised their weapons, but quickly rescinded once they realized they were facing upwards of thirty armed and angry residents. They tossed their guns to the ground and put their hands in the air. The mob corralled them toward the jail.

Holly stepped out of the saloon, "When you boys are done taking care of the bad guys, lunch is ready." She looked at the activity going on all around and smiled. She returned through the saloon door and out of sight.

Luke reached into his pocket and pulled out his credit card sized computer. A small arm flipped out and created a screen from a low powered laser. Then an image was projected from the device onto the screen. It was a menu. He selected *simulation off,* and the entire town with all the people disappeared. He and Raj were now standing in a room where everything was white. The *white room*, as it was known, was located on the first floor of Luke's Evergreen mansion. There was no furniture or anything at all. This too was Sam's invention. He had invented 3D+6 technology, which was simply six 3D video displays, each the size of an entire wall, with an additional surface on the floor and another on the ceiling. Sam's sales of these products were skyrocketing. Theaters across the country were being upgraded to the new system and the motion picture industry had started filming movies utilizing this technology. It was also popular with the simulation and gaming industries. Luke, Holly and Raj used it regularly as a way to exercise their marksmanship and improve their decision making skills.

Luke and Raj walked toward the kitchen. Holly stopped them in their tracks, "Take off the spurs, you guys, they'll scratch the floors." They did as they were instructed.

Lunch was being served on the patio, just outside of the breakfast nook, which was adjacent to the dining room. Luke gave Holly a peck on her cheek, "It looks delicious," he said, "and so do you." They kissed again.

"Ahem," Raj said in a loud firm voice, "in case you haven't noticed, Raj is still over here." He'd recently walked into a few of their impromptu make out sessions which had made him feel a tad bit uncomfortable. He hadn't even been on one date in over four years. He'd just given up and decided that women in general just weren't interested in him. "After all," he tried to rationalize, "what woman would be interested in the same things I'm interested in?" Just like Luke, he was a good guy, but he was also a big kid, who liked super high tech video games and car collecting. He considered Luke to be a lucky man to have found a woman like Holly.

Luke sat down and picked up his fork. Holly tapped her finger above her temple to remind him that he was still wearing his cowboy hat. He removed it and placed it onto a chair off to the side. Raj did the same.

"So, dude," Raj asked, "what's up with the race car in the garage?"

"I'm glad you brought that up," Luke replied. "I'm going to need your help with that. I've decided that I want to take it out and run it in the Vintage Grand Prix series. That's different from most competitive racing because it's designed to be less aggressive. People have a lot of money wrapped up in their cars and most of them are self-sponsored. The promoters want to continue to build up the number of participants, so they've placed strict rules pertaining to aggressive activity that could damage the car or cause harm to the drivers."

"Sounds interesting," said Raj. "How can I help?"

"First of all," Luke said, "You've been an absolute godsend to me with all the work you do around here. Because of you, I now have enough free time to pursue some of my dreams. I'll research the rules and regulations. I want you to round up a couple of good mechanics who could serve as our pit crew. You'll need to locate the Porsche 917 shop manual, as well as any literature put out by Porsche on the proper tuning and setup of the car."

"You know I will," said Raj excitedly. "We'll have this thing on the track in no time."

CHAPTER 10

It wasn't long before all the pieces were in place and Luke was on the racetrack. He would soon find out that he had a knack for it. The first race in the circuit was at the Mid-Ohio Sports Car Course just outside of Lexington, Ohio. He was excited to see his parents there. They only lived about twenty miles from the track. The entire crew would stay at their farm because the house was plenty big enough and Luke's mother, Lillian, wouldn't hear of any other plan. When visiting his parents, Luke and Holly stayed in a cabin on the six hundred acre property located in the midst of a quiet woods.

At the drivers meeting, Luke was given some sound advice from a couple of the more experienced drivers. They told him to get familiar with the track. Don't try to win your first time out. He was experiencing butterflies in the pit of his stomach. He hadn't recalled feeling this way for a very long time. *Okay*, Luke thought, *this is nothing more than the initiation of a new project*. Using his prior experience as a project manager he knew that there were specific tasks to be performed and that he needed to focus on those tasks. Before long he found himself in the *zone*, using a technique that he had developed into what he called a *forced reaction*. He was able to block out everything that was not associated with the immediate task at hand, in this case, it was the race.

His pit crew, led by Raj, had positioned the car inside the assigned garage, in the paddock area. The race officials were making their final rounds, telling the teams to prepare for the start. The team pushed the car into pit row and Luke began the startup procedure. The cars were jockeyed into position based on the results from the time trials that had been run the day before. Luke was starting in position thirteen. He was never much of a superstitious man, but he did think it was a bit disconcerting to win that slot, of all slots for his first race. There were eighteen cars in total.

Holly sat with Luke's parents, James and Lillian. Holly and Lillian were both wringing their hands in exactly the same manner, at the same time, as if it were a choreographed routine. As the racers were preparing to begin, James stood and leaned into the chain link fence. He was nervous for Luke, but couldn't have been more proud of him. He usually met up with a few of his farmer friends for breakfast a couple of days a week and would brag to them about his son becoming a race car driver. Even though anyone who owned a vintage race car was eligible, he conveniently left that part out of the conversation.

The pace car led the way as they circled the track. The track was a 2.4 mile asphalt road course consisting of several twists and turns along the way. Its signature turn was known as the *Esses.* This was located directly in front of the grandstands. Some drivers just referred to it lovingly as *madness.* Many a professional driver had spun out at this difficult spot.

Once the pace car tucked into the pit area, the green flag was waved and the race was on. Coming out of the first turn, Luke missed a gear and was quickly passed by the five cars behind him. *Crap,* he thought, *this puts me in last place.*

He quickly regained momentum and within seconds was back up to speed, hot on their tails. One car seemed to be having engine problems and slowly drifted back to the rear. On the third lap, a few cars spun out at the esses and Luke skillfully weaved past them. At this point, he was becoming much more comfortable with the track and driving with other cars on it. He was learning every nuance, every touch and feel the car had to offer. This gave him an increase in confidence, which permitted him to be a bit more aggressive. He passed two cars on an inside turn known as the *Carousel.* He was now in the twelfth position.

Holly and Lillian were both sitting on the front edge of their seats, leaning forward as if that might somehow help Luke gain speed along the straight sections of the track.

Two hundred and forty miles, one hundred laps in all, was beginning to take a toll on Luke. After doing battle for over two hours, he was nearing the completion of his first vintage race. He had worked his way up to the fifth position, and there were only two laps remaining. "Sharp and steady," he told himself. "I just need to finish. I'm in a good spot, fifth place is respectable. I'm sure I can do better next time with everything I've learned here." As he focused on the last few turns, he saw a small dust cloud kick up over the next hill, just to the right, indicating that someone had spun out. He applied his brakes and crested the hill with caution. Sure enough, a car had spun out. He was sitting sideways with the nose of his car on the track and the rest of it in the runoff area. Luke pulled to the left, maneuvering around him and saw that a second car had run off into a grassy strip adjacent to the track. Luke knew that he had less than a lap to go. He could see his competitors ahead and held the accelerator to the floor in a last ditch attempt to catch them. Luke was working hard to remain steady and a half lap later he crossed the finish line.

He coasted the Porsche into the pit area and followed the documented shutdown procedure. He opened the door and removed his helmet. He didn't appear to be in a huge rush.... that was until a very excited Raj appeared.

"Dude," he said, "You need to hurry up."

Confused, Luke asked, "For what?"

"We need to get you down to the winners circle."

"Winners circle?" Luke had not realized that the final two cars that had spun out were in the first and second position, which had moved him up two spots.

"You placed," Raj said. "You finished third!"

Holly and Lillian hugged one another, while a tear could be seen on James' face. The three worked their way through the crowd and into the winners circle to witness Luke's award presentation. By the time they arrived, Luke, along with the two other winning drivers, were standing on the winners platform. Luke received fallout from Champaign as it was poured over the winners head.

After several handshakes and congratulations, he stepped down and ran over to the waiting Holly, lifting her off her feet. Lillian couldn't resist having them all pose for pictures. She must have taken at least a dozen photos or more. She planned out each shot as if she were a professional photographer. She and James were so proud of their son, and once again Holly felt like the luckiest girl. The one who ended up at the ball with the handsome prince.

As for Luke, he was hooked. He planned to continue with the vintage racing series and see how far he could take it.

After all, he thought, *there's no harm following one's dream…. right?*

INTO THE MINDFIELD

CHAPTER 11

The weekend had arrived and George was at home standing in the middle of what would be his makeshift lab, contemplating the equipment layout as he planned to conduct his own experimentation. It had been almost two weeks since he self-administered the ANT nano transmitter. He had experienced the headaches as expected, but now felt nothing, no side effects at all. He was slightly worried that somehow it didn't take. Perhaps the ANT device failed to attach itself onto the glial cells as programmed, or failed to make its way to the exact coordinates. Even worse, he may have flushed it completely out of his system. He'd find out soon enough. First things first. He needed to get the room set up, then build the receiver.

It was a nice home by anyone's standard, George had purchased it upon the completion of its construction. It was at the end of a street in a development consisting of other homes with similar design features. His was a stucco-sided, three bedroom ranch, similar to the adobe-styled homes of the American southwest. The neighborhood was considered upper middle class, and a welcome addition to the region. Designed with an open floor plan, it felt spacious, yet not uncomfortably large. The foyer overlooked a huge sunken living room. Beyond and to the left was a gourmet kitchen with a formal dining room to its right. Separating the two, was a granite covered breakfast bar, with track lighting extending the full length of it. Stylish drop lights hung from the track to create an elegant ambiance. A breakfast nook extended away from the kitchen in the southwest corner, surrounded by ceiling to floor windows on three sides. To the right of the living room, a hallway led to three traditional bedrooms and two stylish bathrooms. The first door on the right led to the room he'd chosen to be his makeshift laboratory. It was centrally located and convenient to any part of the home. The master suite was located at the end of the hall, which included a walk-in closet and dual French doors leading to a patio that ran two thirds the length of the house, with another set of French doors entering at the dining room.

The lab didn't need to be too elaborate. All he needed was a desk, a small workbench and a sofa. He knew that he'd be spending a lot of time in there, so it had to be a comfortable space. He ordered a new computer that had been built to his specifications. It had arrived earlier that day prompting him to get busy. He now had everything needed to get started.

After a couple of trips to the local furniture store in his new Range Rover, towing his eight foot lawn trailer behind him, he was set. The next day, he set up the custom built computer and copied all the files that he had taken from the cleanroom, which had previously been embedded on his flash drive. The first order of business was to pull up a copy of the schematics that showed the configuration of the components for the ANT receiver. He inventoried the parts and laid them out, according to the diagram, on the small workbench adjacent to the desk. He hadn't had the luxury of acquiring one of the professionally etched circuit boards from SIA, but would make do with the parts at hand. Combining the materials he'd picked up from a local electronics store, he fused them together with the highly sensitive components that had been engineered to extremely tight tolerances. George was able to successfully recreate the receiver using the proper specifications that he and Sam had documented together.

Excitement coursed through his veins as he prepared to power it up for the first time. He quickly ran into the kitchen and selected a wine cooler from the shelf inside the refrigerator door. After all, if he were successful, he would need to toast himself and celebrate his pure genius. On the other hand, if it didn't work, he'd still need a drink, and the troubleshooting process would begin.

He made the final connections, and slid the power switch to the *on* position. The computer immediately recognized the device and initiated a driver uploading sequence. After a few minutes, a message appeared, *your device is now connected,* indicating that the ANT receiver was live. He could hardly stand the anticipation. Only a few more minutes, then he'd know. He'd know if the receiver worked with the transmitter. He'd know if the ANT device was still in his brain, but most importantly, he'd know if all of the ideas and hard work he'd put into this project would prove to be viable.

He launched the ANT software. A menu appeared providing him with multiple options. He chose, *link to ANT.* A spinning wheel consisting of bright green dashes appeared. George tried to remain patient, but that had never been one of his best attributes. The system needed a few minutes to initiate the software and establish a link from the nanobot to the receiver. The wheel continued to spin. Two minutes had passed. "Stay calm," he told himself. "This is the first time the device is being loaded. Naturally it's going to take longer to initiate." He tapped his fingers on the desk. *Or maybe it can't find the device and it will soon time out.* He sat and waited while staring at the screen. *What if this doesn't work?* he pondered. *Then, I've just wasted the past few months of my life. On the other hand, I've been there before. I'd just dust myself off and start over with a different approach.* He didn't dare to even get up to walk down the hall because the computer was looking for the transmitter located inside his head. He figured the range, under optimal conditions, would only be about ten feet. He then felt a slight rush of adrenaline. *But what if it worked, then what?* The anxiety of the waiting caused a tightness in his midsection. He was beginning to feel nauseous.

Glancing between his watch and the computer display, he saw that it had been four minutes and thirty-seven seconds. It was four minutes and thirty-seven seconds of anxiety. Four minutes and thirty-seven seconds felt like an eternity to man who had no patience. Then it happened. A beep rang from the computer as if the liberty bell had been repaired and come back to life. It startled George. He looked up and saw a green indicator with the words he had hoped for.... *Link Successful – ANT active.* As the anticipation ended and the stress of not knowing was finally made clear, George unexpectedly became flushed and immediately ran across the hall toward the bathroom. He had himself worked up into a frenzy and now felt dizzy. He was experiencing tunnel vision and the sound around him faded away as if he were about to pass out. He experienced two rounds of dry heaves, but nothing came up. He ran water in the sink and splashed some on his face, then slowly looked up at the man staring back at him and smiled. "You clever bastard, you." He reached up to pat himself on the back in congratulation.

Once he regained his composure, he reentered the lab and positioned himself in front of the display. He moved the mouse back to the menu. Additional options were available to extract data, run reports, or live interface. He selected, *live Interface*. The screen flickered, then an image appeared. It was an image of the display he was looking at. His heart palpitated as he moved his eyes to the left and right. The image shifted as he moved. Back to the menu, he selected *record*. He then picked up a newspaper from the workbench and read it aloud. He returned to the computer and selected playback. He saw the print from the newspaper appear on the screen and heard his voice through the speakers. Truly, this was turning out to be a great day. Feeling vindicated, he had proven to himself that all of the theory, ideas, and formulas he had worked on for months had paid off, the ANT device was performing as expected. He had beaten Dr. Ackerman to the test and was the only man alive who knew it had worked. *Put me on standby, will you!*

Reveling in the glow of his greatest success, George unscrewed the cap from his wine cooler and took a drink.

To enable a recording of his every move, he slept on the sofa in his homemade laboratory and continued recording throughout the night. The next morning he quickly scanned through the recordings and found that nothing had appeared while he slept. This was a significant finding in itself. He rummaged through an unpacked box in the second bedroom, which appeared to be the fallout of everything he'd owned that didn't need unpacked right away. He pulled out a college ruled notebook, took it back to his desk, and began to document everything that had happened up to this point.

He knew that he had to continue his work at SIA as if nothing had changed. Even though he was busting at the seams, he knew that he couldn't tell anyone what he had done.

CHAPTER 12

"Our first test subject was a student at the University," Dr. Ackerman explained. "This subject was a healthy, active, twenty-two year old male who was a member of the sports medicine program." A picture of the man appeared on the screen. "We'll call him John. He tested with an above average IQ and was in good physical condition. Four hours after the insertion of the ANT device by injection, data was being detected from the nano transmitter. Tests were scheduled to be conducted to determine if various stimulation provided to the subject would have an effect on the data output."

"Our expectation was that we could collect the data and measure it via existing highly sensitive equipment, but the data being received was generating at a much faster rate than the receiver was able to decode. Dr. George Graf, a PhD research scientist at SIA Medical Technologies, came up with the idea to merely capture the data being sent and configure that information into smaller packets similar to how internet data is processed. Then information could be received and saved at the computer. The packets could be fed to the processor at a rate the computer could handle. The end result of this approach was surprising. Once we figured out how to process the data, we immediately had a better understanding of the electrophysiology of the brain. We knew that we would be able to use this information to generate reports. Much to everyone's surprise we found that we could convert this data into images as well."

"Four months after the first experiment, utilizing the same test subject, we were finally able to capture and begin to read the data. We discovered that the video image being sent, emulated everything the subject saw. Other packets were decoded into sound files that emulated everything the subject heard. This was an exciting discovery. We were tapping into information that had been previously unavailable to the scientific community."

The doctor paused for a drink of water. He removed his suit jacket and carefully placed it across the back of the folding metal chair behind and to the right of the podium. He cleared his throat and continued. "We formed a think tank to develop ideas on how this technology could be used. Among the ideas, was the creation of a virtual environment where participants could share this information with certified individuals from their field of specialty, who would then act as their counselors while performing sensitive tasks. For example, imagine a bomb squad technician who had a support team who could see and hear everything the technician does, but doesn't need any special cameras or additional equipment to accomplish this task. Or perhaps a surgeon conducting a sensitive unique procedure that had only been successfully completed by a few people in the entire world. These few people could join him in the operating room even though they might be in another country.

Excitement was high, we knew that we were on the edge of a discovery that would change the world for the better."

INTO THE MINDFIELD

CHAPTER 13

It was turning out to be a gorgeous day. By ten-thirty in the morning, Holly had finished wiping down the patio furniture. Luke was restocking the refrigerator by the pool with an assortment of beverages suitable for adults. A cooler sat beside it to better serve children or anyone who wished to steer away from alcohol. A hog was slowly roasting on a rotisserie in a custom built grill that had been provided by a local catering company specializing in the hosting of large parties and barbeque events. It was tended to by a man and woman who were busy basting the roast to allow time for the flavor to soak in. They had won several blue ribbons and had been showcased on an episode of a nationally syndicated food television series.

The pool was built within a convertible enclosure, so it could be used year round. In the winter it was heated, fully contained within a surround consisting of several glass doors. During the warmer months however, the glass panels folded up into a storage closet that had been built into the walls of the house. The roof panels functioned the same, as they retracted into the space between the first and second floors.

Luke turned to survey the pool area for his final inspection. It was ready for the party. He noticed Holly sitting on the edge of a small side table with her head in her hands. He walked over to her, "You okay, sweetie?" he asked.

She looked up. She had been crying. "I'm fine," she replied.

Luke was a man, and like most men was sometimes accused of not being in touch with their feelings or emotions. He was also an analyzer of sorts. He knew what *fine* looked like, and this was not it.

He gently took her hands and peeled them away from her face. "Seriously," he said, "you can tell me. What can I do to help?" He gently kissed them.

She smiled at the kind gesture, "It's just me," she said. "I was thinking of Eric and just realized that this is the first party I've hosted since Eric died."

Eric had been Holly's first husband. He died on a day similar to this one. Everything seemed perfect until he ran what was supposed to be a quick errand to the grocery store to pick up some last minute party supplies. He never came back. His car was struck broadside by a drunk driver and he was killed instantly.

"I can't bear the thought of ever losing you too," she said.

"I'm not going anywhere," Luke said pointing all around. "We have everything we need." Then he looked directly into her big green eyes, "and I have you." He kissed her on the tip of her nose and then pulled her close. As they held each other, the doorbell rang.

Luke could see through the side-lite of the front door, immediately detecting who it was, but still, he couldn't resist, "Who *is* it?"

"Sam I am," came the expected reply. Luke opened the door, grabbed Sam by the hand, and jerked him into the foyer, following up with a manly hug for his best friend.

"Hi Holly," Sam said. "I brought you something." He presented her with two plastic bags that had been filled to the top. "Well actually, it's for the party. It's a sampling of gourmet breads from around the world. I thought folks might find it interesting."

"Well it certainly interests me," Holly said while giving Sam a welcoming hug and peck on his cheek.

"Where's Raj?" Sam asked.

"He took some of the pool toys into the garage to fill them with air," Holly explained.

"Come on in and make yourself at home," said Luke, "Me Casa… You Casa."

"I don't think that's the way it goes," Sam pointed out.

The doorbell rang again. Luke looked at Sam, shrugged his shoulders, and headed back to the front door.

This time he greeted Marilyn. She and Holly had become the best of friends, almost as soon as they had met. Felicia entered following behind her. She had also become like part of the family. She worked with Marilyn and had recently rented a spare room from her. It was not uncommon to see them at the house or for Holly to run off with them for one of their *girl's night* adventures.

The traffic began to pick-up as more guests arrived. Raj finally made his way back to the pool with an inner-tube around his waist, while balancing a giant rubber duck, and several balls of assorted sizes, teetering as he walked. The dining room opened up into the expanse of the pool area. The aroma of the sweet barbeque filled the air with a fine cloud of hickory smoke lurking about under the noses of the guests.

Several more guests arrived, including Nancy Lawhorn, a former co-worker at TCC, along with her husband Herb. George Graf arrived with two bottles of fine Italian wine in a custom tote. The biggest surprise of the evening was Willis Redman. He had been busy updating his designs for the SkyKar in an attempt to get FAA flight worthiness approval, so it could be sold commercially. He still lived in California, but spent an ample amount of time in Green River. Sam had made him the director of SIA's Aviation division. He had flown his own SkyKar in for the occasion.

Luke switched on some classic rock to help set the mood. He walked around and mingled to ensure that everyone was having a good time. The barbeque was ready at noon and the aroma had piqued everyone's appetite.

After the delicious meal, the guests broke off into smaller groups. Some suited up and jumped into the pool, while others moved chairs around to huddle up in conversation. Some broke away from the masses to have one to one conversations. There must have been thirty guests or more. As Luke walked amongst them, he made note of several separate activities occurring to assure himself that everyone was having a good time.

Marilyn and Holly were in the pool playing a game of volleyball, while watching over the small children in the shallow end.

Raj and Felicia were sitting in lounge chairs alongside of the pool, telling jokes and seeming to be having a blast with one another.

Sam was the center of attention within his small group. They appeared to hang on every word he said. Since he had become successful, it seemed that everyone believed that what he had to say was somehow more interesting, or even more important than before. That each word was somehow carved from a pure nugget of gold. Luke chuckled to himself, "He's still just Sam to me."

Off to the side, George was sitting with Willis, talking about the SkyKar.

"Since it's not actually a car," Willis explained. "It was confusing to the bureaucrats at the FAA. SkyKar might not have been the best choice for the name of it. They kept trying to refer me to the Transportation department. Do you believe that? They thought it was an actual car. I told them, no, it flies, it has wings and everything. It was Holly's father, John McBride, who actually got it straightened out for us. You see he's a general who works at the Pentagon in Washington."

Luke jumped in, "And he doesn't take any guff from anyone either."

"He's in charge of the entire Marine Air Corp," Willis added. "Well maybe not the whole thing, but he *is* over all of the logistics. His team tracks the location of each and every aircraft in the fleet."

George, being a technical geek by nature asked, "How exactly does it work?" He wanted to know the nuts and bolts of everything. He was fascinated by technology and it didn't matter to him what type it was. He had an insatiable thirst for knowledge.

Luke moved on, leaving George and Willis to continue their conversation.

About a half hour later, Luke tapped his glass with a spoon, "Could I have everyone's attention?"

The small crowd stopped what they were doing and looked his way.

"I have a toast I'd like to make," Luke said. "I'd like to toast my friend George Graf. In case you didn't know, I kind of have a thing for old cars." The group, consisting of his best pals, knowing him all too well, gasped and shook their heads in a pretense of disbelief. "Say it isn't so," someone shouted from behind.

"Okay, Okay, let me not bore you with the obvious. Back to George. I have a debt of gratitude to pay to this man." He walked over and placed his hand on George's shoulder. "It was this man who identified the location of my very first car. He found it in a barn where it had been stored for years on a remote farm in Pennsylvania. For that my friend, I thank you." He raised his glass and took a sip. The rest of the guests followed his lead.

"But that's not the whole story," Luke continued, "It's here now.... in the garage. My big news is that the restoration is now complete. If you follow me, I'll be glad to show it to you."

Luke was proud of the fact that he had been able to rescue the old Mustang and bring it back to life. With all of the attention paid to its detail, it was now better than new.

As everyone filed toward the garage, George caught a glimpse of Holly out of the corner of his eye. He knew she was an attractive woman, but he didn't realize until that very moment, how striking she truly was. Becoming aware that he was staring, he quickly diverted his focus and followed the crowd.

The Mustang Mach 1 was perched in the center bay of the garage. It was hidden under a custom made cover with an image of a running horse and the word Mustang printed on it. Luke motioned to Raj to give him a hand. As they pulled the cover back, the car was revealed. Luke was as proud as a new papa, showing off his baby for the first time.

It was beautiful, as nice a restoration as Luke had ever seen, and he'd seen many.

"Ladies and Gentlemen," Luke said, "I'd like you to meet Chuck."

"Chuck?" Nancy asked.

"Well...," Luke explained, "Holly thought we should name the car. So she came up with this idea. This is a

Mach 1, and Holly knew that a man named Chuck Yeager had been the first human to break the sound barrier, the first man to ever travel at Mach 1 speed. Not only did she find that he was still living, but with the help of her father, General McBride, she made contact with him. When Holly flew out to Arlington to visit her father, they actually received permission to go to Chuck Yeager's house and he graciously autographed the glove box door, which she had cleverly stolen…"

"*Borrowed*," Holly shouted from behind.

"Okay, borrowed… from the restoration shop. So, in honor of General Chuck Yeager, we named this car in tribute to him."

Luke lifted the hood and gave a presentation on how the Ram Air system worked as he invited everyone to come in for an up-close examination. Willis and Sam wandered off to the adjacent bay to explore the engineering on Luke's Hennessey F5 and the Porsche 917. They were certainly a bit more *high tech* than the Mustang. Willis signaled to Raj to join them. Raj had acquired an abundance of knowledge about the 917 and was more than happy to share it with them.

Luke had one more announcement to make, "May I have everyone's attention again, please?" Luke asked. Everyone paused and turned toward him. "As you may also know, I've been touring on the Vintage Grand Prix circuit this year, driving this gem over here." He extended his hand toward the 917 race car. "I have won enough races to be a potential finalist for one of the top three spots in the series. The last race of the season will be held next weekend at Laguna Seca Raceway near Monterey,

California. I want you, my closest friends, to all be there with me."

Folks began to look at each other and murmur amongst themselves, discussing the proposal. Each, trying to engineer a plan to support Luke's request. A few would need a babysitter, others were scheduled to work. Then there was the issue of carving a few bucks away from their savings to pay for an unplanned trip.

Holly, witnessing their concern, spoke up, "It's all on us," she said, "We're paying for everything. Luke's already scheduled his jet to take us all there. Transportation, hotel and even meals will be covered. We just want you to have a good time and enjoy yourselves." That changed the tone considerably, removing many of the obstacles.

"To Luke and Holly," Herb Lawhorn said, while raising his drink.

"Good luck, buddy!" Raj shouted, "We'll be cheering for you."

Later that evening as the party died down, the remaining guests were in the pool, all but Sam that was. He couldn't stay much later, but agreed to referee one last volleyball game.

It was boys against girls. On one side was the *manly* team of Luke, Raj, and George. Opposing them was a confident team of women who had already completed a practice round earlier in the evening. This team consisted of Holly, Marilyn, and Felicia.

Sam tossed the ball parallel to the net for the tip off. Luke and George both had a height advantage and spiked the ball into the water just behind their opponents. Raj served first and the boys soon learned that these women were not planning to go down easy. Holly, even though she was shorter at five foot six inches tall, was a powerhouse of energy and agility. Marilyn had the height advantage for the girl's team and was more than capable of working the net. Felicia, was the shortest of them all, but she possessed the skill of precision. Wherever she wanted that ball to go, that's exactly where it went.

After a few rounds, Sam bid farewell. Several rounds later the men conceded their defeat.

One by one they exited the pool. The last two out were Holly and George. Being the gentleman that he was, he motioned her ahead, "Ladies first," he said. She smiled at him as she grabbed the aluminum rails and pulled herself out of the water. George followed closely behind. Luke saw Holly emerging from the pool and mischievously picked up a beach ball firing it directly at her head. To avoid being hit, she quickly retreated, not realizing that George was directly below her. He looked up and saw her rapidly moving in his direction. Instinctively, he raised his hands to catch her. Her bikini clad bottom landed directly into his palms. He was stunned. Not by the surprise from her dodging the ball, but by the way her nicely toned bottom fit perfectly in his hands. She regained her balance and looked down at George, "Oops, sorry," she said blushing, then hurried up and out of the pool. He paused for a second. He'd forgotten what a real woman felt like, and it felt good. He had been divorced for more than a year, but even then, hadn't had any physical contact with his wife for at least a year prior to that. Not only had he enjoyed the *accident*, he was surprisingly aroused by it. Still standing on the bottom rung of the ladder, he stared as Holly walked across the patio. She was the vision of a perfect woman. Her wet skin shimmered under the patio lighting, sparkling with each step. She collected her towel and playfully snapped Luke with it from behind. George continued to watch as the beaded droplets of water fell from her skin. He found himself hypnotized by each movement of her beautiful body in the scant bikini. He watched her backside sway and her breasts jiggle as she playfully bantered with Luke.

Holly suddenly noticed that George was still at the edge of the pool and that he was staring at her through the ladder rails. She quickly wrapped herself in her towel and scampered away.

After all the guests had left, Holly and Luke began cleaning up. "I know you've known George for a long time," she said.

"Seems like forever," Luke replied. He could see that she was struggling to find the right words to say, "Why do you ask?"

"I don't know," she said. "There's just something about him that makes me…. well, a little uneasy. He seems nice enough. Maybe it's about the way he looks at me. I don't know."

"It's just George," Luke said. "I've known him for a long time. Trust me, he's harmless."

INTO THE MINDFIELD

CHAPTER 14

There was much for George to do this morning. He busily scurried around the apartment. After a quick breakfast consisting of an egg sandwich and a glass of milk, he zipped into the bedroom to pack for his trip to California with Luke and the others. He'd need to be at SIA Technologies by ten. It was pushing nine-thirty already and he hadn't documented anything in his journal yet today pertaining to the ANT experiment.

He'd been on many trips and found that he was capable of packing for a full week in less than ten minutes. In this case, he'd only be gone for three days. There'd be no business to conduct for a refreshing change, just leisure. He was looking forward to the break.

He walked into the room now being used as his lab for the experiment. The link between the ANT transmitter and the receiver was working better than ever. It had been twenty-five days since he'd begun, which had given him the opportunity to tweak its performance. Initially the maximum range needed for the receiver to sync up with the transmitter was less than ten feet. He had now increased that range to twenty-five feet and developed a method for it to automatically link to the device whenever he was within range. He found this to be much better than clicking on the menu each time he walked into the room.

Now, he could just glance at the display as he walked past the open door to make sure it was still working as expected, and it was! It was very stable and performed exactly as it should, continuing to display everything George saw and heard. As long as he was within range, it recorded everything, including him making breakfast and packing his bags.

He gathered his remaining toiletries and tossed them into a leather bag that he used as a shaving kit. He neatly packed it into his luggage, secured the house, set the alarm, then out of the door he flew. He figured that he should be right on time. It only took him fifteen minutes to get to work from his house.

George arrived at SIA just as his watch ticked ten o'clock. He had made it before the plane arrived. Sam was in his office and ready to go. He saw George pull in through the gates on one of the thirty security monitors that devoured an entire wall of his office. This had been designed and put into place by the previous owner. Sam, who lived for the latest technology and constantly evolving electronic toys, even thought this was overkill. But it worked, so he left it in place.

A few minutes later, George walked into Sam's office rolling his one piece of luggage behind him. He had a small tote as well, which held his office supplies and electronic notebook. "Ready?" he asked.

"You bet," Sam said. "I've been looking forward to having a few days away from here. Come to think of it, I can't remember the last time I had a vacation." He thought for a minute, then popped up his calendar on his wallet computer. "Nothing," he said with surprise.

"Outside of regularly scheduled holidays, I haven't taken a day off in over three years."

"Then loosen up my friend," George said, "This will be good for us both."

Sam's phone rang. "Sam I am," he answered. "We'll be right there." He turned toward George. "That was the tower, Luke's plane will be on the ground in five minutes."

"Let's do this," George said. They gathered their belongings and headed out to the airfield.

The airplane made its final approach, touching down with ease. The pilot taxied the craft over to a large, one room, two story building, which was the location of the SIA air traffic terminal, as well as the flight business office. It was manned six days a week, but there wasn't a lot of traffic. Maybe you'd see six or seven planes land and take off during the entire day, and even less than that on Saturdays.

The door opened and Luke trotted down the stairs that had been built into the plane as part of the fuselage door. George and Sam greeted him. "What on earth do you have here?" Sam asked pointing to the huge executive jet, "It seems that every time I see you, you have a different plane."

Luke once again explained how his fractional jet ownership agreement gave him access to a whole fleet of aircraft. All he needed to do was reserve the one he wanted and schedule the date. It was a great arrangement for Luke and his millionaire lifestyle.

"All aboard," Luke announced, emulating the role of an old time train conductor.

The plane was magnificent, impressive in every way. It was an Embraer Legacy 650 equipped with seating for twenty. As George and Sam boarded, they saw that most of the seats were filled. Several of the guests who had attended Luke's party the week before had already been seated on the plane. It was another opportunity for a gathering and they were all enjoying their time together.

As George made his way to an open seat, he walked past Holly. She was as beautiful as ever. Her auburn hair flowed bewitchingly over her shoulders. She was reading a book, with a pair of sunglasses resting on top of her head.

"Good Morning." George said. "Lovely day, isn't it?" He thought to himself about how much nicer the day had become since he'd seen her.

She looked up at George in agreement, "Lovely," she politely replied, then immediately focused her attention back to her book. He continued on to his seat.

The next stop would be Monterey, California, a bastion of the aquatic world. They'd find no shortage of things to do in Monterey, everything from the Monterey Bay Aquarium, to Cannery Row and Fisherman's Wharf. Luke had reserved a hotel that would place them within walking distance of these attractions. Nearby, Pebble Beach boasted the most photographed and best known golf courses in the world. He offered to pay the greens fee for anyone in the group who wanted to take up golf, or any other activities for that fact. He knew that his time would be spent at the track in preparation for the race that had been scheduled to be run on Saturday, which was only two days away.

The Porsche 917 was at the track and was ready for them when they arrived. The trailer was just as high tech as the car itself and had been custom built to serve as a portable garage. Any work needing to be done to the car could be completed there. A storage compartment above the work area housed spare parts, as well as oils and lubricants. Raj took charge and assembled the team. They walked through the setup strategy they would use on the car. One that would be specific for this track. Luke would get the opportunity to take the car out on three separate occasions, twice to familiarize himself with the track, and once again for time trials, which would then determine his starting position.

Luke and Holly walked the perimeter of the track so he could get a feel for where the dips and rises in the pavement were. There was one turn in particular he needed to study, the famed *Corkscrew*. "If I have any trouble," Luke said, "it will likely be here. Look at how the track rises to a peak in such a way that the driver can't see over it, and then it immediately cuts to the left, dropping to a steep downhill and then switching back to the right."

"I see why they call it the Corkscrew, that's just what it looks like." Holly replied. Although she supported his racing activities, she remained concerned. "Oh Luke, you be careful out there."

"You know I will," he said. "I will, because I'm getting the top prize today."

"A bit confident, don't you think?" Holly asked.

"Not at all," Luke replied, "because *you* are the top prize." He kissed her on the cheek and smiled. "*That's* how you know I'll be careful out there."

They walked back to the paddock area. Raj ran out to meet them. "Dude, hurry up," he said. "They've called your name."

"What?" Luke replied, "I'm not scheduled for another twenty minutes."

"You got moved up," Raj said. "One of the teams ahead of you were having issues with their car, and can't run during their scheduled time, so everyone got moved up. You need to suit-up, now."

"Gotta run," Luke said to Holly. "Wish me luck."

She gave him a kiss for luck, and headed toward a spot that she had picked out earlier where she could observe the time trials.

Raj helped Luke into the car. "The warm-up procedure has already been completed," he said. "You are ready to go."

"Thanks, buddy," Luke replied. "I sure am glad to have you looking out for me."

He pulled his car out of pit row and onto the track. The first lap was his opportunity to learn the track, get the feel for each turn and the many changes in elevation. He was locking each one into memory and working out a strategy for them. The Corkscrew was just as hair raising as he expected it would be. It was unsettling that he was unable to see what was happening on the track just ahead of him. Sure, during time trials it's fine, but after the rest of the cars were on the track, he knew anything could happen.

"Don't let it psych you out," he told himself. "Just relax and roll with the pavement."

INTO THE MINDFIELD

CHAPTER 15

Race day had arrived. Luke had earned himself a start in the thirteenth position. This was not nearly as good as he had hoped. *And what is it about this number thirteen?* he asked himself. *That's the number I started with in my first race. Actually, it turned out to be okay, because I finished third in that one. I'll just have to work hard to move up to the front.*

Spectators peppered the hillside along the racetrack. They were seated in the grandstand area as well as scattered about the grounds in what each of them hoped was the best strategic location to view the action.

Holly selected her two favorite spots where she thought they'd have the most visibility, the grandstand of course, and the corkscrew view.

Most everyone chose the comfort of the grandstand, which also positioned them to see a larger section of the track than any other location.

Holly, Marilyn, and Felicia decided to head off to the corkscrew view.

It was 2:00 pm as the race began. The pace car led the way for the first full lap, then broke off into the pit area signaling the flagman to wave the green flag, officially starting the race.

They were off. Luke found that racing at Laguna Seca was particularly challenging. Of course there was the *Corkscrew*, but in addition to that, the cars were running the track in a counter clockwise direction. Typically, that shouldn't be an issue for anyone, but it was just enough to make Luke feel like he wasn't on top of his game. He slowed, coming off the *Rahal Straight* leading into the Corkscrew, entering it with caution, and was immediately passed by two cars in the downhill spiral.

His car was running strong, and he found that he was able to gain momentum in the straightaways. He regained the two positions he'd lost in the straight along the grandstands. After pulling through the *Andretti Hairpin*, the tightest turn on the track, he bantered for position with car number twenty-three. They ran side-by-side through turns five and six. Turn seven was at the entrance to the Corkscrew. Luke backed off at the last minute ducking in behind his opponent. At the bottom of the Corkscrew he was passed by car twelve causing him to fall back yet another position.

"Raj," Luke spoke into the microphone. "I need a spotter."

"Sure thing," he replied, "What can I do to help?"

"Give someone a radio and have them monitor the Corkscrew for me." Luke ordered, "I need to know if I can go into it hot, or if I need to back off. Seriously, going into it, I can't see a damn thing."

"I saw Holly and the girls walk over to that side of the track," Raj replied, "I'll have someone run a radio over to them. In the meantime, be careful."

"I can't afford to lose two places every time I drive through it." Luke explained, "I'll finish last."

Entering the Andretti Hairpin, Luke saw dust fly as two cars spun off the track into the runoff area.

"We'll have a spotter in place in about two laps," Raj confirmed.

Once again Luke slowed his car before entering the Corkscrew. Just as before, he was passed by two other cars. This now moved him to seventeenth position. Knowing he was a better driver than that, he knew he'd have to become more aggressive. He once again overtook two cars in the straightaway.

It was an ongoing battle of give and take. There was no secret to winning or losing this race. It was obvious. He needed to overcome his apprehension concerning this one series of turns. He was doing very well at every other point on the track, gaining upon and even overtaking the competition. It was only at the Corkscrew that he lost momentum. This was his first time racing on this track. He needed to come up with a new strategy. On the next lap he chose not to go into it the same way he had done before. This time, he chose to be more aggressive. He knew that he could trust his tires to grip and that he would be able to withstand more lateral G's in the turn.

He downshifted coming off of the straight and immediately accelerated at the crest of the hill. As soon as the nose of his car topped the crest and pivoted downward to where he could see the track, he saw that two cars had tangled in the first part of the turn. They had slid sideways and were now blocking the track. He reacted quickly by hitting the brakes, turning the wheel, and sliding his number five racecar sideways to avoid crashing into them. He stopped the car with less than four inches clearance between them. He looked to the left and saw another car cresting the hill, number seven, and the driver was running at full throttle. By the time that car pivoted into the Corkscrew it was too late for the driver to respond. He drove the nose of his car directly under Luke's left side, almost center between the front and back wheels. He then pushed Luke's car into the side of the two cars that had previously spun out, number twelve and number twenty-three. They'd been scattered across the track blocking any possible passage. The number seven car who was now pushing him, had to have been running near sixty miles per hour at the moment of impact, and it was Luke who was stuck in the middle. That was until he was slammed into the cars that had been sitting still. The nose of the number seven car wedged itself completely under Luke's and then continued under car twenty-three, that was also sitting crossways on the track. This caused Luke's car to flip into the air.

Holly screamed. Her worst nightmare began to unfold right before her eyes. It was sheer terror. Visions of Eric's fatal crash immediately entered her mind.

Luke's car flipped three times before hitting the pavement below. It then rolled one more time before coming to a complete stop, resting on its top.

Holly cried out to Luke. A fire could be seen burning under car number seven and the driver was not responding. The red flag waved as emergency crews were dispatched, pulling onto the track only seconds later. Number seven burst into flames, engulfing not only his car, but also car twenty-three that had originally spun out and was now partially perched on top of him.

Emergency crews arrived at the crash site thirty seconds later. They began to focus on dousing the fire. This was their first priority. They feverishly circled the pile of cars. The driver of number twelve had himself unstrapped and was out of his car in seconds. He climbed onto car twenty three perched on top of car seven, pulled the door open and disconnected the five-point harness that held the driver in place. Flames were shooting up past his ankles and legs. He knew that there were only seconds to spare and hoped that his fire suit would hold out. The driver was unconscious, but he was able to hoist him out of the car and hand him to a rescue worker waiting below.

Holly was frantic and had completely lost control. She was screaming at the rescue workers to help Luke, but they were all busy trying to save the number seven driver who remained trapped in the burning car.

She tried to run onto the track, but was held back by Marilyn and Felicia.

Raj was running across the grass and was now getting his first view of the crash scene. A lump grew in his throat, "Luke," he cried out over the radio, "Say something, buddy." Sam and George had caught up with him from the grandstand and jumped the fence running as fast as they could to help. When they reached the car, they realized how badly torn up it was. It had come to rest on its top, with the rear of the car in the sandy runoff area, and the nose in a grassy strip. They tried to push the car over to no avail. It was just too much for the three of them.

Holly was reliving the day she lost Eric all over again, and couldn't bear the thought of losing Luke too. She buried her face into Marilyn's shoulder, sobbing.

Almost ten minutes had passed. There were still no signs of life coming from Luke's car. Realizing it was still in her possession, Holly located the radio that had been delivered to her and held the button down to talk to Luke in hopes that he could hear her. She spoke about how much she loved him and reminded him that they were getting married soon. She talked about the good times they'd had together, and the many plans they had made for their future. She was begging him to come back to her.

A tow truck arrived and strapped onto the undercarriage of what was left of the Porsche Luke was once so proud to own. They slowly raised one side and turned it over onto its wheels, at least on the two that remained. The emergency medical staff rushed in after the firemen had the door pried open and off of the car.

Holly could see Luke partially hanging out of the opening where the door had once been. She was compelled to go to him, be with him, somehow she needed to help.

Once again Marilyn and Felicia held her back. "Let them do their job, Holly," Marilyn said, gently turning her head, looking directly into her eyes. She'd hoped that Holly would snap out of it and better understand what she was saying.

"But I..." Holly began.

"Shhh," Marilyn interrupted, "He's getting the best help he can right now." Marilyn held her and rubbed her back while Felicia held her hand. Neither of them had a clue what to do, other than to try to keep her calm. Lord only knows how they were able to remain calm themselves.

Four ambulances were on the track, one for Luke and one for each of the other three drivers. The first two left in a hurry with their sirens wailing and lights flashing. The third and fourth pulled away slowly with no sense of urgency.

Holly lifted her head from Marilyn's shoulder, "Which one is Luke in?" she asked in a panic. She was rationalizing why the third and fourth ambulance hadn't left in a hurry. *What else could it be,* Holly thought, *the drivers in those two must be dead. There's no other explanation.*

"It's okay, Holly," Felicia said. "They took him in the first one.

They all found their way to the hospital and were escorted by a nurse into a private waiting area. "The doctor will be in to talk to you shortly."

Holly had gone through at least one full box of tissues. Sam walked over and sat beside her. Felicia and Marilyn were now not so tough; they were consuming tissues at a regular pace as well.

Raj tapped his hand on the wooden arm of the chair he was sitting in. He had a blank look as he stared off into space. George was walking the halls looking for someone, anyone who could tell him something.

After waiting for an hour, the doctor arrived.

Holly leaned forward, "How is he? Please tell me he'll be okay."

The doctor smiled, "He'll be just fine. He has a broken leg and a concussion. We're running a few more tests to make sure there's no internal damage. If all goes well, we should have him out of here in a couple of days."

"Can I see him?" Holly begged. "Please, please, please?"

"Sure," the doctor replied, "You can go in, but keep in mind that he's still in intensive care." He turned to look across the entire group and raised his fingers. "No more than two in the room at one time, okay?"

He gave her the room number and pointed her in the right direction. She walked down the hall and looked around the corner of the doorway to see if she had the right room.

"Hey there, groovy chick," Luke said with half a smirk. He was still in a fog from the medication, but she knew at that instant he'd be okay. She ran over to the bed and cautiously wrapped her arms around him. She was so glad that he was alive, but was afraid to squeeze too hard in fear that she might hurt him. He responded by grabbing her firmly and rolling her onto the bed.

"This was all staged," he explained, slightly slurring his words. "It was part of my brilliant plan. I planned all of this, just to get you into bed."

INTO THE MINDFIELD

CHAPTER 16

With his last burst of energy, George opened the front door and dragged his weary body inside. The plan for three days of rest and relaxation, turned out to be exactly the opposite, hectic and nerve-racking. As he stumbled through the doorway, he took a deep cleansing breath and tossed his keys onto the hall table, along with a copy of the Monterey Herald. The headline read;

Vintage Racer Killed at Grand Prix

A crash at Laguna Seca claimed the life of first year driver, Roger Whitten. Whitten, from Chicago, Illinois, was killed Saturday when he entered the famed Corkscrew, historically the most dangerous turn on the track. While driving his number seven Porsche, he crested the hill and drove his car into three others who had spun out only seconds before. The impact flipped car number five driven by Luke Monroe onto its top. An impact with a second car driven by Carl Langford caused Whitten's car to burst into flames. It took emergency crews several minutes to contain the fire. Whitten was pronounced dead upon arrival at Community Hospital. As of this morning, Monroe and Langford were listed in stable condition.

George was filled with a tiredness that had seeped deep into his bones. It had been a long weekend filled with every possible emotion, some of which one does not care to ever experience. All he was looking forward to now was a nice, hot, steaming shower, followed by a big fluffy pillow. He dragged his luggage down the hall and tossed it onto the bed. Then he froze in his tracks. Something was wrong. A look of confusion washed over his face. Something was definitely different. He wasn't sure exactly what it was, but he had to check it out. He returned up the short hallway and paused just outside of his makeshift lab, slowly peeking around the edge of the half opened door. The room was dark except for the whitish glow of the computer display. It wasn't the display that concerned him. It was what was *being* displayed. He stepped inside and slowly took a seat in his chair while remaining focused on the image displayed on the screen as if he were in a trance.

The display had previously captured everything George had experienced over the past month. It had duplicated everything he saw and recorded everything he had heard. The ANT transmitter had worked flawlessly, but now something had changed. What he saw on the screen was not a duplication of his surroundings. What he saw wasn't even the room that he was sitting in.

The image on the screen was that of an elegant dining room. There was a lavish black table with a top that looked like marble. It contrasted beautifully against a white marble floor. At one end of the room a buffet table was inset into the wall. It had to be at least twelve feet long. Above the buffet table was a mirror as long as the table itself, rising an additional four feet to the ceiling above. The entire opening was framed in mahogany trim made from twelve inch boards. A chandelier hung from a tray ceiling. The ceiling contained soft lighting hidden in the recesses of the trim, which caused it to glow white. The chandelier was wrapped in fabric matching the drapery on the opposing wall. The end wall held one large piece of modern art, displaying a series of brightly colored strokes crossing one another as if they were woven into the canvas.

I know this place, George recalled. *This is the dining room in Luke's house.*

This made absolutely no sense to him. Why would an image of Luke's dining room be on his computer? Luke lived in Denver, Colorado, and he lived in Green River, Wyoming, which was hundreds of miles away. A mantle clock sitting on the buffet table read twenty minutes past eight. He looked at his watch, it too showed eight-twenty. The hair on his arms stood up. It was more than a little eerie. It was just plain creepy.

Unsure what this mysterious image represented, George picked up his pen, opened his journal, and documented the details of what he was now seeing. Experimenting, he adjusted the volume on the speakers to their maximum setting and could actually hear the mantle clock ticking, but nothing else. Beyond the clock, nothing in the room moved. Beyond the clock, there was no other sound. If it wasn't for that clock, it could have been a photograph, but it wasn't.

He rummaged through a box of electronic gear and pulled out an external three terabit hard drive and quickly connected it to his computer. He pulled up the ANT control software and selected the *record* option. In the settings menu, he directed the recordings to the mass storage device. After all, George had always been a rational man. A man of science. He knew that there had to be a perfectly logical explanation. He just needed the time to figure out what it was.

Once the recording began, the indicator on the drive illuminated. The menu disappeared and the display returned to the image of Luke's dining room exactly as it was before.

Stumped, George muttered, "Hmm, I don't get it." He walked outside of the house, beyond the range of the transmitter, to purposely break the ANT link with the receiver. He then returned. The system reacquired the link immediately and once again, there it was, the dining room.... and that damned clock, still ticking away as if to mock him for not having figured it out yet.

He noticed a newspaper lying flat on the opposite end of the table. It was then he received his second shock of the evening. The image on the screen shifted, slowly moving him to the end of the table where the newspaper had been placed. *What the...? This can't be right,* he thought, both startled and perplexed. *The device is a receiver of signals from the nanobot, not a transmitter to it. It's just not possible that I should be able to change an image, just by thinking about it.*

He swiftly jotted the details into the journal. He continued to experiment with other items nearby. Each time he'd focus on a specific object inside the room, the image on the display would move him directly in front of it, just as if he'd walked over there himself, the mantle clock, the light switch on the wall, the mirror.

The mirror! His heart jumped. His breath was taken away as he struggled with what he now saw. Staring back at him was an image. One that he clearly recognized. It was an image of himself. As he desperately tried to understand, he scrunched his eyebrows and squinted. The image in the mirror responded exactly the same. He tried other facial expressions, eyes wide, tongue out, and moving his head from side to side. Each time he moved, his imaged followed in the exact sequence, at the exact same time. It was like he was actually looking into a mirror but, he knew that he wasn't. This was a computer display. He searched his office for a hidden camera, suspecting Sam was playing some kind of twisted high-tech joke on him, but none could be found.

"Okay, okay," he mumbled, while attempting to convince himself. "There's a perfectly logical explanation for this. I'm a scientist, researcher, and an inventor. I'll figure it out."

Shaking off the fog from the trip, it was time to get down to business. *Approach this as you would any experiment.* Outside of documenting what he had witnessed, he had no clue where to start. Then he had an idea, *I know! I'll play back the recording; then I'll know if there's something wrong with the ANT. If it shows me anything other than these images, or if I get a blank display, then I'll know for certain that there's something wrong with the nanobots' transmitter, an error in the device. Sure, that's got to be it!* It was a logical explanation for an illogical situation.

He pulled up the recording file and selected *playback*. His heart sank. Once again he saw the dining room and nothing else. He saved the file to a flash drive, turned off the computer, walked into the master bedroom and removed a laptop from his bag. *If the ANT computer and receiver are powered down, they can't interfere with this machine.* George sat the laptop on the dresser and inserted the flash drive. He found the file and selected it. Immediately he saw the dining room in Luke's house. Perplexed, he flopped down on the bed.

"Okay," he said aloud. "I have proven one thing. The recording is real. Hmm, what can I do...? Where is it coming from?" With further experimentation he set out to prove that the image was coming from the ANT transmitter affixed to the glial cells of his own brain. He set up another recording before powering up the ANT receiver. It recorded a blank image. As soon as the link to the device was confirmed, the image of the dining room reappeared. This was confirmation that it was definitely coming from his brain.

Reasonable deduction, he thought using his scientific acumen. *If I eliminate everything it can't be, then I'll be left with the correct answer.*

George worked late into the night trying every possible configuration his mind could muster. He even loaded the ANT software onto his laptop and moved the transmitter connection over to it, which once again, revealed the same results. He'd been tired when he'd arrived home earlier that night. Now he was way past weary, he was flat-out exhausted. Looking at the clock on the buffet, it read 2:45 am. Checking his watch, he saw that it also read the same. In need of a break, he decided to stretch out on the couch in the lab for ten minutes or so. That should refresh him enough to keep going. Perhaps he could generate some new ideas.

Although he had good intentions, he didn't have the stamina. He nodded off in only a few minutes and didn't wake until nine the next morning. He had slept in his clothes. Rarely would George have mornings where he just couldn't wake up. This was one of them. In a sleep deprived stupor, he staggered across the hall into the bathroom and rotated the knob in the shower to the on position. He automatically launched into his morning routine. Without the effort of thought, he brushed his teeth, shaved, and peeled yesterday's clothes off tossing them onto the floor, then into the shower. After a few minutes of standing under the steady stream of steaming hot water, he began to regain some of the energy that had been lost the night before.

It all started to come back to him.

What an odd dream, he thought. *No, wait.... was it? How strange would that be? I must have eaten something that didn't agree with me to have a dream like that.* He was still unsure.

After the shower, he felt somewhat reenergized. He dumped his dirty clothes into the laundry hamper and walked back to his bedroom for a fresh set. He wandered into the kitchen and found a small bottle of orange juice, popped the cap, turned, and headed back to the lab.

It didn't take but a second to see that this had not been a dream, it was real. Without explanation, the image of the dining room was still being projected from the computer display.

"Let's try a new approach today," George said to himself with a much fresher, semi-rested mind. "Instead of trying to figure out where it's coming from, let's try to interact with it."

He conducted many of the same movements as he'd done the night before. He worked his way through the dining room and was able to walk completely around the table. Looking into the mirror, he waved and could see himself waving back. Just playing around, he reached toward the mirror pretending to straighten his collar. That's when he saw an image of his hand extending from his own vantage point. But it was inside the display. It was as if he were actually there, standing in that room, at that moment. His excitement escalated as he continued to unravel the possibilities.

The next experiment he devised was to see if he could use his hands to actually touch objects in the room. He walked over to the buffet table, extended his arms and grabbed the mantle clock. He could actually feel the grain in the wood, the smooth polished surface, and the sharp edges leading from the side to the face. He picked it up and moved it six inches to the right. When he released it, he could see that it remained in its new location. He quickly wrote his findings into his journal. He rose and once again walked to the end of the table to see if he could pick up the newspaper.

As he reached forward, his hand once again came into view. He picked up the paper and held it up as he would if he were reading any paper. It was the Monterey Herald. He read the headline.

Vintage Racer Killed at Grand Prix

A crash at Laguna Seca claimed the life of first year driver, Luke Monroe.

With a gasp, George dropped the paper and fell back into his chair. He rubbed his eyes, regrouped his thoughts, and continued.

Monroe, from Denver, Colorado, was killed Saturday when he entered the famed Corkscrew, historically the most dangerous turn on the track. While driving his number five Porsche 917, he crested the hill and slid his car sideways to avoid hitting two others who had spun out only seconds before. A fourth car driven by Roger Whitten crested the hill striking Monroe in the side. The impact flipped Monroe's car into the air causing it to land onto its top. An impact with a second car driven by Carl Langford caused Whitten's car to burst into flame. It took emergency crews several minutes to contain the fire. Monroe was pronounced dead upon arrival at Community Hospital. As of this morning, Whitten and Langford were listed in stable condition.

"What the hell!" George yelled. He ran into the hall and picked up the newspaper that he'd tossed on the table the night before, the one that he personally had carried back from California himself. It looked to be exactly the same as the one on Luke's table. The headline read the same, but the story was different.

How can this be?

Sitting on the sofa for the next hour and a half, George felt numb as he stared into space. He was more confused than ever. He considered himself to be a logical man, but just couldn't find the logic in any of this. He returned to the computer to see if he could uncover more clues.

The only item in the room that wasn't part of the home's décor was the newspaper. George read it again to make sure he had seen it correctly. Sure enough, it explained how it was Luke who had been killed in the crash and not Roger Whitten from Chicago. He compared the two newspapers side by side. They still, in fact, represented different outcomes. He stood and once again walked around the table.

Wait, he thought, *am I just restricted to only the dining room? Let's see if I can move to other areas of the house.*

He made his way to an opening, leading to what he knew to be the living room.

As he stepped through the doorway, his legs weakened causing him to fall against the mahogany trim. A cold chill made the hair stand up on the back of his neck. He swallowed hard.

What he saw were Luke's family and friends. The same group he had just spent time with in California. The group he had flown with, attended the race with, and together visited Luke in the hospital.

After regaining his composure, he cautiously took a step closer.

Holly was seated in a chair with her back to George. Sam, Raj, Marilyn and Felicia were all seated on the sofas and chairs that were gathered around a coffee table in the center of the arrangement. There were papers and pictures scattered all around the area. Each person had a small pile of their own sitting on their lap.

"What's going on here?" George asked himself out loud.

Immediately, Sam raised his head from his stack of papers and looked directly at George, "Oh, hi George," he said, "we're going through some of Luke's old papers and photographs for the memoriam."

George's heart began to palpitate out of rhythm. *How could Sam hear me? Furthermore, how could he speak to me? Can it be true? Am I interacting with a software program, perhaps a hallucination?*

"What…. Why? " George asked.

"For the funeral," Raj said. "Luke's funeral."

"No," George said defiantly, "He isn't dead. I just spoke to him last night. He's okay."

Marilyn broke down in tears, "Oh, George," she said sympathetically. She apparently thought that he was in denial of the tragedy they had just been handed. She ran over and wrapped her arms around him. "He's left us, George. He's gone for good."

George shuddered. He could feel Marilyn's arms pulled tightly around him. He could feel the dampness of her tears on his shirt. Not knowing if it was fear or just an unwillingness to accept what was happening as even a remote possibility, he pushed her away and ran back into the dining room.

Digging through a pile of papers on the desk in his lab, he shoved them to the side, after finding the number he was searching for. He dialed.

"Sam I am," he responded cheerfully, answering in his usual way.

"Sam, this is George. Have you heard anything from Luke today? I'm worried that something bad has happened."

"No, I haven't heard anything," Sam said. "But let's conference Holly in to be sure." There was click followed by another. "George, I have Holly on the line."

"What's up guys?" she asked.

"I'm just worried about Luke," George said. "Is he okay?"

"He's fine, George," Holly confirmed, "I just left his room a few minutes ago. The doctor said he should be getting out in the next day or so. It's nice of you to think about him, but I assure you he's doing great."

George didn't quite know what to say. He felt confused, maybe even a little embarrassed. He thanked both her and Sam for indulging him and asked them to keep him updated should anything change.

After the call, he looked back to the display. He looked into the mirror at a man who, for the most part was capable and confident, but today he was baffled and felt inadequate. He was trying to find answers, but there didn't seem to be any. He thought that a man such as himself, should always be able to keep it together. He was used to a world where everything could be explained. He didn't like this confusion and for the first time experienced a tinge of fear that he might never figure it out. He felt as if he were walking ever so gingerly through a virtual minefield, where a new experience could explode at any moment, one chocked full of unexplainable events, events that were slowly taking control of his emotions. He once again looked into the mirror. Trying to untangle a wide range of emotions, a tear ran down his cheek. Holly entered the room. He could see her reflection as she approached him from behind. Even in his confused state, he was still mesmerized by her beauty.

"Are you going to be alright?" she asked. She could see the tear, and surmised that he had been crying about Luke.

He turned to look at her and said, "I'm just a bit confused right now."

"We all are, George," she said as she took her tissue and wiped the tear from his face. She wrapped her arms around him. "You are a very sweet man, George." Then buried her face in his chest.

He could feel the heat from her face. He wrapped his arms around her and could feel her as if she were there in the room with him. The touch of her skin, the texture of her blouse. It was amazing. Even though he was caught up in the moment, he knew that he had to persevere and find out the truth about what was happening here.

Holly took his hand, "Come on, we've got work to do." She led him into the living room, picked up a stack of photographs and handed them to him. "I need you to help me through this."

INTO THE MINDFIELD

CHAPTER 17

It was Monday morning and George was in his office at SIA finding it impossible to keep his mind focused on work. He was tilted back in his chair, twirling a paper clip on the tip of his pen. He'd been distracted all morning thinking about the unexplainable events from the night before. After all, how was it possible to witness someone else's life on a computer? Furthermore, how could Luke's accident have had two separate outcomes? Then again, how was he able to record images from as far away as Denver? Where was all of this coming from? There were countless questions to be answered.

One thing was for certain. He knew that it could not be a hallucination. The fact that it had been captured, recorded, and could be played back, proved that whatever it was, it was real. George was baffled. His mind was running in a continuous circular loop, that wasn't locking onto any possible options. He was a rational man, always had been, and was proud of it. He also knew that by following some basic universal rules, he'd eventually get to the bottom of any problem facing him. Why should he treat this any differently than any other experiment he'd administered? After a bit of pondering, he decided to create a list. The list consisted of four columns. In the first column he wrote facts that he knew to be true. In the second column he captured notes that would provide written justification that would prove his conclusion for that item. Column three listed items that were not yet resolved, followed by a fourth to capture possible options needing to be researched. This was a technique that he had used regularly as a research scientist to help him clear up unresolved issues. In the first column he validated his findings.

The ANT device had been installed in his brain and was working. This could be validated by the equipment set up in his lab at home. The signal indicator worked and images appeared on the screen.

The nature of the experiment had changed. The ANT data being received was providing a different view than what had been previously generated.

Prior to yesterday, the equipment only measured what George had seen and heard. Upon his return from California the experiment had changed without any direct input from him that might have caused it to do so.

Information pertaining to a single event had shown results with two separate outcomes. In reality, Luke had been in an accident and had escaped harm, with only a few minor exceptions. This had been confirmed by a call to Holly at the hospital, which had been witnessed by Sam, indicating that Luke was okay.

The ANT had shown that he had been killed and that his friends and family were grieving. The ANT image was being captured in real-time. This had been confirmed by the time shown on the mantle clock in the dining room. It had been synchronized with the time shown on his wrist watch outside of the experiment.

In the third column, he began to document items that he could not confirm.

Where was this signal originating? We can confirm that it is coming from the ANT, but where does it pick up this information? How could there possibly be two separate interpretations of what happened? Of course there's reality, we can't dispute that. However, the events taking place through the ANT seem to be disturbingly convincing and are following a logical pattern as well.

Due to his profession, George had been the subject of many psychological tests over the past several years, which had all concluded that he was as sane and stable as they come. His ability to find rational solutions had been a key component, enabling him to uncover the correct answers, where others had failed.

It was nearly 10:00 am, the usual time slated for the monthly SIA division meeting. This meeting gave the division heads the opportunity to showcase their advances to the rest of the executive leadership. The executive team consisted of George, representing the SIA Medical Technologies group, Willis Redman, in charge of the SIA Aviation Technologies and Sam, leading the SIA Computer Technologies division, as well as serving in the role of CEO for the entire company. This meeting provided each division director the opportunity to discuss challenges and potential roadblocks and to receive valuable input from the others. Additionally, the meeting included project managers and administrative assistants, depending on the material to be covered that day.

The conference room boasted a modern motif with recessed lighting encompassing the perimeter of the room. Three large circular lights hung over the huge conference table made of aircraft grade aluminum and fitted with a smoked glass top. The end wall was stacked full of the latest high tech multimedia equipment which included a floor-to-ceiling screen made out of Sam's favorite material, the electrically conductive polymer he used in many of his inventions. As a result, no projector was needed to make these presentations.

"Gentlemen," Sam began, "we have a lot to cover today, so let's get started. Mr. Redman, we'll begin with you." In keeping with the tradition of this fairly young company, everyone had an opportunity to present their items and issues.

"Good morning," Willis began, "I have a couple of items to discuss today." He initiated a PowerPoint presentation and picked up a remote control to switch the slides. "Last week we submitted the final designs for the SkyKar to the Federal Aviation Administration. Our team is ready to respond to letters of clarification as they arrive. Indicators are positive that we should have approval by the end of the year. We are working on modifications to our interactive canopy designs that will give pilots more control while improving the safety of the aircraft. We are moving past mere detection of air traffic and are adding automatic avoidance features, which as you know, is a huge advancement when applied to small aircraft. Finally, we have started the initial design process for the prototype of SkyKar2. This design will have a more complex gyroscope system and will be able to carry additional passengers and payload, fly at a higher altitude, and travel at a greater speed than our current model."

Sam was excited about Willis's report, as was everyone else in the room. After discussing some of the specifics surrounding the activity in the aviation division, Willis returned to his seat.

Then it was George's turn, "In the Medical Technologies Division, we delivered the completed version of the ANT unit to Cornell University. Upon the installation of the first ever ANT device into a human being, Dr. Ackerman reported difficulty in decoding the data. An analysis of the equipment showed that the data was being collected faster than it could be stored. My team and I devised a method to capture the data in smaller packets that could be sent to a mass storage device. Then these packets could be buffered into the computer at a rate that it was able to process. We've been told that this procedure was successful, but as of today, we've not seen any details on how the experiment is progressing."

"Of course," Sam nodded, "we were all disappointed that Dr. Ackerman chose not to include us in the experiment. I remain confident that the information will trickle back to us in good time. Does anyone have any questions for Dr. Graf?" No one spoke up.

"Okay," he continued. "Here's what I have for you today." He sat a small box on the table and reached inside, pulling out a half dozen pairs of what appeared to be ordinary sunglasses. The group responded by analyzing them just as they would any product. They shook them, checked the rigidity of the frames, and tried them on.

"Sunglasses, huh?" Willis spouted. "You created a pair of sunglasses?" He showed signs of confusion, as did everyone else in the room.

"Yes, they are a form of sunglasses," Sam explained. "Sunglasses, equipped with polarized lenses as well. If you bear with me, however, I'm sure you'll approve. Please put them on." They did as instructed and put them in place. "Now, lean back and close your eyes." Everyone played along. "Imagine yourself in a faraway paradise, perhaps on a beach in Hawaii. The breeze is gently blowing through the palm trees."

George had been through relaxation sessions before, but coming from Sam, thought this was just weird.

"If you listen carefully, you can hear the ebb and flow of the water washing up onto the sand and just as quickly returning back to the sea. Imagine hearing the voices of the people on the beach, each of them following their own recreational ritual." It was eerie, but the small group in the conference room that day began to actually hear those voices, the waves crashing, and the wind rustling the leaves of the palm trees. It became louder and then even louder as each member had the sensation that they were being transported onto that beach.

"Now open your eyes," Sam ordered. There were gasps from around the room as people began to realize that they appeared to actually be on that beach. At least they had the sensation as if they were. They looked around the all-encompassing, panoramic, three hundred and sixty degree view. Even for this highly educated group, it was a mind-blowing departure. George lifted his glasses long enough to see that he was still in the conference room with the rest of the leadership team, but when the glasses were on, his mind told him that there was no doubt; he was at that beach.

"May I introduce you to our next evolution of 3D+6 technology? I call this the VR-720-PX, or 'X-Specs' for short. This is the first completely integrated four dimensional experience ever developed. The experience you are now having is a result of combining six, three dimensional cameras with the images sewn together into a seamless view, no matter which direction you choose to look. The sound comes from four micro-speakers hidden within the frames providing a complete surround sound experience. You'll notice that the lenses are configured in a wraparound design removing any part of the frame from your line of sight."

Questions were fired from every direction, and they were plentiful.

"What software do you use to drive it?"

"Is it linked to the system using Bluetooth technology?"

"Can it run on any computer?"

"What's the range?"

"How difficult is it to set up?"

"Can it be integrated into older technology?"

"Okay, slow down," Sam said. "There will be plenty of time to answer your questions, but for now, the most important thing for you to know is that we intend to roll it out next month at the International Technology Convention in Hong Kong. So it's *top secret* until then, understand? What I need from each of you now, is to start thinking about how this technology could be used in your fields of specialty. Willis, how can we tie this invention into navigating an airplane or reading the instruments?"

"I'm way ahead of you, boss," Willis responded. "I've got at least three things in mind already."

"George, I need you to do the same."

"I'm on it," George quipped, and he was too. But not for the reason anyone on the team might think. He was beginning to think about how he could use it to solve the issue with his own ANT experiment. The one he had set up in his home. The one he had never been authorized to conduct.

"Each of you can take a pair of these with you. Study them. Play with them. See if you can break them. We need to know their limitations as well as their promise. I'll send you the drivers and software this afternoon. We'll review your ideas in two weeks. That'll give us enough time to tweak our presentation before the convention." Sam adjourned the meeting just in time for lunch.

CHAPTER 18

He let out a loud groan as he fell back into his chair. "Good Lord!" Luke exclaimed. "I sound just like an old man." Holly placed a pillow on the coffee table and helped position his leg so he would be nice and comfy. The cast ran the entire length of his leg and shrouded his foot with only his toes exposed to the cool air. Comfort, for Luke, was subject to interpretation. He didn't think anyone could be *comfortable* with their leg encapsulated in concrete.

"I don't know if I can do this for six weeks," he fussed. It would prove to be more than just a little difficult for him. Luke had always been an active man. He was constantly involved in something, relentlessly on the go. That would obviously have to change for at least the next six weeks, maybe longer. The cast extended his leg as straight as an arrow, making it difficult for him to navigate freely. Seemingly simple tasks that had been previously conducted without any contemplation, would now require a strategy. Something as simple as taking a shower would now become a big ordeal. "I don't like this one bit."

"Stop your whining," Holly said as she tapped the tip of his nose. "The way I see it is that you don't have much of a say in the matter. Besides, if you behave like a good little boy, there might be some ice cream in it for you."

"Oh, I see how it is," he quipped, pretending to be offended. "You're going to take advantage of me because I'm a helpless invalid with a major disability, unable to fend for myself."

She leaned in nose to nose. "You bet your cute little tushy I am. You're under my control now, and there's nothing you can do about it." She kissed him. He responded by pulling her onto his one good leg while continuously maintaining contact with her soft warm lips.

"I guess there could be worse things," he conceded.

As they engaged in a passionate exchange that had the likely potential of leading elsewhere, they heard the side door click shut, followed by a rustling as Raj removed his shoes in the back hall. "We need to hang a cow bell on that boy," Luke said with a sideways grin.

Having Raj in the house was a non-issue as far as both of them were concerned. They had been through a lot together, and to them, he was just another member of the family.

He entered the room and headed to his favorite spot on the sofa. "How you doing, buddy?" he asked.

Luke pointed to Holly as if to tattle, "She won't let me whine."

"That seems a bit unreasonable, don't you think? If anyone has earned the right... besides, you've been whining for years."

Luke sat up straight with an inquisitive look, gesturing with his palms open, "Whose side are you on anyway?"

"Well… how bad is it?" Luke quickly changed the subject. Raj had been in the garage surveying the damage to the Porsche.

"It looks pretty bad on the surface. Virtually every body panel is shot. The suspension on the left front is beyond repair, and the rear axle has broken through the transmission housing. The roll cage was damaged in multiple places. On a positive note the right side remains intact. Until it's completely torn down, it's hard to tell what other damage we'll find, but I think it's repairable."

"We've got all winter before next year's season starts," said Luke. "It's a lot of work, but we should be able to have it completed by then."

Luke could see apprehension on Holly's face. He knew that she was particularly fearful of losing someone she loved. "Don't worry, sweetheart. I've learned a lot from this experience. The biggest lesson is to never race into a blind corner without having a spotter in place. I'll *never* repeat that mistake again."

"I thought I'd lost you," Holly replied. "I don't ever want to go through that again."

Luke rubbed Holly's back. "If I'm not allowed to whine, then you're not allowed to worry… deal?"

She took a deep breath, followed by a heavy sigh. "Deal."

~

George couldn't wait to get home. He'd spent the afternoon locked inside his office, learning everything he could about the X-Specs. He was curious to see how it could interact with the ANT system, and desperately wanted to try it out. If this device provided better visibility into the environment, he could conceivably see something that he'd previously missed. He was anxious to get started, but had to remain cautious so that no one would find out about his experimentation.

VR-720-PX stood for 'Virtual Reality, 720 degree, Panoramic Experience'. It sounded like a mouthful, but Sam wanted to make sure the acronym was in alignment with what the device actually did. He explained it as a virtual world where 720 degrees represented two intersecting 360 degree views, one horizontal and one vertical, completely engulfing the user.

It was designed to connect to any Bluetooth compatible computer, but could only function with the proprietary software designed specifically for it. Although it was capable of enhancing traditional 3D games and movies, it could not expand them into anything more than what would normally be displayed on a standard television screen. The complete 720 degree experience could only be created via a recording generated by another one of Sam's inventions; the 3D+6 camera array.

A digital compass was imbedded in the glasses, inside the bridge of the frame, which provided information to show the computer which direction the user was actually facing. It would make immediate changes to the image seen by the user as they moved about. Another miniaturized device was located inside the frame on the temple near the hinge. Sam's design had been inspired by the way a flight level indicator worked in an airplane. Conveniently he just happened to have one lying around that he could dissect for the purpose of reverse engineering. This device would sense the angle at which the user held their head. Were they looking up or down? It would send that information to the control software, which would immediately make adjustments to the image accordingly.

It was an impressive device. George wondered how Sam had been able to keep it a secret all this time. After all, with this level of sophistication, it must have taken at least a couple of years just to get a prototype completed. These were developed far past the prototype stage. It appeared that they were ready for market.

It was five-thirty in the evening. George decided to skip dinner because he had a lot to do. He fumbled with his keys as he hurried to unlock the door. It seemed that whenever he was in a rush, everything took twice as long. He pushed the door open and dashed into the house making a beeline path directly to the lab. He bumped the hall table as he zipped by, nearly causing a decorative vase to fall. It wobbled back and forth eventually returning to its original position. In his right hand, he carried the glasses and a flash drive containing the required software. He quickly settled into his chair and approached the keyboard. With one series of strokes, he closed the ANT program, then loaded the X-Specs software, followed by a reboot of the machine. Once it returned to life, the link to the ANT, as well as the connection to the X-Specs glasses, were established. "All systems are go," he said aloud as he lifted the glasses to put them on.

"YES!" he shouted unable to contain his excitement. "They work!" And work they did. They worked so well in fact, it was as if he were actually transported there. Upon entering the alternate reality, he turned his head to one side. The image changed his perspective as he moved. He looked up. The view followed his movements.

Standing in an unfamiliar place, he was on a landing above a series of concrete steps leading to a parking lot overflowing with traffic. Additional cars were being parked along the street. Still experimenting with the glasses, George turned to face the rear. Behind him was an enormous double oak doorway rising at least twelve feet to the top. Six ornate panels had been carved across the face of it. The doors hung on massive brass hinges that had been kept to a nicely polished finish, giving the appearance that they were new. He looked down and surprisingly saw his own feet. This just wasn't possible on a mere computer display. He slowly reached out to touch one of the massive pillars in front of him. The pillar was used to hold up the roof of a portico-like structure that led to the sizable entrance. He was startled as he could actually feel the coolness and texture of the column.

He felt a tug on his sleeve, "George... George," It was Holly. She had noticed that he was distracted and appeared to be unable to focus. "Are you okay?" She whispered.

He redirected his attention to her. She was as beautiful as he had ever seen her. She wore a black dress adorned with a black belt and was carrying a matching clutch. It was a look he'd not seen on her before. It was elegant, yet not over the top.

"Uh... Yeah," he replied. "I'm just trying to get used to all of this." Of course he was referring to the X-Specs, but Holly seemed to interpret it as him trying to come to terms with the loss of Luke.

She wrapped her arms around him and squeezed, "You sweet, sweet man. Come, let's go inside." As they approached the door, he froze. He now saw the brass nameplate mounted to the left side of the doorway. It read 'Waterhouse Funeral Home'.

Holly took his hand. She was shaking, with tears in her eyes, "Oh, George, this is hard for me too. How about we help each other through it?"

"You know I'll be here for you, Holly," he replied looking into her eyes while placing his hand on top of hers. He then removed his handkerchief from his suit pocket, dabbed her eyes and offered it to her. With Holly under his wing, they reluctantly made it through the doorway.

Shaken, George removed the X-Specs. This was *far* too real. It was seriously intense. More than he could have ever imagined. He was compelled to stay to help Holly with her grief, but knew that the alternate version of himself would always be there in his absence. Realizing that he was merely a research scientist, he conceded that this was only an experiment. He found that he was beginning to get too wrapped up in the events taking place. There was an immense sense of emotion, at least for a minute, then he quickly shook it off. *This is silly.* He reminded himself that the task at hand was to figure out the source of this alternate path. *That's it! Nothing more.*

"Note to self," George spoke as he wrote. "Tell Sam that the VR-720-PX kicks ass."

CHAPTER 19

For the remainder of the week, George intentionally limited the amount of time he spent logged into the ANT system. Although he was intrigued by everything happening in that environment, he didn't feel that it was leading him to a solution. He needed to be able to explain the source of the data. Not only that, but to explain it in true, scientific terms. He would lose all credibility if he were to leave anything to speculation or conjecture. It had to be based on logic and scientific fact. There could be no exception.

He'd been spending the majority of his time on websites to see if he could uncover clues that would take him to the next step. So far, nothing. He visited some familiar sites he'd previously used while conducting neurologic brain research, as well as several college and university websites to see if any recent discoveries had been made. He checked the trade, science and medical journals to find articles that might help.

Then he stumbled onto an article pertaining to *Quantum Mechanics*. This was certainly outside of his area of expertise. As he read, he began to take notes. The Delft University of Technology, located in the Netherlands, had completed an experiment that proved a theory related to *Quantum Entanglement*.

In this experiment, they had measured two electrons that were encased within diamonds placed more than one and a half miles apart. When the electron at one end was triggered to rotate in one direction, the other would automatically rotate in the opposite direction. Their theory stated that the distance didn't matter, it could be across the room or across the galaxy. Whatever happened to one, would always affect the other. This experiment proved once and for all that the theory was correct.

George rationalized that if one electron behaved in this manner, it would be a given conclusion that others would do the same. He drew a chart to help himself visualize the concept.

"All matter is made up of electrons, protons and neutrons," he mumbled as he wrote. "These all come together to form atoms. So if the atoms make up the molecules, which are the building blocks for everything else... *Oh my God! That's it!*"

Once, perhaps twice in a researcher's life, would he truly have an epiphany, a real *eureka* moment, and *this* would be his. He finally understood. It was as clear as finely polished crystal. He may have just proven that alternate universes might actually exist, and that it was he, Dr. George Graf, who had figured it out.

"Contain your excitement, big guy," he said to himself. "You're a scientist, let's confirm if you're interpreting it correctly." He located the number to the University and checked the time zone map. "Damn," he barked. He'd have to wait until morning. The Netherlands were seven hours ahead of Mountain Standard Time.

He wasn't about to wait until morning. As soon as the clock struck 1:00 am he dialed the phone. The attendant directed him to Dr. Reginald Easterling, who was one of the staff assigned to lead the experiment. George had several questions that would be carefully masked so the doctor couldn't detect why he was asking. He didn't want to give away his discovery allowing someone else to have all of the glory. His final question would validate all of his assumptions, "Based on the outcome of your experiment, does it prove the existence of alternate universes?"

Clearing his throat, Dr. Easterling responded, "It's a *big* leap to get to that point. From where we are today, at the smallest microscopic level, I suppose it does open the possibility, but it's still just a theory."

George thanked him for his time and hung up the phone. *Theory my ass.* He had the proof Dr. Easterling would need to take that leap. *In due time*, he thought.

George worked through the remainder of the morning, organizing his notes so that he could best explain his discovery.

It was mindboggling to think that his brain was directly connected to another version of himself in an alternate universe. He'd previously believed that this kind of thing was nothing more than science fiction. Something imagined, completely made up in the mind of an unstable author and seen only in late night movies. On the other hand, he found it difficult not to let his thoughts get away from him, as this alternate world could be lightyears away, on another planet, just like earth, with copies of everything in exact detail. The electron experiment had shown the reverse effect on the second electron, which made perfect sense to George. In one world, Luke survived the crash, and in the other he didn't, just like the experiment had proven. It was exciting that his creation, the ANT device, was the only missing part that would permit him to tap into the brain cells that were linked to this alternate existence.

He sat down at his desk and connected to the ANT while placing the glasses firmly against his nose.

He found himself lying on the couch in Luke's living room. By this time it was 4:00 am.

He got up and quietly wandered through the house, not knowing what, if anything, he was looking for. He could feel the plush carpet caress his feet with each step. He studied each room as he passed by, taking in everything that could be seen with the only source of illumination being the moon and the dim lights shining through the windows from the courtyard. There was a click as he slowly turned the knob on the door leading to the master suite. He pushed it open, just a crack at first and peeked in. Holly was sound asleep on the right side of the bed. He opened the door further and stepped in. Carefully, he made his way to the bed in total silence. His curiosity led him there. He couldn't explain it, he just needed to take a closer look. She was wearing what appeared to be a pair of Luke's pajamas. They were blue in color and far too big for her small frame. Restless, she repositioned herself, pulling her leg forward, curling into a semi-fetal position. He paused for only a second, then touched the sheets near the foot of the bed where her leg had been lying. It was still warm from the heat of her body. George watched her, sleeping like an angel. One that had been sent to him from heaven by God himself. A lock of her hair lay across her face which flipped every time she exhaled. It seemed as if he could feel the pure essence of her soul and longed for the day they could be together. Seeing her this time felt different, because *this* time, he knew she was real.

He watched her for what could have been five minutes. For all he knew, it could have been an hour. He lost all track of time. Still restless, she rolled onto her left side and burrowed her face into the pillow. Startled, afraid he might be discovered, he quickly made his way back to the door and slipped out. He returned to the living room and stretched out. "Theory my ass," he mumbled once again.

At the same time, he laid back on the couch in his lab wondering where this discovery would ultimately take him. Oh sure, he pictured fame and fortune, but there was no hurry. It wasn't the right time for that. What he needed to do now, was to interact with the environment, record every minute of it, and document it in detail.

~

The phone rang. George made his way to the desk where he had attached it to a charger the night before. "Yo," he uttered, lacking the necessary energy to even say as much as *hello*.

"It's nine forty-five." Sam announced. "No one in the office has heard from you today. I'm just checking in to see if you're okay."

"Sorry, Sam," George replied, trying to regain his senses. "I must have come down with something. I've been up all night and just fell asleep a couple of hours ago. I don't think I'm going to make it in today."

At least some of it was true, he had been up all night, and he certainly would not be in today. Sam accepted his explanation and told him to get some rest, take care of himself and he'd see him tomorrow.

Over the next several weeks, George logged into the system as much as he possibly dared. He'd go home for lunch, leave work early, and show up late. Now that he knew *this* world was just as real as the one he'd lived in his entire life, he felt a need, *no*, an obligation, to be there. Be there to help Holly through her grief. To help her with odd jobs around the house. To be that sounding board in case she just needed someone to talk to. He found that she liked having him around too. She didn't want to be left alone in that big house all by herself. She even asked if he'd set himself up in one of the spare bedrooms so he'd be nearby.

~

At SIA, Sam noticed that George's work was suffering. They regularly attended dinner a couple of times a week, but lately, George always seemed to have something else he had to do. It was common for him to spend time in Sam's office during lunch to discuss strategies on how they would leverage the company to the next level. That activity had ceased as well. Sam started to receive complaints from the staff that George was not attentive and difficult to contact. In the event contact could be made, there was little effort on his part to follow up. This was unlike George, not at all what Sam had come to expect. He assumed that George was going through something personal and felt that his position was to talk to him to see if there was anything he could do to help, or if there was anything he needed.

Of course George told him that everything was just fine. He was convinced that it was.

~

It was Saturday afternoon and George was in his usual spot in the lab at his house. He was logged into the system and found himself mowing Holly's yard. He had worked up a sweat, after all there were over five acres of finished lawn to take care of. He saw Holly step out of the house onto the patio and motion him to join her. She was carrying two tall glasses of lemonade on a tray, and placed them onto the garden table located about one hundred feet past the pool. It was in the center of an area she called the 'flower pot'. This was her personal flower garden. Since Luke's death, she'd spent a fair amount of her free time here, tending to the lush plants. It had been over seven months since the accident. She was very proud of the variety of plants she'd collected from countries all around the world. The combination of plants created a fragrance that was unlike anything George had known before. She had begun her collection by first studying mountainous geographical areas with a climate similar to hers. Just outside of Evergreen, Colorado, the altitude was 7,220 feet above sea level. By searching for indigenous plants that thrived at that altitude, she had acquired a collection that was truly world class. She joined a garden club where she picked up a lot of good tips from the other members.

George made his way to the garden. He was beaten down by the hot sun and out of breath. Holly offered him a lemonade. There'd be no argument from him. He took the ice cold glass and tipped his head back. Black rings of dirt followed the creases along the lines of his neck. His hair was disheveled and his shirt was soaked.

"Oh yeah," he proclaimed as he smacked his lips, "that hit the spot. Just what I needed."

"What you need," Holly said, "is a bath. Look at you."

"This is my rugged, *tough guy* look. What do you think?"

"What do I think?" She repeated, "I'll tell you what I think." She stood and slowly started to make her way toward a row of fruit trees that lined one side of the garden.

"What are you up to?" George asked, raising his brow suspiciously.

"Nothin'," She replied, acting coy. Then she suddenly burst into a mad dash, taking hold of a water hose lying along the edge of the lawn. Turning toward him, she squeezed the nozzle. With nowhere to run, he looked for a place that could shield him from the surprise attack. As he turned, he saw a similar hose on the opposite side of the garden, and took an aggressive stance. The battle was on, it was to be a fight to the end. Both were drenched in the cold mountain water. As the battle closed in, they were only a few feet apart when Holly ran in, grabbed George's belt, and shoved the nozzle into his pants. He turned to get away, but instead pulled her closer, as the hose wrapped around her waist. Relentlessly, she would not release her grip, the nozzle would stay right where it was. The cold water made George squirm. He continued to spin around in an attempt to escape. By this time they had both become so intertwined with the hoses that they could no longer remain standing. George fell to the ground with Holly on top of him. They were both laughing uncontrollably. She had thought that she would get the best of him, but hadn't counted on his retaliation.

"Looks like we're both losers." She laughed with her wet hair hanging down into his face.

He looked up at her, and became lost in her big, beautiful, emerald-green eyes. He pulled her close and gently kissed her. "From my point of view," he said. "Looks like we're both *winners*."

Pushing back, she looked at him expressionlessly, pausing for only a moment, not quite sure what to say. Instead, she refocused her attention toward untangling herself from the hose. She shook herself off, then headed back to the house without uttering as much as a single word.

George fretted that he had just screwed up, a major *faux pas*. He obviously came on too strong. "Dumb ass." He muttered to himself. "That was a bone head move. She's not ready for that. Give her some space."

He returned to his seat at the garden table to finish his lemonade…. alone.

~

Back at home in his lab, George removed the X-Specs and rubbed his eyes. He was tired, worn down from trying to maintain two lives, and it was taking a toll on him. He had skipped most of his lunches throughout the week and hadn't taken the time to properly prepare healthy meals. Fast food had become the norm, along with bags of chips, cookies, and anything else he could drag into the lab. His health and overall well-being was at risk. He hadn't shaved for at least four months and was now sporting a full beard. He hadn't cleaned the house during that time either. Things had been thrown about everywhere and his home now looked as if it had been robbed and vandalized. An odor of dirty laundry filled the air throughout the residence.

Eventually, he lost his job at SIA. Sam had been left with no choice, but to let him go. George had reached a point where work was no longer a priority and he just stopped showing up.

None of these things were important to him anymore. The only thing that was important to him was taking care of Holly. Worldly things in *this* reality were no longer necessary. He had everything he'd ever need in Holly's world.

CHAPTER 20

George had always maintained a stellar reputation for being responsible, and was well-respected for taking care of those things needing taken care of. When it came to Holly, he always made sure that everything was in order. He didn't want her to be concerned over petty tasks such as cleaning, household maintenance, or other mundane responsibilities. He believed that she'd be happier doing the things she *wanted* to do, not just the things she *had* to do. Certainly, there were things they enjoyed doing together, like trying out new recipes in the kitchen. It was fun for both of them. It had gotten to the point where she jokingly referred to him as her *manservant*.

Unfortunately, George was not as responsible in his *own* world. He cherished every moment he had with Holly in hers, but had recently begun to think about how long he could continue that relationship. After all, he was no longer receiving a paycheck. He knew that at his current rate of spending, he'd be out of cash soon and was not sure how he'd survive. Survival in Holly's world would not be an issue. They had an agreement whereby he would take care of the estate, in return, she would take care of his financial needs and would provide him with a place to stay. It was a satisfactory arrangement for both of them. She didn't know anything about his other reality, nor could she have done anything about it had she known.

That was something George needed to gain control of on his own.

Realizing this, George decided to put a plan together. It had to be the type of plan that would last a lifetime, because a lifetime was exactly what he wanted to share with Holly. He had already made the decision not to disclose the results of his experiment to the scientific community. It had become far too personal for him now, and he wanted to keep it that way.

He made a list of those things that were necessary for his basic survival, like electricity, food, and shelter. After all, without electricity, he wouldn't be able to power up his equipment, which was what enabled him to connect with Holly's world. He decided that he'd just call it *Holly's world,* instead of alternate universe or alternate reality. It just felt a bit more casual, a lot less stuffy.

Determining his needs to be minimal, it was time to execute his plan. The first step would be to sell all of his personal possessions. He consigned with a local auction house and delivered everything to them that was to be sold. This, he felt would be the quickest way. Much to his surprise, he discovered that he had a baseball card collection from his childhood that turned out to be quite valuable. The 1952 Mickey Mantle rookie card alone brought fifty thousand dollars. The complete collection generated almost one hundred and twenty-five thousand dollars. All that remained in the house after the sale were the few items in his makeshift laboratory and a bed. He sold his Range Rover and listed the house with a local realtor. It sold only four months later. He even parted with his beloved '56 Chevy, the one that he'd had since college. He rationalized, if it wasn't on his list, he really didn't need it. In total, counting all of the items sold, along with the investments that had been made prior to his failed marriage, he generated cash in the amount of two hundred and fifty thousand dollars.

He still required transportation to support his new lifestyle, so he invested in an old Pontiac Firebird. He chose that model for no other reason than it was cheap. The cost was six hundred dollars. To say it was worth every penny, was a bit overstated. The paint was faded in the places where paint still existed. The right headlight remained locked in the *up* position, while the left wouldn't raise at all. There was a dent in the passenger side door, and the plastic trim on that side was missing. The interior looked as though it had once been used as a den for a pack of wolves. It was covered in rust and appeared to be sagging in the middle. One good sized pot hole might be all it would need to break it in half. But it ran, and that's what George cared about.

Next, he needed a place to live. In the spirit of keeping his costs as low as possible, he only looked at the *total* expense of the apartment. Perhaps, one that included utilities would make sense, then he'd know what to budget each month. He figured if he could keep his spending under ten thousand dollars per year, he'd have enough set aside to last him twenty five years. That would get him to the point where his retirement would kick in, and he could live off of that moving forward. It was a great plan. Oh sure, it had a couple of major holes in it. For instance, he'd chosen not to have any kind of health insurance. He was in good health now, and would just have to ensure it stayed that way.

George decided to live in Denver, because it was close to Evergreen, which was where he and Holly lived in *her* world. He found exactly what he was looking for. It was an upstairs, one room efficiency apartment, located above an abandoned storefront, in a place that could most kindly be described as a *sleazy* neighborhood. The rent was only three hundred dollars per month, which included all utilities. It was an eyesore at best, for certain it would be classified as a distressed property. The windows in the lower part of the structure were clad with iron bars on the outside, which were also covered in rust. In many towns, it would have been condemned, but it had electricity and running water, which suited his purposes just fine.

His mattress and desk had been strapped to the roof of his car. His chair was lashed to the wing attached to the trunk lid. They were all waiting to be taken into their new home. Everything else, all that he owned, was crammed inside the somewhat small car. He was now ready to begin what was sure to be the start of a perfect life.

Upon settling into the apartment, George looked around and concluded that even for his purposes, this felt a bit drab. The countertop was chipped along the leading edge, and had discolored due to years of abuse. The porcelain in the sink had been chipped, revealing the cast iron beneath it. It was consumed by rust at the drain and near the faucets. In a valiant attempt to spiff the place up, he printed several pictures of Holly that he had collected from the hours of recordings he'd maintained. His printer was capable of handling paper up to eleven by seventeen inches, which he discovered came in quite handy to cover a couple of the larger holes in the wall.

He chuckled to himself as he thought about his family, colleagues, and friends from the past, *If only they could see me now.*

One expense George hadn't planned for was air freshener, but after being inside the cramped space for the past two hours, it was promptly added to his list of necessities. He discovered a few more items were still needed to make the apartment livable. Completing a quick inventory, he added things like a towel bar and toilet paper holder. A couple of throw rugs would help to cover the spots where the linoleum was missing, as well as to hide the burn in the carpet from a clothes iron that had obviously been laid face down while turned on. He also decided to stock up on groceries while he was out and made a list.

George jumped into the Pontiac and pulled the door shut. The entire car rattled as if it had just crossed a series of uneven railroad tracks. He inserted the key into the ignition and turned it to the right. It started immediately. He smiled, satisfied that he had made a good choice, while pulling onto Colfax Avenue near downtown. Not being familiar with the area, he thought he would explore a bit while he was out, but not very long, because he was eager to get back and log onto the system as soon as possible. He told Holly that he'd gone fishing with some of his old work buddies He wanted to get home early enough to connect with the alternate George in Holly's world, before *he* returned from that trip.

He reveled in how clever he was, not only as the creator of the ANT device, but how he had used this technology to better his own life. Before long, he found himself entering the shopping district at Pleasant View, near the town of Golden. He spotted a home center that would be sure to have everything he needed and pulled in. Upon entering the lot, he immediately noticed a familiar car heading toward the exit. It was one that he knew all too well, because he had regularly driven it himself. It was Luke's white '71 Mustang Mach 1. Behind the wheel was Luke himself. He hadn't seen Luke since the accident. As they passed one another George stared into the window to get a better look. Sure enough, in the passenger's seat, sat Holly. She was talking to Luke and had a big bright smile on her face. Temporarily distracted, George slammed on the brakes, just missing a rear-end collision with the car in front of him.

It was a disturbing sight. Of course, he knew that Luke survived the accident, and it was logical that he and Holly were still together. However, he hadn't expected that he would actually see them, and he certainly wasn't prepared for it. A surge of jealousy shot through his veins. He was personally offended. How dare he? Luke didn't belong with her, it just wasn't right. After a few minutes he calmed down, reminding himself that he was the only man in Holly's world, and he remained hopeful that once she was past the grieving, she'd be able to see him as more than just her manservant.

After making his final selections, he paid for the items and loaded them into his car. Once again the Firebird fired immediately and he smiled at its consistency.

Returning to his crusty apartment, he unloaded the supplies and carried them up the creaky staircase.

After performing the necessary handyman tasks, he positioned his desk into its desired location, and connected the computer equipment. He logged in and carefully placed the X-Specs over his eyes.

~

Once again connected with his alternate self, he stepped into the kitchen. Holly was chopping some vegetables as she prepared dinner.

"There you are," she said. "I was beginning to wonder about you. Did you and the boys catch anything?"

George flashed back to the parking lot. He couldn't get that awful image of her with Luke out of his head.

"George," Holly said a bit louder.

"Huh, what?" he replied.

"Did you and the boys catch anything?"

"No, nothing," he muttered, then walked into the living room.

Holly followed, "Something on your mind?"

"Just thinking," he was clearly distant from the conversation.

"Is it one of the guys?" She asked.

He only responded by staring at the floor and shaking his head no.

"Okay, if you need some time by yourself, I get it." She was always warm and understanding. "If you change your mind, I'll be in the kitchen."

George was faced with a dilemma. He knew that Luke was alive, and that Holly was a big part of his life. He also knew, just as *that* was real, so was the world where he and Holly were together. The only difference was where he was *physically* located. He knew that he really belonged in the non-electrically stimulated world, and could only visit Holly's world through the ANT equipment, which was somehow streaming data through the portal in his brain. When he was in Holly's world, it was as real as if he were there without the system connected. He morally questioned if it were ok to live his life this way, or was he somehow cheating the greater design of the universe. Perhaps he was interfering with God himself? These were much larger philosophical issues than he was prepared to deal with at this time.

After dinner, he excused himself early, and headed off to bed.

He stared at the ceiling for what seemed to be an eternity. The clock passed nine, then ten. It was ten twenty-two when Holly tapped on the door. "Are you awake?"

"Yes."

She opened the door a crack, "May I come in?"

"Sure," he replied. He felt guilty for ignoring her all evening. He knew that she didn't know why, and he most definitely couldn't tell her. "Come on in."

She was wearing a terry cloth bath robe. Her hair was wet, indicating that she had just finished her shower and had been getting ready for bed herself. George was under the covers dressed as usual for bedtime, wearing nothing but a pair of boxer shorts.

"I need to talk to you, George." She was nervously fidgeting with her hair brush as she tried to speak.

In an attempt to ease her angst, he placed his hand on top of hers and noticed that she was trembling, "Look, I am so sorry about how I acted this evening."

"No George, It's not that. I want to apologize to you. It's me. I feel like I've been taking advantage of your good nature. You must feel that I'm only using you."

"No, not at all. Where is this coming from? I assure you, I'm not doing anything that I don't *want* to do." He slid over to make room on the edge of the bed, "Please, sit," he said while lightly patting the sheet with his hand.

She began, "I've been thinking a lot lately about where my life is headed. I've accepted the fact that Luke is gone and won't be coming back. Until now, I've been living one day at a time, just getting by. I don't think I could have made it without your help."

"It's been my pleasure." he interrupted.

"Shush," she pressed her finger against his lips. "Please let me get this off my chest. It's taken me a while to drum up the courage to have this talk, I just need to get through it. I realized earlier today that it just can't wait any longer. It's been on my mind for at least six months. It started the day we had the water fight in the garden, the day you kissed me. I treated you poorly by walking away, for that, I'm sorry, you didn't deserve it. Since then I've been thinking about how good we are for each other, and that maybe, just like you said, we really *are* winners. I thought you should know that I've grown more than just a little fond of you, I've developed feelings for you. I've known for some time that you have feelings for me, but was afraid to say anything. I was worried what you might think if I were to reveal those feelings too soon after Luke was gone. It's been a year now, you're still here and I still feel this way. You don't have to say anything now, just sleep on it. We can talk more tomorrow." It came out just as if it had been rehearsed. She stood, took a deep breath, seeming to be relieved that she had finally said it, and stepped toward the door.

"Wait," George said as he sat up on the edge of the bed. "I don't have to sleep on it, I feel exactly the same. It may sound silly, but I was afraid if I told you how I felt, that I'd ruin everything and scare you away." He now stood facing her, taking her hands. "The truth is, I've grown to love you and it's my hope that someday, you'll feel the same about me."

Her big green eyes began to tear up. She stepped forward, wrapping her arms around him, and squeezed tight. "I do George! I really do love you."

They kissed.

CHAPTER 21

George woke just as the morning light peeked through a slit between the curtains, drawing a bright line of sunshine across the carpet, running the full length of the room. He was the happiest man on earth, or any other planet for that matter. He was lying in bed with Holly, the love of his life, next to him. Her head snuggled firmly against his shoulder. He could smell the strawberry scent from the shampoo she had used the night before. Her right hand laid still on his hair covered chest and her leg crossed over his, seemingly to lock him in place. Yes indeed, it was a perfect morning. He remained careful not to disturb her sleep. He treasured the feel of her body next to his and wanted it to last forever, knowing from here on, things would never be the same between them. All he could do was smile.

Staring at the ceiling, he began to think about the night before; about how he'd felt when he saw Luke in the car with Holly. He certainly surprised himself by how he'd reacted to it emotionally. Up to now, his plan to win her over had worked just as he had envisioned. The only part that wasn't exactly ideal was that this was in *her* world, a totally different place. The connection he shared with her was strong, but he knew it was somewhat artificial. Not the love that he felt for her. No, that was genuine and rock solid. The connection he was concerned with was the method in which he was able to enter her world. That was artificial... it was electrically enabled. It was like he was cheating fate somehow. But there was no way he would ever give up on her, or disconnect this relationship. He only wished that they could live in the *same* world. *The only way that could ever happen,* he thought, *would be if Luke were out of the picture.* Then he'd have Holly all to himself, here or there, no matter what, but that wasn't likely to happen anytime soon.

Holly stirred and began to wake. She wiped her eyes and looked at George. "Good morning, beautiful," he said.

She smiled, gave him a kiss, and wiggled up tightly against him with a sigh. "Yes it is," she replied, "an absolutely undeniably, wonderfully fantastic morning."

Things were different for them after that. They continued to grow closer and felt more comfortable around each other. It was as if it were meant to be. A perfect relationship with a perfect partner. *If ever there were a case study that highlighted the true meaning of bliss,* George thought, *this would be it.* He was sure she felt the same.

They cherished each and every day they spent together. Days became weeks, and weeks became months. They had become inseparable, and could regularly be seen driving around town in Luke's old Mustang.

George had come to the point where he spent virtually all of his time logged into the ANT system, day and night. It was rare that he ever left Holly's side, but he also made a promise to himself that he'd take care of his health in his current world. Of course he needed to eat and take periodic health breaks, so he created a system where he'd log off from time to time, but never for too long. This gave him the time he needed to run his errands, do his shopping, and finish his chores around the rundown apartment. He became very efficient and found that all of this could be completed with minimal time away from Holly. To keep himself from losing muscle from the many hours of inactivity, he'd take breaks to get some exercise, and would regularly take a run through the neighborhood, or if the weather was bad, run the stairs inside of his building for twenty minutes.

One day, he was doing just that, and noticed that one of his neighbors hadn't picked up their newspapers in a few days. They were beginning to pile up. He knocked on the door, eventually coming to the conclusion that no one was home. Being a good neighbor, he scooped the papers up and took them into his apartment. He'd keep an eye out and deliver them when his neighbors returned. Shoot, after seeing them coming and going in the hall for months, he realized that he didn't even know their names.

He tossed the papers onto the table and picked up the Sunday edition from the stack. It was thicker than the rest, mainly due to all the ads stuffed inside. It would be good to take a break for ten minutes as he caught his breath from the morning run. Then, he would log back into the system where he and Holly had been making vacation plans.

Opening the paper to the lifestyles section, his jaw dropped. He couldn't believe what he was seeing. The title read, "Lottery Winners to Tie the Knot". It showed a picture of Luke standing with his arms around Holly. Along the side was a story about how they had met at a convention for lottery winners, fell in love, and were now engaged to be married. His heart sank. He tossed the paper down in disgust, unable to risk another look at that *dreadful* picture, reminding himself that it was *he* who Holly loved, and that *he* was the only one. Understanding there were two separate realities, he knew that in *this* world she was with Luke. Needing to accept that fact, he conceded that he would probably see them from time to time. *But I don't have to like it*, he groused.

He rationalized that he'd have Holly for the rest of his life in her world, and Luke would in his. It would be a reality that would continue unbroken, forever.

Suddenly, he became flushed with a heightened sense of anxiety.

Unbroken? he thought... *Forever?* The world he'd come to know, his entire life with Holly was contingent upon one thing: the equipment *must* remain working. He hadn't considered what would happen if something actually broke. The ANT transmitter would need to continue to transmit data for the rest of his natural life, as would the receiver. It could *not* be allowed to break. Typically, computer equipment wears out and is promptly replaced. The computer he ran the software on wasn't necessarily a concern to him, it could easily be replaced. What couldn't be replaced, were the unique components used in the nanobot and ANT receiver. The four-dimensional glasses were a prototype. These had been developed by Sam, in the lab at SIA. He couldn't just go in to the office and say, "I'd like an ANT neurotransmitter and receiver please." He shouldn't even have the one that was in his possession now. He had stolen it. Surely he'd go to jail for that alone.

Without access to parts, he feared it was only a matter of time. The system *would* fail. It was inevitable. The question was when. It could be a year from now, or ten years from now, but the odds were that it *would* fail. His life with Holly would be tragically cut short. They would never get the opportunity to experience growing old together. He would no longer enjoy the taste of her soft sweet lips, or how it made him feel when he held her body firmly against his.

"Wait one damned minute," he said defiantly, "I'm the inventor of this thing, and I can recreate it." The reality was however, that he just wasn't capable. Yes, his name *was* on the patent, but SIA was working from a multi-million dollar grant, employing a team of researchers, scientists, and technicians. This was much larger than George could handle alone. He certainly didn't have that amount of funding. His anxiety soon turned into panic. *What if it were to fail tomorrow?* he wondered. *We'd never be together again.*

His panic quickly turned into depression. He couldn't bear the thought of it. In need of a long term plan, he decided to go back to his standard, basic approach of simply making a list. It had never failed him in the past. A big dose of *rational thought* was what he needed at this point. As a researcher, he should be able to remove his personal emotions from the equation. This would have to be no different. At a minimum, it should give him a place to start.

George stared blankly out of the window through a pane, with a crack resembling a curved spider web. The edges of the crack refracted the many colors of the rainbow. Like a crystal, it sparkled brightly in an otherwise shamefully drab existence, trying desperately to bring life back into the room. He remained frozen in that position for over an hour, doing nothing else, just staring at that section of cracked glass. His mind was cycling through a field of possible options. He was desperately searching for the one that would resolve his issue. Unfortunately, that's all he was doing, cycling. He was unable to find a solution he could lock into, not one single option to explore... nothing!

Shoving the paper to the center of the table, he stood, shaking his head. It was unlike him to draw a blank. *The best thing to do,* he thought, *is to sleep on it. I'll eventually figure it out.* He returned to the computer and logged back into the ANT system.

~

Disconnecting his call with Sam, Luke looked up at Raj. "I just don't get it."

"What's that?" Raj asked.

"I still don't get how a man who's worked hard building a career his entire life, can just walk away from it like that."

"You must be talking about George?" Raj replied, "No one's heard from him?"

Luke shook his head, "No, not a word. It's like he's dropped off the face of the earth. I hope nothing's happened to him."

"Sam fired him months ago," Raj pointed out. "You can't expect him stay in town without a job. I doubt there are too many opportunities for neuroscientists in Green River, Wyoming."

"I suppose you're right." Luke saw the logic in it. "I just can't figure out what went wrong. I'd ask him myself, but he's moved out of his house, to who knows where? His phone was disconnected. He hasn't spoken to Sam since he was let go from SIA. I certainly don't blame Sam for any of this. He merely acted as he needed for the benefit of the company. I would have done the same. Maybe it's just my curiosity, but I care about what happens to him. We've been friends for a long time."

"If he wants to be found," Raj pointed out, "he will be." Try sending him a letter by mail. Then you'll know if he left a forwarding address with the post office."

"How'd you get to be such a wise man?" Luke asked, "That's exactly what I'll do."

~

It had been almost a week and George was lost, still no closer to finding a solution. Even though he thought about it often, the list that he'd placed on the table was still blank. He ran down the stairs to begin his morning jog. It gave him the opportunity to clear his mind and provided him with the time to think. He was happy and embraced how complete he felt with Holly in his life. The worry he had, that the equipment could fail, was a valid concern. Even worse, if the equipment failed, he would lose access to Holly and the life they shared together forever.

Wouldn't it be nice, he thought, *if Luke was actually out of the picture? That would be perfect*. He imagined Luke clenching his chest while falling over from an apparent heart attack. *If he were out of the picture, I'd have direct access to Holly in this world. I could be there for her. To help her pick up the pieces of her broken life. She'd fall in love with me all over again, just like she has already done. I know it would work, but there's Luke, healthy as an ox. Nothing like that would ever happen to him.*

A sinister thought crossed his mind, *Maybe I could help? Help him have an accident.*

He immediately came back to his senses, but was unable to let go of that one menacing thought. A seed had been planted, and he wasn't able to dig it up to get rid of it.

George talked to himself during the final ten minutes of his jog. He rationalized that he had always been a fine upstanding citizen, and had been raised a Christian. One does not take the life of another for *any* reason. It's just not done. Besides, he had the personality of a man who in good conscience, could never actually go through with something like that anyhow, so why even think about it. "You're just wasting your time George," he said to himself.

It would be ingenious though, a clever way to have Holly all to myself forever. If Luke were to have an accident because of something like his brakes failing, no one would be the wiser.

"Stop it!" he shouted as he passed a man who was sitting on a park bench wondering what he had just done wrong. He continued to mutter to himself along the way, "You are not that kind of man. Luke is your friend. It's not in your DNA. It's outside of your limitations."

He began to wonder what his *limitations* really were. *How far would I honestly go? How can that even be measured? If I had a gun, could I actually shoot someone? Probably not. What if that someone was going to cause me physical harm or try to kill me? Absolutely, I could. That's different. It's justifiable. What if someone was stealing from me? No, I don't think so. What if someone was causing harm to my family or someone I love? Once again... justifiable. I would protect them.*

After clearing his mind, George returned to his apartment. He felt refreshed and had gotten out most of his frustrations. He grabbed his mail and continued inside.

The mail consisted of two letters. One was an offer for a supplemental life insurance policy, which promptly landed in the trash. The other however was from Luke. He placed it on the table and looked at it for a few minutes, wondering what he could possibly have to say to him. "Had he seen me at the home center?" Or even worse yet, "Does he know about my relationship with Holly? Only one way to find out." He opened the letter.

Dear George,

I hope this letter finds you well. No one's heard from you in months and we've been wondering what you've been up to. Holly and Raj said to tell you hello.

As you know after the accident last year, we had to postpone our wedding because I couldn't walk. The physical therapy took longer than we expected. I'm through it now. The doctor says I'm fit as a fiddle (whatever that means). To us that means that the wedding is back on track and moving forward. We'll be sending invitations out in the next five or six weeks.

Holly and I would both love to see you attend. It's hard to put into words how much I absolutely love her. I sincerely hope you can make it.

Let's not lose touch like we did before.

Your friend,
Luke

He folded the letter and stuffed it back into the envelope. Deeply pondering the whole idea, he began to tap his finger on the table. After a few minutes, he noticed the blank paper that he had intended to use as a list to solve his current dilemma, one that had become even more crucial upon reading Luke's letter. He slid the paper over, picked up his pen, and wrote on it. Pushing himself away from the table, he grabbed an apple from a plastic bag and took a bite. Robotically, he returned back to the computer and logged on.

The list that had been blank for almost a week, now had two words written on it. Two words that defined a plan. Two words that would give George the direction he needed to fix everything. Two words that would become his call to action.

Kill Luke!

CHAPTER 22

Twice a year Luke was required to travel to Washington, D.C., to meet with the Lottery Oversite Committee. It was the first week in July, and *this* would be the final day of his week-long trip. He finished up all of the procedural meetings, and had concluded with his detailed report to Congress earlier that day. At first, he found it intimidating to speak before Congress. It was awe-inspiring to be standing in the same room where presidents and dignitaries had delivered history altering speeches, and where the future history of the country was being molded daily, with the passage of each bill. Luke felt that in some small way he had contributed to this history through the *state of the lottery* reports. After repeating this exercise a few times, he found himself becoming more comfortable and at ease.

Holly was proud of Luke. She swelled with pride, as she watched from the public gallery located in the balcony above.

They had both been to Washington several times, always finding something new and interesting to see. On this trip it would be the National Building Museum. They were both fascinated with architecture, and had been on several trips to Europe, touring some of the many castles planted along the valleys and peppered into the mountainsides.

Luke had even proposed to Holly at Neuschwanstein Castle in Bavaria, Germany.

Holly, with her insatiable thirst for facts and statistics, picked up a museum brochure as soon as they were inside. "It says here that the Great Hall is over three hundred and sixteen feet long."

"Are you sure?" Luke questioned. "That's longer than a football field."

"The support columns must give an illusion that it's not that big," She said. "Just look at us, we're like ants in here."

The Corinthian columns were among the tallest in the world, and served not only to support the roof, but to divide the Grand Hall into three separate courts. Natural light entered from the windows above, flooding the vast floor below. Spanning twenty-eight feet across, a fountain stood in the center of the hall, consisting of the original terra cotta trim from the 1880's.

"This would be a great place to use one of Sam's cameras," Luke observed. "The size alone is overwhelming. The style of architecture is unbelievable." They sat on the floor at the base of one of the columns, waiting for the next tour to begin.

"It states here that the ceiling is one hundred and fifty-nine feet at its highest point," Holly quoted as she scanned the brochure.

Several minutes later, a small group gathered at an information desk, and the tour began. Luke found the exhibition on concrete to be especially fascinating. On display were several variations of the material with differing textures and densities. Each one had been used for a specific purpose. There were two samples so unique that they hooked him immediately. The first, was a sample of concrete that would actually float. It was buoyant, lighter than water. He didn't know that such a thing existed. Even more fascinating, was a wall that had been made out of *Transparent Concrete*. At least that's what they called it. It didn't have the appearance of being invisible at all. It could be seen and it looked like any other concrete wall. But when a light source illuminated from the opposite side, it could be seen shining through. Holly passed along the side that contained the light and Luke could see her shadow just as if it had been shining through a thin curtain. Further discussion with the tour guide explained how this was accomplished. When the wall was poured, hundreds of tiny fiber optic strands were added to the mold. The result was a solid concrete wall which allowed light to pass through it. Luke wondered how it could be incorporated into traditional building designs.

After the tour, they met Holly's parents for dinner. As they made their way toward their preselected restaurant, Holly had an uneasy feeling that they were being watched.

The sign proudly displayed in front of the old colonial-styled building read, *'Franklin's'*. Established in nineteen-twenty as a locally owned bar and grill, it specialized in American cuisine. The walls were covered with portraits of Benjamin Franklin. Famous quotes were scattered about, purportedly coming from the mind of the infamous politician through one of his many publications,

Poor Richard's Almanac. A pair of bifocals were encased in a shadow box claiming to be one of the many inventions produced by Franklin.

Holly's father, General John McBride, the head of logistics for the Marine Air Corps, worked in the Pentagon. His role was to identify and track the location of every Marine aircraft at all times. His team also developed strategies for tracking oversees deployment of these expensive government assets. Holly just called him Daddy. Her mother, Miriam, took care of things at home and had recently published a cookbook full of recipes she had collected in their many travels from around the world. Even though she was a relatively shy person, she had recently attended her first book signing event.

After the meal arrived, the general inquired, "How are the wedding plans progressing?"

Holly tilted her head to the side, "Wedding?"

"Yes," Luke interrupted, "didn't I tell you that I was marrying the most beautiful woman in the world?" He leaned in, touching his head against hers.

"Um, you might have mentioned it." The truth was that she just loved to hear him say it. She also felt that they were the perfect match for each other.

Her parents liked him as well. Luke was one of the few people who'd ever had the permission to call the general by his nickname, 'Big Mac'. He had a lot of respect for Luke even if he was only a civilian.

"I must admit," Luke said, taking Holly's hand, "I feel guilty for not spending more time on the plans with you."

"Nonsense," Holly replied. "We discussed this and I have it well under control. My sister Hannah will be on leave next week. We have plans to hook up with Marilyn to go into the city and pick out the dress, meet with our event planner, and then the caterer. We'll also pick out a design for the cake and ice sculpture. I've been in contact with a couple of entertainment candidates as well. I've got it all mapped out in this." She held up her daily calendar/planner. "This goes with me everywhere."

"I'm impressed," Luke said. "Maybe *you* should have been a project manager."

As they chatted, Luke began to feel a sharp pain in his stomach. Apparently, he'd eaten something that hadn't agreed with him. He began to look pale, and Miriam noticed his discomfort. "Are you okay?"

"Must have been something I ate. Just give me a few minutes, I'll be fine."

But that wasn't to be the case. He continued to feel worse. He began sweating and leaned his head against the back of the booth. Holly began to worry. She hadn't seen him sick before. He'd always been healthy and strong.

The general spoke up, "Come on boy, I'll walk you to the rest room. You need some cold water on your face." He didn't have the best bed side manner, but his heart was in the right place.

As General McBride stood, Luke doubled over, clenching his abdomen. He winced in pain. He took a deep breath and doubled over again, this time rolling out of the booth and onto the floor. Miriam and Holly both raced to his side. They were at a loss, not knowing exactly what they should do. The general dialed 9-1-1. Patrons throughout the restaurant gawked to see what was happening. Some dropped their utensils and pushed their plates away, not knowing if they might be affected the same way.

Holly dabbed ice water from her drinking glass, and stroked it gently onto Luke's forehead and upper lip, in a futile attempt to keep his temperature down. Drenched in sweat, he began to shake and was becoming incoherent. Even though he was still able to detect that things were happening around him, they were becoming more distant and unclear. His eyes began to roll back as he fought to remain conscious.

Holly and her mother were both in tears by the time the paramedics arrived. They were asked to step aside and reluctantly obliged. Holly wanted to help, but finally came to the conclusion that the best way for her to help was to let the professionals do their job. Her mother held her as they watched.

After strapping him onto a gurney, they connected him to an IV, placed an oxygen mask over his nose, and wheeled him outside to an awaiting ambulance. People everywhere were straining to see what was happening. The kitchen door in the alley was held open a crack, as a pair of eyes peered at the unfolding scene in front of the building.

"You go with him," The general ordered Holly. "Mom and I will meet you at the hospital."

As the ambulance pulled away with the lights flashing and the siren wailing, the kitchen door flew open. George ran into the street. He too was beginning to feel nauseous, not because of anything he'd eaten, but because of what he'd just done. After all, Luke had been his friend, but he was convinced that he had been left with no choice. It just had to be this way. Undetected, he ran the opposite direction, down the narrow alley, disappearing into the night.

INTO THE MINDFIELD

CHAPTER 23

"To make our experiments more conclusive," Dr. Ackerman continued, "we needed to see similar results from other test subjects. Our second test subject was a thirty two year old female, who worked as an administrative assistant for one of the board members at the college. She also tested with an above average IQ. For this discussion, we'll refer to her as Jane." A picture of the woman appeared on the screen. "The results associated with data from this subject, we discovered, would be quite different than the subject we had previously observed. We were careful to perform each step *exactly* as it had been done on the first subject. The method of insertion was the same and the final location of the ANT device was confirmed to be affixed to the same position within the brain. Our results, however, would be dramatically different. Once images became available on the screen, we realized that we were looking at images that were completely different from what *she* was seeing. What we saw was a series of disturbing images that appeared to be from the subject's point of view, containing information thought to be from prior traumatic events that we suspected had happened at some point in her life. We believed that she had somehow slipped through our strict screening process. Events flashed by quickly, such as a head-on automobile crash, a man repeatedly striking her in the face, falling from the rooftop of a house, being trapped in a burning room, and an underwater scene where she was struggling to resurface. During this observation, the subject remained calm and seemed to be unaware that these events were being transmitted; directly transmitted from her brain."

Dr. Ackerman shuffled through his folder at the podium and found a report printed on yellow paper. He held it up for the audience to see. "Inside your packets," he proceeded, "you'll find a copy of the psycho-evaluation performed on Jane that afternoon. The interesting point here is that as she was being interviewed, she had no recollection that any of these events had ever taken place. The next step was to determine if she was masking these seemingly deep rooted traumatic events, or were we picking up images from her memory that had been generated from outside stimuli, such as scenes from a movie she had once watched."

"After some discussion, we decided to show her these images in real-time. This, we felt, would trigger her memory one way or the other. We were not even slightly prepared for what happened next. As the technician turned the display toward her, she had an immediate negative reaction. It started with an elevation of her heart rate and a surge in her adrenal levels. As the images passed by, she seemed to experience each event as they happened. She began to thrash around as if trying to protect her face from injury while she struggled for air. Then her arms and legs began to flail as she tried to find something to grab on to. It was as if she were trying to prevent herself from falling. Her body temperature was rising rapidly, as though it had an exterior heat source. She seemed to be experiencing each event as if they were all happening to her simultaneously. She was quickly sedated and after a few minutes was brought down to an acceptable level. We researched her medical records, but could find no signs of trauma or scarring on her body. After a few hours of sleep she was interviewed a second time. This time she remembered each event, but claimed that this was the first time she had ever seen these images. Nothing like this had ever happened in her past. She couldn't explain the terror she felt when they were presented to her. She had never experienced an episode like this before."

INTO THE MINDFIELD

CHAPTER 24

Back in Evergreen, Luke and Holly brought Raj up to date about the events that had occurred while in D.C.

"We waited for what seemed like forever before anyone came to talk to us. When the doctor finally arrived, I think I saw *Kevorkian* on his nametag," Holly chuckled.

"Dr. Death?" Luke interrupted, "the guy who helped people commit suicide? Good grief, I'm glad it wasn't him. This guy's name was Dr. Kovovetz."

"Okay," she said, rolling her eyes, "Dr. *Kovovetz* came in and told us that Luke had been poisoned. They pumped his stomach and filled him with fluid to help flush it out. I asked if they knew what kind of poison it was. He said it was likely something in the food, although no one else at the restaurant had complained of any symptoms. They won't know for sure until the toxicology report comes back."

"Sounds awful," Raj said. "I'm sure glad I didn't have to go through it."

"It was not pleasant, my friend." Luke confirmed, while patting him on the shoulder. "I don't *ever* want to experience anything like that again."

The doorbell rang. Holly ran to answer it. It was Hannah, Holly's twin sister. They were identical in almost every way. Only the keenest of eyes could tell them apart. For Luke, it was simple, Holly's hair flowed just past her shoulders while Hannah kept hers a bit shorter, and she had a few more freckles.

Holly rarely got the opportunity to see her sister since she'd enlisted in the Marines several years earlier. The day they became of age, she and Holly visited the recruiter's office and signed their commitment papers together. They had both planned to make a lifelong career of it, just as their father had done, but Holly retired after winning the lottery. Hannah refused an offer from Holly to retire along with her. She was committed to finishing what she had started.

Raj had never met Hannah, but he felt like he had just been cast under some kind of wizard's spell. He couldn't help himself from staring at her. It was like looking at Holly through an ancient mystical mirror that duplicated not just images; but duplicated actual people. Oh sure, he'd met twins before, but it was strange to see a carbon copy of a close friend, someone he'd known for a long time. "Weird," he whispered to Luke.

Like many twins throughout history, Holly and Hannah were mischievous at times. When they were children, they'd often play tricks, targeting easy unsuspecting prey. One would find an innocent victim and fool him into believing she could do magnificent feats. Pretending to be a magician, Holly would duck behind a chair or sofa on one end of the room, only to have Hannah appear at the opposite end. They'd laugh for hours recounting the blank looks that appeared on their targeted victim's faces, who, up until this point, had remained completely unaware that Holly was actually a twin. Now they were both older and more mature, each focused on a life of her own. Oh sure, they were still connected as sisters, they always would be. All through their teenage years, their mother, Miriam, joked about how interchangeable they were. She'd say, "They were fungible, with the primary emphasis on FUN". A common trait they shared was that no matter how long they'd been apart, it would only take a minute to re-bond and pick up where they had last left off. "The chattering shall now commence," Luke whispered back to Raj.

After the initial greeting, Holly introduced Hannah to Raj, who responded with a gentlemanly handshake. Luke, who had met her previously on at least three other occasions, held out his hand as well. She pushed it to the side almost knocking Luke off balance and zeroed in for a hug. "We're family now," Hannah said, "well, almost."

She turned to Holly, "So, do I get a tour of this place or what?"

She had the same pleasant, outgoing personality as Holly, and Luke knew how happy they both were to be able to spend the week together. Holly grabbed her by the arm and quickly led her down the hall.

As the cab drove away, Luke noticed that Hannah's bags had been neatly stacked in a pile near the center of the courtyard.

"Give me a hand?" he asked, as he stepped out the front door. Without answering, Raj followed suit.

The next morning they gathered in the kitchen. Holly and Hannah were discussing their plans for the day. It would be a day of preparation for the upcoming wedding. It was particularly special for Holly because she had never gotten to experience the big fancy wedding that she'd dreamed of since she was little. She'd play with her dolls and set up their wedding scene, but never actually had the opportunity to experience it for herself. She had been married before, but her wedding to Eric took place on a base in Afghanistan. It was not exactly what she had imagined when she was young. Now she had the opportunity to do it right and had the budget to pull it off.

Holly and Luke were to be married in less than three months. It had been originally scheduled a year earlier, but was postponed due to Luke's accident. After months of therapy, Luke was back to his old self again and the wedding was back on the calendar. They were both excited to finally have their day of commitment, for all of their friends and family to witness.

It had been a fairy tale story for Holly. She often referred to Luke as her handsome prince. Certainly he thought of her as his princess, but he saw many layers beyond that. There was the first layer, the surface layer. There'd be no argument, she was strikingly beautiful, and very pleasant to look at. Her facial features resembled those of an expensive limited edition doll, which would be the envy of most any collector. Also, being in great physical condition, she remained diligent with her daily exercise regime, and kept a close watch on her diet. The end result was a body that resembled a finely crafted work of art. Over the years, she'd become accustomed to men, and women alike, staring at her as she passed by, but it was all new to Luke. When he was with her, he was as proud as any man could be. He was well grounded and never egotistical, but there were times he'd give a nod to those gawkers, as if to say, "Yeah, she's with me."

The second layer of beauty, was her mind. She was intelligent and thoughtful, always wanting to do what's right, believing that far too many people had lost that ability. She was an impeccable sounding board for Luke, offering him objective opinions and new ideas. She was witty and smart, and knew how to use those skills to make everyone around her feel happy and welcome. To Luke, her mind was equally as beautiful as her outward appearance.

Then, there was the third layer, her heart. It was no secret that she had a soft spot for children, especially children who had been hospitalized. She'd seen the fear in their eyes as they wondered what was happening to them, or if they'd ever be well again. She saw their tears when they learned the details of their disease, desperately struggling to understand if they'd even survive. It was this passion that caused her and Luke to create a charitable foundation in support of these kids. Not only had they personally managed it, they donated one million dollars to it annually. For all of these reasons, Luke knew that under every layer, she was the perfect woman. To live up to his vision of her, he strived to be a better man.

The doorbell rang. "That must be Marilyn," Holly said, as she made her way to answer it. Today, was to be a girls' day out. Holly had created a long list of items that she expected to complete. They'd meet with the caterer and spend the day shopping at the many stores and boutiques scattered throughout downtown Denver. This day was particularly exciting, because this was to be *the* day. The day she would select her wedding gown.

In a hurry, Holly kissed Luke goodbye, "Gotta run!" The girls headed into the courtyard and excitedly piled into the awaiting Mustang. Hannah chose the back seat, allowing Marilyn to ride *shotgun*. As they drove down the long winding lane and onto the street below, they discussed where they'd have lunch while in the city. No one paid any attention to the old Pontiac sitting along the side of the street. To them it was just an old broken down car. As they drove by, George crouched deep into the seat trying to remain undetected. He looked into the mirror and watched as the Mustang vanished out of sight.

~

Luke and Raj planned to spend the day in the garage, preparing the Porsche for the race that was to be held the following weekend. After that, they intended to survey Luke's latest acquisition, a 1933 Packard Twelve. In need of total restoration, they'd create a parts list of items that were in restorable condition. Another list would be used to identify and track new versus used parts that must be either located or custom made.

Luke received a tip from a man he met at a regional car show about an old car he'd seen in a barn near Aspen. He hadn't been sure of the make or model, but it had obviously impressed him enough to want to talk about it, even to total strangers. Car show participants heard stories like this regularly, and for the most part they shared in the conversation, then usually didn't give it another thought. Luke was conversing as usual, but it wasn't until the man began to explain what the car looked like, that his ears perked up.

"I went to look at this 1963 Studebaker Hawk," the man said, identifying himself as Herbert Renshaw. "I saw this ad explainin' it was all original and had less than ten thousand miles on it. Shoot, that's not something you read every day. I figured I better check it out."

"I certainly would have," Luke replied, in agreement.

"So I go out there, and I meet up with this eighty-three year old guy." Herbert continued, "Richard was his name, but he wanted to be called Buck. So I called him Buck. He took me out to a barn at the back of his property. Way back! Seemed like we wasn't ever goin' to get there. We go inside and there I see about fifteen old cars, all kinds of makes and models. I check out the Studebaker. When he said it was original, he wasn't just blowin' smoke. Shoot, it still had the original tires on it. Two of them still had air in them. Do you believe that?"

"That certainly sounds impressive," Luke said, engaging in polite conversation. "I assume you bought it?"

"You bet your boots I did. I took it with me that day. I'm thinkin' I'll go back and get another one. He had an old Desoto I put my eye on. I think I'll get that next. He had a few older cars, like from the thirties. They didn't interest me that much, I don't do anything older than 1948."

"Ah," Luke replied, "You're a post-war collector. What else did he have?"

"I don't know what it was, but he had this *big honkin'* car. I figured it was built somewhere in the thirties. It had wire wheels on it. Much older than that, it would have been wooden spoke. Newer, it might have had steel wheels or hub caps." The man continued, "It was a pretty thing, kind of off white, course it was kinda hard to tell through all the dirt. I knew it wasn't something I was interested in, but couldn't help lookin' at it. It had these big fenders that swooped back into the running board. The interesting part was the spare tires. There were two of them, one mounted on each side, kinda half stuck in the fender. Oh, and the mirrors were strapped onto the tires. I thought that was kinda odd."

That was it, the words that got Luke's attention. "Mirrors strapped onto the tires." That description could fit a number of pre-war classics, but few had spares on both sides of the car and even fewer had the mirrors mounted on them. He knew that there would be something special about it. Herbert wrote down Buck's phone number. Luke made a call and met up with him the next day.

"He must have been talking about my Packard," Buck said. "It's been in the family since it was new. It hasn't seen the light of day in lord knows how long, since I was a young man myself. Maybe fifty years ago. I'm retiring and need to clear out some of this stuff. My wife's had some health issues and can't take the cold winters anymore, so we're headed to Arizona."

He unlocked the door, and they walked inside. Luke noticed it immediately, partially tarped in the far back corner. Rays shooting from between the slats of the wooden barn siding, striped the old car in light. His excitement rose. It was indeed a Packard, 1933 to be precise. Known as the Packard Twelve, it was powered by a V-12 engine that was housed under a hood that had to be at least half the length of the entire car. It was a two seat convertible with an added *rumble* seat in the rear. At the far rear, a steel rack held a trunk. It had the appearance of an old steamer trunk, but had been factory built and painted to match the exterior color of the car. Luke spit on his thumb and rubbed on a section of the paint hoping to expose its true color. It was a creamy off white, one of sophistication and elegance, reserved for only the most elite of brands. Extremely rare for the period.

It wasn't until after Luke made the purchase and returned home, that he realized just how rare this car truly was. His research had shown that only fifty Packard Twelve convertibles were ever built. Of these, only sixteen were known to survive. *I know of at least one more,* he chuckled.

INTO THE MINDFIELD

CHAPTER 25

They'd been getting a lot of their tasks completed, and were having a wonderful time doing it. Holly always enjoyed her time with Marilyn, but today she had her sister as well. She was elated and couldn't have asked for a better day, even the weather was perfect. The meeting with the caterer flew by quicker than expected, so they decided on a little shopping before lunch. Two doors from the restaurant stood *Stone's Jewelers,* a family owned business, now in its thirty-seventh year. They decided to check it out. Holly had already selected the jewelry that she would wear for the wedding, but Marilyn and Hannah, as her maids of honor, were still looking for that one special item that was *just right.* Following tradition, Holly would pay for this piece of course, but she would let each woman make her own selection. She felt that it would be much more personal for them if they did. Marilyn decided upon a diamond chipped locket. Its entire face sparkled in the light. Most lockets of this type, she had found, consisted of a single heart in which photos could be placed in each half. This one was different. It was designed as a double heart, with room when opened, for a single photo on one side and for an engraving on the other. *Besides,* Marilyn thought, *it will be perfect with the gown.*

Hannah looked, but didn't commit. She wanted to check out a few other stores before making her final decision.

They all ordered a salad for lunch and laughed about how eating this *one* salad could possibly make any difference whatsoever for them to look their best on the day of the wedding.

"Being in the wedding party," Marilyn began. "Or should I say as the *old maid* of honor, we've got some things we need to discuss."

"Oh stop it," Holly insisted, while lightly smacking the back of her hand.

"We need to talk about the bachelorette party," Marilyn said. "As of now, I don't have many ideas." She had ruled out the traditional drinking and male strippers; that was for a different crowd. Besides, she wanted to come up with something extra special for her best friend.

"Oh, I've got it!" Hannah shouted. "Once when we were around fourteen, our mom took us to a horse farm. We spent an entire week riding and learning to take care of the animals, remember?"

"That was a great time," Holly replied. "I remember bugging mom for a horse for weeks after that, but we just didn't have a place for one, not on the Marine base."

Hannah looked at Marilyn, "She even cried when it was time to go home. I must admit, I had grown fond of those horses as well, and felt sad leaving the farm."

"Horses?" Holly said, "I didn't cry because of the horses. It was the cute boys on the ranch that I didn't want to leave behind."

They all burst into laughter.

"I've never ridden a horse," Marilyn said with a concerned look washing across her face. "I wouldn't know how."

"They'll teach you," Holly said, "You'll love it, I promise. Although I'll warn you in advance, you'll feel a bit stiff the next day."

"Then we'll need to follow up with one of *my* favorite activities," insisted Marilyn. "A massage and day spa."

"Perfect," Holly confirmed. "Let's make it a two day event, just the three of us."

Hannah had been thinking about the locket and asked Marilyn if she could see it again. "Why a locket?" she asked.

"Simple," Marilyn replied, "I'll put a picture of Luke and Holly in here and engrave the date over here. That will be a keepsake I'll treasure forever."

"Oh my God," Hannah said, as the bulb lit. "I hadn't thought of that. What an awesome idea. I'm going back to Stone's to get one after lunch."

After finishing their meals, Holly and Marilyn decided to stop by the church to pick up a pre-marriage counseling package from the minister while Hannah would swing by the jewelers only two doors down. It should only take each of them a few minutes because the church was only two blocks away. They decided to meet up at the car which had been conveniently parked between them.

As they walked toward the church, they passed an alley where a few unsavory characters appeared to be using it as a place to hang out. They began shouting lewd comments and whistling at the two women as they made their way down the street.

"You girls lookin' for a good time?" one said. "I got just what you need."

"Just keep walking," Holly whispered to Marilyn.

"Hey," he yelled. "I'm talkin' to you stuck up bitches. I said, I can show you a good time."

They kept walking, offering no acknowledgement.

Dashing out of the alley, the men ran at them from an angle that would purposely cut off their path on the sidewalk. There were four men in total now surrounding them. Two were on the sidewalk directly in front, and two were behind. One man, who appeared to be the leader of the obnoxious foursome, was particularly large, standing around six foot, six inches tall. He appeared to be covered in tattoos from head to toe, including some questionable artwork residing on his shaven head. He was acting like a textbook tough guy, but Holly could tell that it was all for show, most likely just to impress his buddies. Being familiar with years of actual hand-to-hand combat, she observed that he had little muscle mass in his long lanky arms, and that he was overweight to the point of his belly lapping over his belt. Personal hygiene was non-existent. Holly could smell his stench from over six feet away.

"What is it that you fine gentlemen would like to discuss?" Holly asked, attempting to defuse the situation.

"I would like," he paused. No one had actually ever asked him that before. "I would like to show you bitches a good time."

"And what does a *good time* look like with you?" she questioned.

Once again he paused. The fact was, he hadn't ever thought about it. "A good time is, you and me, back in that alley, takin' care of business." He winked at his buddies, chuckled, and stepped in closer. He wasn't preparing to back down and Holly knew this altercation showed signs that it could escalate to the next level.

"What kind of business do you run back there?" she calmly asked, pretending not to understand what he meant.

He was starting to become agitated. He had expected her to be intimidated by him and that she'd do as she was told. "You are just going to have to go back there to see." He took another step.

As politely as she could, Holly made yet another attempt to end the confrontation, "Well, thank you very much for your offer, but my friend and I have a lot to do today, and just don't have the time. Perhaps another day?"

He didn't intend to take *no* for an answer. Reaching behind him, he pulled a .38 caliber semi-automatic pistol from his belt. "I said we are going to have a good time."

"Take it easy Moose!" the man to his right shouted.

Upon seeing the gun, Holly immediately stepped in front of Marilyn. "Are you sure you want to do this?"

"You'll do what I say," he responded. "Now, hands where I can see them and turn around."

She complied as instructed. Now facing Marilyn, her hands were raised with her purse hanging from the thumb of her left hand, and a shopping bag hanging from the right.

"And you too," he ordered Marilyn, as he shoved the muzzle of the gun into Holly's back.

Marilyn just stood there. She knew that things were about to get ugly. She'd seen Holly in a similar situation and sort of felt bad for the man's ignorance. He had no idea what was about to happen to him.

Holly looked at Marilyn, "Is he in my *personal* space?" Marilyn nodded in the affirmative. "I hate when someone comes into my personal space without being invited." She winked. That was the signal for Marilyn to get ready. Holly released the purse and shopping bag simultaneously while stepping back and spinning to the right deflecting the barrel of the gun away from them. Marilyn grabbed the bags before they hit the ground, swinging them in the opposite direction, using them as a makeshift weapon. She made contact with each of the men standing behind her, impacting their faces, causing them to lose balance. Holly jammed her right elbow to the inside of the assailants' arm and used her other hand to grip the top of the gun. It fired, landing a bullet into the shin of one of the two that were standing behind Marilyn. He fell, screaming in pain. Because Holly had gripped the gun around the slide mechanism *before* it was fired, it couldn't cock. It would not be fired again until it could be manually pulled back to load another bullet into the chamber. With his index finger still inside the trigger guard, Holly used the gun as a lever to break his finger. He released his grip and the gun fell. Screaming in pain, he backed up two steps. The man standing beside him lunged toward her. She spun completely around with her leg extended. As she did, Marilyn dropped to the sidewalk to scoop up the gun. Holly's foot landed directly in the center of the man's face, promptly breaking his nose. He dropped to his knees, both hands now covering his face. Moose, the big, bald smelly guy with the broken finger, attempted to punch Holly in the face. She pulled back and cupped her hand around his fist, redirecting the blow downward, while using the other hand to apply pressure against his elbow. Maintaining her grip, she circled around behind him. She felt the pressure release as his arm snapped, and he too fell to the ground.

The one remaining, and only uninjured thug, was now frozen in place. He wasn't sure what to do. He'd just seen the toughest guy he'd ever known get his ass kicked.... by a girl no less. He raised his hands into the air and cried, "Truce." Holly took an aggressive step toward him. He turned and ran in the opposite direction. *Pouring on the coal,* he sprinted at full speed for at least two blocks before slowing, feeling certain that he was at a safe distance. He took a break to catch his breath while leaning against a light post in front of a local store, *Stone Jewelers*. Hannah stepped through the doorway. Panic once again surged through his veins immediately upon seeing her. This was now a familiar face to him, one which would forever represent imminent danger. He bolted, running as fast as he could, while screaming, until he was completely out of sight.

That was weird, Hannah thought.

"Well, Mr. Moose," Holly said, "I suppose an apology is in order."

"Sorry, lady!" he shouted, while cradling his arm, sitting on the edge of the sidewalk. He was thoroughly disgusted with himself for letting this woman emasculate him in public. Until this incident, this had been *his* territory. *He* was the one who called the shots. It was he and his minions who were in control. Once word got around about this, his reputation would be lost for certain.

"Oh no," she said. "It is *I* who should apologize to *you*."

He looked at her with a blank stare, wondering what the hell she was talking about.

"You certainly *do* know how to show a girl a good time. I had a lot of fun."

CHAPTER 26

It had been two weeks since his return from D.C. George realized that although it had been an excellent plan, it had failed miserably. Luke had survived. He'd wasted a great deal of time planning for it, and faced numerous expenses that had not been intended as part of his grand budget. They would have been justified, of course, had the trip been a success. But it hadn't been. Time and money had been wasted, with nothing to show for it. *All Luke got from it was a stupid tummy ache*, he grumbled, as he envisioned the level of sympathy Holly must have poured over him. George knew that Holly was a compassionate, caring person, who would have done anything for Luke to make him feel better. He shuddered. It was a distasteful notion.

George was now on a new mission. His decision had been made. There was no other choice available to him, but to see it through. He didn't dare try poison again, as that would most certainly raise unwanted suspicion. It had to look like an accident. He also knew that for this plan to work in his favor, Holly must never learn of his involvement. If she suspected that George had anything to do with it, she'd shun him for sure. He'd not be able to play the part of the hero who came to her side when she most needed one. He began to daydream about how wonderful their lives would be together. Just as they shared their love for one another in the *other* world, they would be able to in this world as well.

His head was pounding as he downed two extra-strength aspirins. Thinking about what to do, and what not to do, had produced a whopper of a headache. He knew that Holly would help alleviate the pressure. He logged onto the ANT and found himself stretched out on the sofa.

"There you are," Holly said. "I've been looking all over for you, and here you are taking a nap, you sleepy bear." She knelt beside him.

"I'm not napping," he replied. "I've just got a headache and thought I'd lie down for a while."

"Poor baby, let me help you. Is it here?" She kissed his temple.

"No."

"Here?" She planted a soft gentle kiss on his forehead.

"No."

"How about here?" She said, as she kissed the tip of is nose.

"Not there either," he moaned.

"Then it must be here," she said seductively, as she traced the tip of her finger around his mouth. She licked her lips and leaned in for a kiss.

By this time George had completely forgotten about his headache. He was now caught up in the moment. Lured in by Holly's affectionate behavior, he sat up, grabbed her hand, and led her into the bedroom. She giggled the entire way, "But George, I thought you weren't feeling well."

"I'm cured," he said. "It's a miracle!" He scooped her into the air and tossed her onto the bed. She held her arms wide open, reaching toward him, inviting him in.

Two hours later, they remained naked, cuddling under the sheets.

"I want your thoughts on something," George asked.

"Anything," she rolled over to face him. "But you do have a tendency to make good girls have *bad* thoughts." She smiled and gave him another quick peck on the lips.

"Oh, it's no big deal," he said. "I was just wondering something."

"Okay, fire away."

"With your extensive military experience in the Marine Special Forces," he hesitated, "have you ever actually killed anyone?"

"What an odd question," she answered as she sat up. "Why do you ask?"

"I was just wondering what it was like."

"Well, yes," she hesitantly replied, seeming to worry that George would somehow think less of her for it. "It was my job. It was what I had trained for most of my life. Although women weren't permitted in the Marine Special Operations Command, I was given an exception. I had won multiple national competitions in martial arts. My skills were advanced well beyond the other new recruits. My father's influence as a commander didn't hurt either. It was decided that I could fill a niche area, which allowed me to infiltrate people and places that the guys were not exactly equipped to, if you know what I mean. I was very effective. So yes, I killed people."

"How many?" George was still inquisitive.

Holly took a deep breath and held it for a second. With her eyes closed, she slowly replied, "Seven," she paused, "teen." She opened one eye to see if George had been appalled by what he'd just heard. She seemed to be afraid that it may scare him off.

But it didn't, he was more interested now than ever. "So, tell me," he asked. "If you wanted to kill someone, how would you go about it?"

"Every situation was different," she replied. "We'd gather intelligence to find a pattern allowing us to predict where the target would be on a specific day and time. Then we'd plan our operation around that. We had contingency plans in the event any of our assumptions turned out to be wrong. It was the same routine each time. There were only a couple of times I can recall not being successful. That was only because the target never showed up where we expected he'd be."

"Did you ever have to dispose of a body?" George inquired. It was a dark topic for him, but kind of exciting too.

"Sometimes," she seemed bewildered by where this line of questioning was taking her. "There were times when we were instructed to eliminate the body because of concern that the target would be used as a martyr. That could have the reverse effect, resulting in more violence instead of less."

Still prying, George asked, "What's the best way to hide a body so it would never be found?"

"I suppose you would take it to a remote location and bury it," she said. "The more remote, the better. Hey, why all the questions? Are you afraid I might try to get rid of you and bury your body?"

"Something like that," he followed with a fake chuckle.

"Well, don't you worry your handsome self about it," she said as she wrapped her arms tightly around him. "I don't *ever* intend to let you go."

Later that evening, after Holly was sound asleep, George removed the X-Specs and logged off the system. He walked over to the flaking and rotted counter top to fix a cup of coffee. He picked up his pen and jotted on the notepad that sat near the edge of the table. *Number one*, he started. *Know where your target will be.* This made sense. He had previously followed Luke all the way to Washington, like some kind of deranged stalker. It was strictly by chance that he found an opportunity to act. What he needed now was information, or to devise a plan that would put Luke exactly where he wanted him to be. *Number two*, he wrote. *The more remote, the better.* An unassuming Holly had provided him with simple, yet valuable advice. She was not even slightly aware that George intended to use what he'd learned to eliminate Luke. From her perspective, Luke was already dead.

The following morning, with a newly devised plan in hand, he dialed the phone.

It was answered. "This is Luke."

"Luc-ass," George replied. He needed to act as if nothing were wrong, but had to be careful not to overplay his hand.

There was an awkward pause, "George?"

"Yeah, it's me. I thought I'd check in to see what you've been up to."

"Same old stuff," Luke replied, "but what about you? Nobody's heard from you in almost a year. You just dropped off of the radar. Sam couldn't even tell me what happened."

George had a plan, but hadn't considered that anyone would ask questions. He wasn't sure what to tell him. He certainly couldn't tell Luke that he'd been living in his house, driving his cars and sleeping with Holly. He needed time to think this through.

"I guess I was going through some personal stuff," George ambiguously replied. "We should get together and I'll tell you all about it." *That's the way to approach it*, he thought. *Ha... still able to think on my feet.*

"Sure, maybe we could meet for lunch somewhere," Luke suggested. He was more than a little curious about why George had abandoned his job and moved away.

"Why don't we just make a day of it?" George replied, "I know this place up in the mountains about twenty miles from Walden. We could do some rafting on the North Platte River."

"I haven't been in a raft in what seems like forever," Luke said. It was odd that he hadn't heard from George in months, and now, here he was, acting like nothing had ever been wrong, like no time had passed, and that it was just another day. "I don't know, George."

"Come on," George begged. "It'll be fun."

"I guess I could carve out a day," Luke hesitantly replied. "I'll call Sam. We can all go together."

"NO!" George shouted abruptly. He panicked at the idea that someone else might be there. He knew what needed to be done and couldn't have any witnesses.

Luke was surprised by George's abruptness, "Did you and Sam have some kind of falling out? I hadn't heard anything from him that would lead me to think that."

Drawing a blank, George replied, "I'll tell you all about it when we meet."

Accepting it as a reasonable response, Luke agreed to take the trip. They set a date and decided to meet at Northgate Canyon.

Perfect, George thought, as they ended the call. He had followed Holly's advice to the letter. He now knew where his target would be, when he would be there, and had arranged to meet him in an extremely remote area.

~

After days of nervous anticipation, the time for the trip had arrived. It would be a trip with ill-fated consequences for one Mr. Luke Monroe. George was not looking forward to performing the deed he was required to do, but *was* looking forward to consoling Holly and to receiving all of the benefits resulting from his kindness. It was simply a task that needed to be done, one that would finally set the universe straight.

At an elevation of eight thousand feet, the road narrowed and the old Pontiac Firebird entered the Northgate Canyon. It was approximately forty miles north of the Rocky Mountain National Park. Running north, along the Medicine Bow Mountain range was the North Platte River. It was cited as one of the most scenic class-four rivers in the United States. As he pulled into the parking area, George saw a black Porsche Cayenne with Luke sitting comfortably behind the wheel. He rolled up beside him. Luke lowered the window, but George was unable to respond with the same simple task. His window, much like a number of other items on his car, didn't work. He opened the door a few inches and craned his neck backward. "Hey buddy, are you ready for this?"

"Let's go," Luke replied. "The weather's perfect." It was expected to reach a high of eighty-five degrees in the late afternoon, which was a perfect day to navigate down the river in the cool mountain water.

Luke stepped out of his car, "Where on earth did you find that clunker?" referring to his old beater. Luke never imagined that George would ever be caught dead in a disgrace like this. He'd always been a rather classy guy.

"It was cheap," George said. "I haven't worked since I left SIA."

Luke was aghast, "You haven't worked for a year? How are you getting by?"

"No problem," he explained, "I have plenty in savings, and I've drastically cut back on my lifestyle."

"*Apparently,*" Luke said, once again pointing at the car.

"Come on, let's get our gear." George was eager to get this over with. He had been thinking it through for days. He imagined how it should be choreographed. Everything had to be staged perfectly for it to appear as an accident.

They selected a two-man raft, after declining a river guide that had been assigned to assist them. There were two styles of oars. One was constructed of aluminum with paddles attached on both ends. It was best used by the person at the rear of the boat for the flexibility gained while steering. The other type was made of wood. It was much longer and heavier, equipped with a paddle on only one end. It was to be used for powering the boat in a forward motion. George selected this style. Even though it was in the process of being phased out by the rental company, there were still a few scattered about. The staff assisted them with their life vests and helmets. They pulled the raft to the water's edge and dropped it in. The staff then helped the two men into the boat and provided them with some last minute instructions. They pushed away from the dock and were soon captured by the current, sending them downstream.

"This is relaxing," Luke noted. "I'm glad you talked me into it."

Minutes later they entered the first set of rapids. They were milder than expected. George surmised it was likely because it was late summer and most of the heavy runoff from the melting snow had already cascaded down the mountain. What would have been labeled as a class-five rapid, at best, would only measure a three or four. *No matter*, he thought. *I still have a job to do, and I can use this to my advantage.*

To initiate his plan, he leveraged this fact and promptly removed his life vest and helmet. "Ah, that's much better," he said to Luke. "The sun feels great. You should do the same. This time of year, the water runs slow. That rapid we just went through was the worst one on the entire river, and you saw how mild it was." He showed Luke the river map.

With some apprehension for safety, Luke agreed with George's logic and soon followed his lead.

Excellent! George thought. The stage was now set. All he needed to do was wait. Only a few miles downriver, and it would be all over. He had studied that map every day since formulating this plan. The spot he had chosen for the deed was in a place known to the locals as *Cowpie Rapid.*

"Okay, so you haven't been working for the past year," Luke wondered. "What have you been doing?"

George was better prepared for these kind of questions, now that he'd had plenty of time to think about them. "I only work on freelance projects these days. They keep me quite busy."

"What kind of projects?" he queried, "Who do you work for?"

The answer, George thought, *was pure genius. A work of art, but one that would put the questions to rest once and for all.* "I'm afraid I'm not at liberty to say. It's top secret. I could be arrested if I said anything about it at all."

"Got it. I won't pry," Luke said. He was at a loss for the purpose of this trip. George was adamant about getting together, but he didn't seem to be willing to talk, certainly not about his work. He didn't offer any personal tidbits to explain why he left SIA. *And what's up with this lifestyle change?*

"What should we talk about?" Luke asked.

George responded with a shrug, "I don't know." His thoughts were elsewhere.

They spent the next several minutes in an uncomfortable state of silence. Luke picked up the scent of burgers being charred, and saw a family getting ready for a picnic not far from the water's edge. Their grill was ablaze and was being managed by what seemed to be an amateur grill master.

It wouldn't be long now, only one more bend. George's nerves had reached their limit. Could he actually do it? He had to, there was no other way to have Holly to himself forever. It had to be done.

There it was, Cowpie Rapid. This would be it. George focused on the water ahead. He looked back to make sure he knew Luke's exact position as they entered the choppy water. Luke was talking, but George couldn't hear him. He saw his mouth moving, but had blocked out all sound. He was focused on following through with the task at hand, and only that task. Nothing else mattered. The choppiness of the water increased as they neared the rapid. A large rock protruded from the center of the river directly ahead. That's the spot. That's where he'd do it. He rehearsed his plan in his mind one last time. Just as the raft brushed up against the rock, George tightened his grip on the oar and sprang into action. He partially stood and acted as if he were off balance. Stiffening his arm, he swung the oar to his right and behind him with as much force as he could muster. The oar made contact with the side of Luke's head near his temple. There was a cracking sound resembling that of a falling tree limb in an otherwise quiet woods.

Just as George had choreographed it in his mind, Luke dropped over the side of the raft and into the river. George, no longer standing, twisted his body toward the rear of the boat desperately trying to catch a glimpse of Luke in the water to determine if his dastardly deed had been successful. He had lost all control of the raft as it mercilessly bounced from one large rock to another. Then he saw Luke out of the corner of his eye. Bouncing off the rocks in the violent water, he didn't appear to be struggling at all. His head slammed into a boulder driven by the raging current, and completely vanished from view.

George watched for several minutes to see if he would emerge… nothing. He experienced a burst of anxiety not knowing Luke's fate, yet strangely excited because he'd completed the most important step in his plan. He moved to the rear of the raft where Luke had once sat and laid back. The raft floated out of the rough water. It was now gliding along the slow current, smooth as silk.

Luke's right, he thought, *this is relaxing.*

INTO THE MINDFIELD

CHAPTER 27

It was perhaps George's greatest performance. Returning to the rental office, he emerged with tears in his eyes, explaining how his best friend fell out of the raft and disappeared from sight. *Surely,* he thought, *this was an academy award winning moment.*

The staff quickly jumped into action by sending out a search and rescue team. They had trained for such an event and appeared to be well prepared for it. George was instructed to find a place to relax while the river was searched. He asked one of the staffers if it would be alright for him to rest in his car. They consoled him by explaining that they'll do everything possible to find his friend, and sent him out of the office.

Once out of site, George grinned, as he headed toward the parking area, mulling over the best approach to tell Holly that Luke was gone. It needed to be just right. It needed to be *perfect*.

I'll tell her he fell out of the raft, George thought, *and that he hit his head on a rock and I never saw him again after that. I looked everywhere, reported it to the staff and everything. He was just nowhere to be found.*

Even still, he had to treat it with the greatest finesse. This was the most critical step in his entire plan. If he played it right, he'd endear himself to her forever. If he played it wrong, he'd surely chase her away.

Maybe I'll just be with her when they find the body, he thought. *Then I'll console her in her time of need. Yeah, that's it.*

As he drew closer to the car, he saw someone sitting in Luke's Porsche. He squinted trying to get a better look. *What the... is someone trying to steal Luke's car?* Then he had an inspiration. *How awesome would that be? Not only would I get away with killing Luke, I'd have someone else to pin it on.* He picked up his pace arriving at the parked automobiles less than a minute later. Peeking into the deeply tinted window, his heart jumped. It was Luke! He was alive!

Luke was fully reclined in the driver's seat, when he saw George peering in. He raised his seat back to its normal position and pressed the button to lower the window.

George became lightheaded and dropped to one knee, "You're alive!" he cried in disbelief. "I'm so sorry. It was an accident, I swear." But he wasn't sorry, the groveling was yet another theatrical presentation to keep him from being suspected or getting caught.

Luke had a cut on the upper side of his right cheek bone which was beginning to form a huge shiner. He had a bump on the left side of his forehead, with a small scrape in the center. "I know it was an accident, George. Why didn't you listen to me when I told you to stay seated?"

Still confused, George asked, "How did you get back? I looked everywhere for you."

"Remember that family we saw having a picnic?" Luke explained, "after pulling myself out of the water and onto the bank, I walked back to their camp. They offered me a burger, then drove me back here. They were real nice people."

"Let me make it up to you." George was desperately trying to get his mind around this and think ahead. "How about we get together next weekend?"

"No," Luke replied. "I've got a race scheduled."

"How about the weekend after?" George was searching for a plan. He needed to know where his *target* would be.

"Maybe," Luke said, "but right now I need to get some ice on this thing." He lightly touched his cheek. A rescue vehicle flew by. "I suppose one of us should tell them I'm okay."

~

Upon arriving home, Luke walked into the garage to see how Raj was coming along with the Porsche. He had loaded it onto the trailer, preparing it for the long trip ahead. They were headed to the Pocono International Raceway, which was located in eastern Pennsylvania. The pit crew usually handled transportation, but one of them had a bad case of the flu and couldn't make it. Secretly, Raj enjoyed driving the big truck anyhow. He volunteered every chance he got.

"What happened to you?" Raj asked, immediately noticing Luke's battered face.

"It was George," Luke replied. "He stood up in the raft, lost his balance, and I took an oar across the face."

"You have got to stop this," Raj pointed out. "Lately, it seems you've either been hurt or sick on a weekly basis."

"Yeah," Luke laughed. "Seems like the safest place for me these days is on the racetrack." There was some truth to that statement. Luke had been having a great year on the track and was holding onto the number two spot for the series. During *this* season, he hadn't experienced a single incident.

Holly was preparing to meet Marilyn and Felicia for lunch. As she stepped out of the front door, she noticed that Luke's car was in the driveway. Curious, she walked into the garage.

"Hey," Holly said. "I expected you to be spending the day on the river."

His back was facing the open door. He slowly turned, revealing the mess that his face had become.

"Oh my God," She ran to him. "Are you okay? What happened?"

Luke knew that Holly didn't have the highest opinion of George, so he certainly didn't want to say that George was the cause of all of this. He shrugged his shoulders and offered a sheepish grin, "I fell out of the raft. We weren't on the river for more than thirty minutes."

"Is there anything I can do for you before I go?"

"You go have fun with the girls," Raj said. "I'll see that he's taken care of."

She reluctantly agreed, headed to the Mustang, climbed in, fired it up, and took off.

Raj looked at Luke inquisitively, "Isn't that *your* car?"

"It used to be," Luke laughed.

~

George was at his wits end. How could he have botched it the way he did? He'd lost the perfect opportunity. His plan had been executed to the letter, just as he'd rehearsed. He began to analyze each step.

Step one, the phone call to Luke had achieved its desired result. He had accepted the offer to spend the day on the river. Step two, the proper selection of rafting equipment. Just as planned, George was able to select the proper raft, the correct oars, and even got Luke to agree to enter the river without a guide. Step three, was to get Luke into the rear of the boat... check! Step four, get Luke to remove his safety gear. It took a little convincing, but he had pulled that off as well. Step five, the take down. George swung the oar like a professional golfer executing the perfect backswing. Everything had worked just as he had planned. Everything, except for the most important thing: Luke didn't die.

After dwelling on it during the drive back to Denver, he decided to put it behind him. It hadn't worked, and that's all there was to it. What he needed now, was to come up with a new plan. He once again repeated the advice Holly had offered him. *Know where your target will be.*

"Come on George," he said to himself. "Where will he be?" He remembered Luke saying something about having a race this weekend. *But where?* Maybe he didn't say, or maybe, due to all of the excitement, he just couldn't remember.

Maybe it doesn't matter where he'll be. He had an epiphany, *what matters is where he won't be next weekend. He won't be at home. George, you are a genius!*

Now satisfied that he had a plan in place, he knew that all of the specific details would need to be worked out later. He still had a few days to think them through. *What I need now, is to unwind.* He tipped his head back into his chair and placed the X-Specs over his eyes.

~

Holly had just finished potting some plants and was preparing to walk out to the garden. Her face was smudged with the dark potting soil and her hands were totally black. Her blouse prominently displayed black rings around her midsection where she had leaned into the workbench. Her jeans reflected imprints of her own hands along the sides and across her rear where she had wiped them off. She owned gloves for this type of work, but never actually liked to use them. She preferred to dig in and feel what she was doing.

George stepped into the garden shed and reached around her from behind. "You are a dirty girl," he said mischievously. She craned her head over her shoulder and kissed him.

"Do you love me?" he asked. The tension between them was finally gone. They were now free to say whatever they wanted to each other and free to be as flirtatious as they desired. They were in love and were acting like love struck teenagers.

"More than the sun and the moon," she replied. "Do you love me?"

"More than all of the stars in the sky," George countered.

"Great," she said. "Then grab some of these pots. I've got some work for you."

"I've been duped!" he said as he pulled her hair off her shoulder and kissed the nape of her neck, "Taken in by your charms."

~

Luke held the number two position for the series, and this was the second to the last race of the season. Pocono Raceway was a two and one-half mile track formed in the shape of a triangle. Known as the *Tricky Triangle* in the racing circuit, it had a long rich history which included the first five hundred mile Indy race on a two and one-half mile track. It also held the title as the first track to host a five hundred mile NASCAR race. Today's race would be four hundred miles, one hundred and sixty laps in all. The number of pit stops would be determined by track conditions and the number of red or yellow flags occurring during the race.

The smell of high octane fuel filled the air. Luke had a good run during the time trials held the previous day, and had won the number one pole position, placing him in front of the pack. This was a different type of track than Luke had grown accustomed to. He had become familiar with road circuits consisting of numerous changes in elevation, with lots of twists and turns. He was excited about this race because his car had a history of running strong in the straightaways. *Consistency*, he thought, *that will be the key word of the day.*

The drivers took their places next to each car as the national anthem played. The lineup was announced, and the drivers were strapped into their seats. The engines came to life as the pace car exited pit row, with the entire field of racecars following close behind. Even though Luke had done well this season, this was the first time he actually got to follow the pace car onto the track. It seemed more exciting to him somehow.

~

George parked his car on the street near the entrance to Luke's house. He knew there were multiple security cameras and had studied the grounds enough to feel confident that he'd located them all. By systematically disabling each, one at a time, he would be sure to remain undetected.

He certainly wasn't pressed for time, he'd have all of that he would need. Everyone had gone to the race, he'd have the entire weekend if he wanted.

In his chosen profession as a research scientist, he'd become accustomed to working with miniature devices. Over the years, he'd acquired several tools that he found to be quite useful. Among these tools, he had a professional lock pick set, just like one that would be used by a locksmith to open doors for customers who had regretfully lost their keys. He wasn't particularly skilled at using them to open locks, but he had watched a couple of how-to videos online, and had practiced on a few locks at home. He felt confident that his skills would be good enough to do the job he had planned for the day.

Kneeling in front of the door, George inserted the pick. Carefully manipulating the pins inside the tumbler, he applied pressure using a tension wrench. Once all the pins were aligned, the cylinder rotated to the right, releasing the deadbolt. Humming as he worked, George repeated the steps a second time to release the lock centered in the doorknob. Turning the knob, he heard a click, followed by a squeak as he pushed the door open.

Needs a little oil, he thought as he stepped inside. Feeling around on the wall to the right of the door, he found a light switch and toggled it upward. The fluorescent bulbs flickered as they became energized. He sat a canvas tool bag on the concrete floor and closed the door behind him.

There it stood in front of him, the project he had planned for the day. The bright white paint reflected the fluorescent lighting causing it to sparkle like a tree decorated for Christmas. The red stripes contrasted sharply against the black trim. It was an impressive looking machine.

INTO THE MINDFIELD

It was Luke's SkyKar.

~

After the first pace lap, two of the participants were in the wrong position according to the official line up. After making the adjustment to slot them into their proper starting locations, and upon the completion of the second lap, the pace car exited the track and the green flag waved. Luke, starting in the lead position, accelerated, pushing the Porsche 917 to its limit. His goal was to remain in the lead, hopefully for the entire race. He knew that he'd fall back during pit stops, but that lag would only be temporary because the rest of the field would have to do the same. The key was to keep the time in the pit to an absolute minimum.

Holly and Marilyn chose a spot near the top of the grandstands. There, they could get the best view of the entire track. It was exciting to see Luke leading the pack. Everything was progressing as planned. Luke remained in the lead through his first two pit stops. The third pit stop arrived on lap one hundred and thirty two. During this stop, he'd receive a new set of tires. Tire changes had been practiced relentlessly by his crew. They now had it down to only twenty seconds. Other teams had been meeting similar times. Perfect execution would be critical to the outcome of the race. A single jack was slid underneath as soon as the car had come to a complete stop. It lifted the entire car into the air, allowing the tire crew to do their job. Once all four tires were replaced and tightened, the car dropped and the jack was removed. Upon hearing the word, CLEAR, Luke would be free to pull the car back onto the racetrack.

This time it had gone without a hitch. A timer showed that Luke was *clear* in only 18.7 seconds. That was until car number forty-two arrived for *his* pit stop. The driver was to pull into the pit area directly in front of Luke. His eagerness to get in quickly caused him to cut too sharp and clip the right front corner of Luke's car. He hit with enough force to bounce the front of the car two feet to the left, knocking one of the crew members to the ground. The Porsche's fiberglass fender was shattered and partially lying on the pavement. The headlight was leaning against the nose of the car with the wires still attached. The crew immediately surveyed the damage and cut the loose parts off with a reciprocating saw. Another crewman snipped the wires and tossed the headlight off to the side. The remaining damage was deemed to be only superficial. Unfortunately another forty seconds had been lost. Once all the drivers had completed their pit stops, it was determined that Luke was now in fifth place.

Back on the track, Luke immediately sensed that something was wrong. The impact had knocked his wheels out of alignment causing the steering to pull hard to the left. Oddly, this worked to his advantage in the turns, but on the straightaways, he had to constantly fight it to keep from turning.

"Raj," Luke spoke into his helmet microphone, "The car is fighting me. Something is bent in the steering. It's taking everything I've got to keep it straight."

"This is going to have to be your call," Raj replied. "To fix it, you'll need to bring it back in, or you can try to fight it and finish the race near the front. What I can't tell from here is how much your tire is in tow. That will determine how quickly it wears."

"There are only twenty-six laps remaining," Luke commented. "Let's roll the dice, I say we go for it."

"You're in fifth place now, see if you can hang onto it."

"Hang on to it? I intend to win this thing."

The remaining twenty-six laps were the hardest sixty-five miles Luke had ever driven. He was losing the blood flow in his hands and his arms were stiff and tired from constantly pulling the wheel to the right. He found that he could run strong in the turns, and it was there that he was able to overtake his competitors. One by one, he picked them off, regaining the lead only seconds before crossing the finish line.

~

Now whistling, George packed up his tool bag and wiped the SkyKar down to ensure that he'd left no fingerprints behind. He turned off the lights and locked the door using the pick set to slide the deadbolt back into its locked position. After placing the tools into the trunk of his car, he reconnected each of the security cameras.

We wouldn't want any trespassers to get in, he chuckled to himself. *Something really bad could happen.*

CHAPTER 28

Finding the perfect spot, Luke placed the winning trophy on the shelf. He couldn't have been any happier. He was nearing the end of a winning season with only one more race to go. In addition, he and Holly were going to be married on September 4th, Labor Day weekend. That was only six weeks out and he could feel the excitement building. He had been deeply in love with Holly for over two years, but knew from the day they met that they were meant for each other.

He'd been struggling to come up with an idea for her wedding gift, one that would be personal and unique. She was the best thing that had ever happened to him, and he wanted only the best for her. He had spent hours on line, but had never found exactly what he was looking for. Sure, there were a bunch of over-the-top, expensive ideas that were restricted to people within his income range. That all seemed like unnecessary *flash* to Luke, superficial at best. There were the luxurious gifts, trips, shows and concerts, but nothing that felt *just right*.

A few weeks earlier, he'd asked Sam to help him find something creative. Luke knew if anyone could, it would be him. Then Sam called.

"Are you in a place where you can talk privately?" he asked, "I've got something I think you'll like."

"Holly's in the next room," Luke replied. "I'll head to the garage, it'll be safe out there." He slipped out the door undetected and into the garage where he had created a sitting area for Raj and the team. "All clear."

"I didn't want to talk to you about this prematurely," Sam began. "I wanted to make sure that I could get it to work first." Like most of Sam's ideas, Luke could tell he was excited about it.

"Do you remember seeing those little glass blocks with laser etched 3D images inside them?"

"Yeah, they're everywhere," Luke noted.

"Well imagine this," Sam explained, "a 3D holographic image *moving* inside a crystal block that can *even* speak."

"Sounds pretty cool," Luke said. "But how does that become the perfect wedding gift?"

"Let me break it down for you," Sam continued. "I figured out a way to use the 3D+6 technology in reverse. Instead of using six cameras in a cluster all pointing outward to create a 3D image, I used the same six cameras and pointed them inward toward a single object. In this case, that object would be you."

"Okay," Luke said, "Then you end up with a 3D image of me in a cube of crystal. I suppose that's better than a photograph. I'm sure she'd like it, but I'd still need something else."

"You're not getting it," Sam said. "Imagine that single image of you moving around in the cube. Then, with a micro-speaker attached to the bottom, it could be played back, and she could hear what you've recorded. In your case, you'll be looking directly at her while reciting your wedding vows. She'll have a pocket sized version of you that she can look at and play back as she wishes. What woman wouldn't love something like that?"

"So it will look just like me?" Luke asked.

"It will *be* you, in ultra-high definition, just as if you'd been shrunk down to a four inch version of yourself. Every detail exact, in every way. Let me show you, just a minute." There was silence on the opposite end of the phone with the exception of a few mouse clicks and a beep or two. "There," Sam said. "I just sent you a file."

Luke powered up his pocket computer and opened the file. He found it amusing. It was Sam. He was about three inches tall encased in a crystal cube. The only thing he saw in the cube with him was a chair. He sat on the chair then stood and walked to the cube's edge pretending to lean against the glass wall. Then he returned to the seat again.

"As usual Sam, you've blown me away."

"This was my first prototype," Sam acknowledged. "I've since added the sound component to it."

"It's perfect!" Luke said. "This is *exactly* what I've been looking for."

"Great," Sam replied. "I'll need to get you here so we can do the recording, I'll take it from there. I assume you have your vows written?"

"They are, but I'll need to cut them back a bit, I sort of got carried away."

Luke and Sam agreed to meet at SIA the following Tuesday.

~

It had been a week since George tampered with the SkyKar. He was anxious to know if Luke had attempted to fly it since. If so, what had been the outcome? He expected that it would be catastrophic... at least for Luke. Pacing the floor, he couldn't take it any longer, he had to know. Picking up the phone, he dialed.

"This is Luke," came the answer from the connecting end.

Damn, George thought to himself.

"Luc-ass," He said with his undeniably familiar greeting.

"Double G, what's up?"

"Uh," He said, while drawing a blank. He certainly couldn't just *blatantly* ask him what he really wanted to know, *Why aren't you dead yet?* Instead, he opted for something a little more subtle, "I was wondering if we were getting together next week. I thought I'd check in with you after you returned from the race."

"Oh yeah," Luke replied, "we did talk about that. What were you thinking?"

"I'm thinking we could go fishing," George explained. "We could drive up to the lake, rent a cabin, and get an early start the next morning." Of course George knew that it would not likely happen, because Luke would have already been killed in a horrific airplane crash. "How does Tuesday sound?"

"I can't do Tuesday," Luke said. "I'm meeting Sam in Green River for the day."

Bingo! George now knew when Luke had planned to fly next.

"I can do Wednesday night, if that's good for you, but let's be clear, I won't get into a boat with you."

"Perfect!" George replied.

~

Tuesday rolled around just like any other day. Luke was preparing for his trip to SIA to meet with Sam and begin work on the *special gift* he had planned for Holly. Holly knew something was up because Luke would rarely go to Green River without her. She didn't mind though. She knew he had a good reason. Besides, she felt that Sam and Luke needed some *guy* time together without her. This would be good for everyone.

Luke pulled the SkyKar out of the hangar and was preparing it for the trip. He ran through the preflight checklist, inspecting the fuel level as well as the other fluids. He filed a flight plan as usual. He had some extra time and decided to wipe it down and apply a fresh coat of wax. Finally, he checked the air pressure in the tires, vacuumed the interior and cleaned the windows.

"When you finish with that," Holly said, walking across the courtyard, "you can start on my car." She was headed into town for a noon meeting with her garden club. She said her goodbyes to Luke and reminded him of a concert they had planned to attend at the Red Rocks Amphitheater later that evening.

She climbed into the Cayenne and exited the driveway. Once out of sight, Luke positioned himself into the cockpit of the SkyKar and powered it up. Following the normal routine, the electric motors provided the required torque to lift the craft into the air. Once altitude was reached, Luke transitioned the props to a forty-five degree angle. Upon reaching I-70, he flipped a switch to start the fuel powered engine. It started, sputtered for a few seconds and then died out. He tried a second time and it came to life. Transitioning the propellers to a full ninety degrees, the helicopter became an airplane. He adjusted his heading toward Green River and climbed to three thousand feet.

The trip was mostly uneventful. Arriving exactly one and a half hours later he landed at SIA and taxied the SkyKar over to a hanger attached to the building and coasted inside. He shut down the engines and secured the craft before heading to Sam's office.

Sam, always glad to see Luke, presented him with a lively handshake and *man* hug. "Follow me," He said. They walked down a short corridor into a small room that Sam used as a photography studio. It was already set up with the 3D+6 cameras locked in their desired position. Luke changed into his tuxedo and recited his vows as Sam recorded the event.

"Well, that's about it," Sam said.

"I flew one and a half hours to do something that lasted less than ten minutes?" Luke asked, even though he was absolutely fine with it. In keeping with tradition, Luke and Sam always had to give each other a hard time.

"I had hoped we'd run into town for lunch," Sam suggested.

"Well…. Okay," Luke agreed. "That will help me justify the trip." He laughed as he patted Sam on the back. "You're buying, right?"

During lunch, Luke brought Sam up to date about George.

"So he just called you out of the blue and asked you to go rafting with him," Sam asked, "for no particular reason?"

"That's about the size of it," Luke replied. "Outside of taking an unexpected swim, it was uneventful. I still don't understand what the heck he wanted. It felt like something was on his mind, but he couldn't seem to say it."

"You keep an eye on him," Sam said. "He's not the same old George he used to be."

Upon assuring him that he would, they headed back to SIA. Luke thanked Sam again for helping him with the awesome wedding gift. They bid each other adieu, and Luke climbed aboard the SkyKar. Following the same procedure as he'd done countless times before, Luke powered it up.

Because he was not in a residential area, he was not required to lift off using the electric motors. He had a full sized airport runway and could take off like any other aircraft. He started the Continental engine and taxied into position at the end of the runway. Once permission was granted he throttled up, gaining enough speed to lift the craft into the air. After climbing to an altitude of one thousand feet, the engine unexpectedly sputtered and died. The configuration of the aircraft design didn't permit it to function well as a glider. It fell quickly. Luke switched over to the electric motors. They too failed to start. With little time to find an alternate solution, Luke prepared for impact. Upon hitting the ground, the left side main running gear collapsed, sliding the wing directly into a large boulder in the middle of an open field. It sheared off approximately half of the wing, along with the left rotor assembly and motor, spinning the SkyKar around one hundred and eighty degrees. It was now sliding backward. While slowing to around twenty miles per hour, the tail end of the craft dropped into a large hole appearing to have been created by a meteorite. This caused the tail to dig in, forcing the SkyKar to flip over backward. The plane came to rest on its top. Luke released his harness and fell onto the canopy which was now under him. He kicked at it until it broke free, cutting a three inch gash in his ankle in the process. The design of the aircraft didn't permit any other means of escape should it somehow turn over onto its top. After breaking the canopy, Luke dug the ground from underneath using a stainless steel coffee mug, until a small tunnel could be created that was large enough for him to shimmy through. Covered from head to toe in the sandy Wyoming dirt, he slowly limped back to SIA and into Sam's office.

Sam looked up from his desk, stunned by what he saw.

"Two things," Luke announced. "I need a bandage, and a ride to Evergreen, Colorado."

INTO THE MINDFIELD

.

CHAPTER 29

Wednesday morning while finishing breakfast, George pondered what his new life with Holly would be like. *It will be just like the one I have now,* he thought, *I just wouldn't be tethered to the computer anymore.* He felt a tinge of guilt that he would soon leave Holly, in Holly's world, but was justified in knowing it was for the best. *Besides, the other version of me will continue to handle things after I'm gone.* He'd soon be handling things for Holly in this world, which is where he ultimately felt he belonged.

He recently began thinking of her as *my* Holly, a possessive term, indicating that she somehow belonged to him, that he was, in fact, entitled to her. It was also a way for him to think of her without Luke being in the picture.

Luke, George thought. *He should be gone by now.* But, he needed to know for sure.

While dialing the phone, he had visions of Holly answering in tears, and that he'd tell her he'd be right there. He pictured himself coming to her rescue, and that she'd respond positively, embracing him, eventually falling in love with him. That's not what happened. The phone was answered, but not by Holly.

"This is Luke," the familiar voice said.

It grated on George like fingernails on a chalkboard. This was not at all what he expected to hear. *Why won't this guy die?* he questioned himself in disbelief. *He's like some kind of mutant cockroach that can't seem to be eliminated no matter what I try.*

"So are we going fishing, or what?" George asked abruptly. He was not at all happy about this and it reflected in his voice.

Luke paused, surprised by George's tone, "To my knowledge the plan hasn't changed."

"Okay then," George snipped, "I'll meet you at your house." He hung up without even giving Luke the opportunity to respond.

Luke sat at his desk with a perplexed look washed over his face. He didn't understand what the issue was. It couldn't have been anything he had done. Maybe George was just having a bad day. Holly walked by. "Who was that?" she asked.

"George," Luke replied, shaking his head. "That's one very strange man."

Holly nodded with her palm extended as if to say she was in total agreement. It wasn't in her nature to say, *See, I told you so.* Those words would never be spoken.

~

Still peeved at Luke for not being dead, George collected his mail from downstairs and took it back to his apartment. As if to purposely add fuel to the fire, there it was, Luke and Holly's wedding invitation. He didn't open it. He could only imagine what kind of disgusting message was written inside. *It would be some happy bullshit about how honored they'd be to have me as their guest. About how freaking happy they are together, and that they'll spend all of eternity with one another. I guarantee that's not going to happen.* George pounded his fist on the table while shouting, "She belongs to *me*!" He tore the invitation into small pieces and callously tossed them onto the floor. He'd had enough. He'd personally see to it that today would be Luke's last day on earth. No more excuses.

To clear his mind, George suited up for his daily run. He couldn't stop thinking about it. He was well beyond angry. Luke was the only thing standing in the way of his lifetime of happiness. As he stepped out of the apartment building, he decided to plot a different route, one that would take him away from the park. His intent would be to try to engage one of the local gangs to get some urgently needed assistance. He'd noticed a few places where some of them regularly hung out. This would be the place where he'd likely find the one tool that he didn't have stashed inside his tool bag.

George slowly entered an alley where he expected to find them. There didn't appear to be anything special about this alley. It looked like most any other he'd seen in the neighborhood. The only difference was that he'd personally seen some crude, rough looking guys hanging around here, always appearing to be looking for trouble. Then, out of nowhere, he was blindsided, struck in the face with an object thrown from behind a stack of trash cans. Before he could react, a man rushed him, pinning him against the brick wall with his forearm jammed tightly against his throat. He was not an attractive man. He had several missing teeth and long greasy hair that looked as though it hadn't been washed in years. The smell of rotting garbage was overpowered only by this man's stench.

"What the hell you doin' here?" the man shouted, spitting in George's face as he spoke. "You lookin' for trouble mister? Well you just found some."

George couldn't speak but was trying to explain that he needed to talk to someone in charge. He closed his eyes in an attempt to protect himself from this man's spray.

Three more shady characters appeared in the shadows behind the dumpster.

The man eased off of his throat slightly, to where George could speak. He panted, "There's a one hundred dollar bill in my right front pocket. Take it. There's more, if you can help me out."

The three men stepped into the light. Their appearance took George by surprise. One man, rather large, had a bald head that was covered in tattoos. His left arm was in a cast, lying in a sling hanging from his neck. He also had a splint on his right index finger. A second man, much smaller, had a cast on his left leg and walked with a single crutch. The third man sported a metal bridge taped across his nose with a small amount of gauze protruding from his nostrils. Both of his eyes had been blackened.

The long haired man dived into George's pocket to retrieve the hundred. After verifying it was in fact there, he plucked it out and backed off. The four men surrounded him.

Looking them over, George wondered if he had made the right choice, "What happened to you guys?"

They looked at each other, then the bald guy spoke, "Street fight." The other men agreed with that angle and all chimed in.

"Yeah, street fight, gang related, a real bad one."

"There had to be at least twenty guys."

"I counted twenty-five."

"You think we look bad, you should see them. Sent them all to the hospital."

"All of them?" George asked.

"Every last stinkin' one."

"Hey! Why all the questions," Baldy asked. "You a cop? What the hell do you want?"

"Well," George proceeded gingerly, choosing his words with care, "I sort of have a rodent problem. I'm looking for a way to take care of it, once and for all. I need a little firepower, if you know what I mean."

"When do you need it?"

"By three o'clock today."

"That's not much time. All I got right now is a .38 special, which is mine... not for sale. Hey, Marco, you still got that two-shot, .22 derringer?"

Marco was the man with the broken nose. He explained that he'd accidentally left it at his grandmother's house the weekend before. "I'm sorry, Moose," he said, "I just forgot it."

"You dumb shit," Moose replied, while kicking him in the leg. Marco cursed under his breath as he walked over to a box where he sat down and began to rub his shin. Moose was the nickname of the man with the tattooed bald head. He began the negotiation. "I know a guy, but he ain't cheap. I could get you a .22 for about five hundred."

"I'm not sure that will do the job," George replied, confident that they were now on the same page. "This rodent is a big one. Ugly too."

Moose nodded his head, "I think I can fix you up for a grand. Just meet me back here at three, *with* the money."

"I can do that," George agreed. "Deal."

His day was starting to improve. He jogged through the park as he made his way back to the apartment. "She's got no business marrying him. She should be marrying me," he mumbled. That generated another idea, *Why not? I'll just marry her in her world, Luke can't touch me there.* He rushed home and logged into the system where he and Holly had just returned from the grocery store.

They had been unloading bags from the Mustang and carting them into the kitchen. Each time they passed one another, they'd smile or wink, flirting as if they'd just met. Once inside, they each selected a bag and began to place the items in the cupboards where they belonged. Interrupting the steady flow, George backed Holly against the counter.

"I've been thinking," he said. "We should get married."

She looked surprised, as this came out of nowhere. George knew that she was the type of girl who would have expected to be asked such a question while being romanced in a nice restaurant, or on a dream vacation, not in the kitchen surrounded by bags of unpacked groceries. He was however, content in knowing that they were deeply in love with each other. It seemed that marriage would be the next logical step. "Thinking always gets you into trouble," Holly said, while poking him in the stomach. "So are you *thinking* a spring wedding?"

"I'm thinking we should do it right away," George replied. "There's no point in waiting. I love you more now than ever. I'd say no later than... Labor Day weekend."

"But that's only three weeks away," Holly explained. "How can we arrange a wedding by then? There's the reception, and the food. What about the cake? We'd need a church. What about my parents? I don't have any brides' maids, and you don't have groomsmen." Her head was spinning.

George calmly leaned in and kissed her, "We'll figure it out. Just let our love be our guide. How about it?"

Even though George made it sound a bit corny, she had to know he was right. If they truly loved each other, they'd find a way. She smiled and looked into his chocolate brown eyes, "Yes George, I *will* marry you."

Satisfied that he had *that* deal sewn up, George's thoughts drifted to his planned *fishing* trip with Luke. He logged off and leaned back in his chair. Everything would be over soon. Glancing at his watch, he saw that it was 2:30 pm, time to meet with Moose and see what he had come up with.

He made his way back to the same alley where they had met earlier. No one appeared to be around. George became concerned that they may have taken the hundred and blown it on booze or something. An old van pulled up at the end of the alley and the side door slid open. Marco was inside, "Come on, come on," he said impatiently. George ran up to the door and Marco pulled him in. The door closed behind him. Moose and his gang were all there.

"What did you find for me?" George asked.

"Not so fast," Moose said, "You got the rest of the money?"

George pulled out a wad of one hundred dollar bills, carefully straightening them and laying them out on the console side by side. "Nine hundred dollars. What have *you* got for me?"

Moose unwrapped a plastic shopping bag and pulled out the merchandise. It was a 9mm semi-automatic. It was much more than George expected to see.

"The cops like these," Moose said, presenting what he believed to be a savvy sales pitch.

Made by Walther, it was a model PPX M1. Just like Moose had said, it was popular among many law enforcement agencies. The slide mechanism was machined out of stainless steel. It came with a sixteen round magazine and a full box of bullets. "I figured you was gonna need these." Moose said.

"It's perfect," George replied, "This should take care of my rodent problem for good."

The van circled the block one more time, just to make sure there were no signs of any cops. They let George out where they had picked him up. He tucked the shopping bag under his arm and headed back to his apartment. Throwing a quick overnight gym bag together, he tucked the gun and bullets inside the shoe compartment. Securing the apartment, he ran downstairs. Tossing the bag onto the passenger seat of the Pontiac, he settled in behind the wheel and started the car.

"Tonight is going to be your night, Mr. Monroe." George said as he patted the top of his gym bag.

INTO THE MINDFIELD

CHAPTER 30

Forty-five minutes later, George pulled through the entrance gate of Luke's stately home. The old Pontiac sputtered as it rolled up the long winding lane. Luke was loading his gear into the Cayenne when George pulled up beside him. Luke wasn't sure what to expect from him after the curt phone conversation earlier in the day.

"Luc-ass," he cheerfully addressed him. "I'm ready, you ready?" He seemed to be happy to be there. In fact he was, but not for the reason Luke would suspect. Luke believed that he was happy to be going on the trip with him, basically to spend a little time bonding with him and to get away from it all for a day.

George, on the other hand, was happy to be there, if only to finish the job that he had failed so many times before to bring to an end. He was now ready and excited that it would soon be over.

"Hi, George," Luke said. "Good to see you in an upbeat mood. I wasn't sure after our call this morning if you'd even show up."

"Are you kidding?" George asked, "There's no way I'd miss this. Sorry about the call this morning, I had something else on my mind. It's all good now. I've been thinking about this all day."

"Do you have your gear?" Luke asked.

"Yeah, sure do," George confirmed. "I can drive if you like."

Luke scanned over the beat down Firebird wondering, not only if it were road worthy, but how the heck it was still running. "I'll drive! Just park yours over there." He pointed toward a spot in front of the garage.

"It leaks a bit," George explained. "Do you have an oil pan we could keep under it? I wouldn't want it to stain the concrete."

"Just park it in the grass beside the hangar," Luke directed him to the correct spot. "It should be fine over there."

He moved the car into position as instructed and stepped out. He pulled the blue gym bag from the passenger seat and sat it on the ground. With both hands, slammed the door hard, startling Luke. "That's the only way it'll stay shut," George explained.

Luke had everything laid out in the courtyard, and had been taking inventory before loading it into the high performance SUV. Having been a project manager for several years, this was just how he believed things should be done. Compulsive, not really. Obsessive, you bet.

George assisted him with the inventory. Luke read from his checklist and George confirmed.

"Suit case?"
"Check."

"Propane grill?"

"Check."

"Fishing pole?"

"Check."

"Tackle?"

"Check."

"Ice chest, packed with food items?"

"Check."

"Ice chest, packed with beverages?"

"Check."

"Deck of cards?"

"Deck of cards?" George asked.

"In case of rain."

"Okay, check."

"Now let's go over your stuff," Luke said.

"Suit case?"

"Overnight bag, check."

"Fishing pole?"

There was no answer. Luke glanced up and saw George standing there with a blank look. He seemed to have forgotten his fishing gear.

"You do realize this is a *fishing* trip, right?"

George was somewhat embarrassed. How could he have forgotten to bring at least the most basic of items along? Then he laughed as he thought that Luke actually believed this *was* a fishing trip.

"Alright," Luke said. "I've got enough spare gear here to fix you up with a set. He walked into the garage, returning a few minutes later with another pole and a tackle box.

He held them up for George to see, "I hope you like pink. These belong to Holly."

As far as George was concerned, anything affiliated with Holly was perfectly fine with him. He nodded in the affirmative.

Once the inventory was complete, they finished loading the vehicle and closed the hatch.

Holly stepped outside to wish them good luck. "Hello George," she said, being cordial.

George felt unusually awkward, and couldn't bring himself to look her in the eye, not with Luke standing right there. He looked at the ground and shuffled his feet. "Hello," was all he could get out. With his eyes focused on the ground, he slowly walked to the opposite side of the SUV.

Holly walked over to Luke, and wrapped her arms around him to give him a proper send off. "You be careful," she insisted. This would be the first night they'd spent apart since she moved in with him over a year ago.

"You know I will," he replied. "I already wish it were tomorrow." They kissed.

George peered through the window from the far side of the SUV. He saw them kiss. He was infuriated by it. First by the kiss itself. It just wasn't right to see the woman he was about to marry kiss another man. Second, he became more enraged the longer the kiss took. Seconds to George seemed like minutes. He couldn't hold back any longer.

"Hey," he shouted, "We better get going. We're running out of time"

"Someone's getting restless," Holly whispered to Luke. "You should go."

One final peck, and Luke turned toward the SUV. He climbed in as Holly walked in the other direction toward the house. He rolled the window down, "Excuse me, Ms. Vaughn," Luke said.

She did a half turn, looking over her shoulder and said, "It won't be Ms. Vaughn for much longer."

You got that right, George thought.

"I was just admiring the swing on your back porch," Luke said with a mischievous grin. She smiled.

George was insulted. *How dare he! He was talking about her ass.*

Luke started the car and Holly blew a kiss, "You guys have fun."

George knew deep down that the kiss was meant for him.

They had a four and a half hour drive ahead of them. George had selected the lake and rented the cabin. Without Luke's knowledge, he even rented a boat that he intended to use later to dispose of the body.

It was 4:30 in the afternoon, which should put them at the lake by 9:00 pm. It would be dark by then. George was satisfied that he'd found the most remote cabin available, one where he'd be certain not to be disturbed.

"So what's the name of this place?" Luke asked.

"Lake Purgatory," George replied, snickering to himself. He thought that it was the perfect name, especially for this trip. "I have a map and brochure with directions. It says here that it's a seventeen acre lake that's full of several species of trout. They're busy year round, with skiing in the winter, hiking and fishing in the summer. It got its name in 1776 when a party of Spanish explorers became lost in this area, never to be found again. They were said to have been cast into purgatory."

Stopping for fuel, they each picked up a soda and snack for the road.

It was a long trip, but not because of the distance. It was a long trip because neither of them seemed to have anything to say to one another. Luke didn't know what to ask George. He'd tried several topics, but George wasn't very talkative. The only thing he could think to do was talk about his life and things he had been up to.

George knew the real purpose for the trip and understood that he'd be coming back home alone. He didn't care to hear about anything Luke had to say, not about his racing, nor his involvement with the lottery commission. He certainly didn't want to hear about the upcoming wedding. He reclined the seat and closed his eyes.

CHAPTER 31

D_{r.} Ackerman projected an image of the human brain onto the screen. "Even though we programed the ANT device to attach itself to a specific region of the brain, we found that the data received was not necessarily from that region. The ANT was programmed to attach itself toward the rear of the temporal lobe. This is the area of the brain where sound files are stored and recalled for recognition.

In the case of our first test subject, John, synaptic bridges were built by the brain to communicate directly to the Nano transmitter. A bridge, by its very nature, is a structure that permits one to span over obstructions to get directly to a specific destination. Synaptic bridges work very much the same way. It allows neurons to span over parts of the brain providing connections to their destination. Over time, the link targeting that specific part of the brain would grow stronger and could be better controlled. As a result, our equipment picked up sound and visual data, even though sound and vision functions are from entirely different sectors of the brain. Vision originates from the visual cortex, located here." He used a laser pointer to show the location of the occipital lobe. Then moving the laser toward the front and near the top of the temporal lobe he continued, "This is the auditory cortex, where we process sound. You'll notice that while one is located at the rear of the brain, the other is just forward of the center. Yet in the case of this test subject, synaptic bridges were built to each location. We still do not understand why the brain chose that specific pattern."

"When we reviewed the second test subject, Jane, her brain had chosen a different path. The bridge was built from here…" as Dr. Ackerman once again showed where the ANT device was located, "all the way to here," moving the pointer to the far front. "This is the prefrontal cortex which controls routine functions like planning, emotion, and judgement. In Jane's case, it connected to a deeper form of emotion focusing on fear. The images we witnessed were those things that she feared the most. Being imbedded deeply inside this area of the brain, there was no logical reason for it to be brought into her span of awareness. But there it was. We have no solid scientific explanation for this phenomenon, which is now known as the Graf-Jenkins effect, named after the devices creators."

CHAPTER 32

Luke took charge of the map and drove on, wondering why George had even invited him on this trip. Forging ahead, the hours passed. It was 8:45 pm when they arrived at the lake. George sat up and helped Luke navigate to the remote cabin. Once it was located, they unloaded the SUV and placed their belongings inside. The cabin sat partially on the mountainside overlooking the lake from afar. They were high above it, but it could still be seen off in the distance.

"Why so far away from the lake?" Luke asked.

"It's all they had available." George replied. He was fully prepared with the answer, knowing that Luke would ask the question. He knew that this was not the case, there were several cabins available at the water's edge. This cabin, being more remote, would far better suit his purpose.

They were both famished because they hadn't stopped for dinner anywhere along the way.

"Let's fix something to eat," Luke said as he began to set up the propane stove a few feet outside of the cabin door.

"I'll get a fire started," George volunteered. He began to gather wood to start a campfire in the iron ringed pit. He collected a small pile of kindling, about the size of a football. Luke loaned him a hatchet to cut larger pieces of wood from trees that had previously fallen. He stood these pieces in a circle, all leaning into one another resembling a teepee. Then he gathered some pine needles and shoved them into the bottom of the stack. Once he applied fire from Luke's handheld grill lighter, the needles caught immediately and in less than a minute, the kindling was burning as well. Five minutes later, George had a nice, well-evened fire, perfect for roasting wieners and marshmallows.

As he worked on the fire, he planned *how* he'd actually do it. Although he had never fired a gun before, he knew that he'd be successful. How hard could it be? When would he do it? Should he wait until Luke was asleep? That hardly seemed fair. He at least owed him an explanation on why it had to be done. He'd be sure to understand.

Then it hit him. He had been in such a rush to get to Luke's house that he'd forgotten to take the time to load the gun. What good would a gun be to him this way? The gym bag was in the cabin and Luke had already lit the lanterns inside. *That's no good, he'd see me in there for sure.* There was an outhouse behind the cabin. He could do it there, but would need to take a flashlight with him. *I guess that's it.*

Grabbing his gym bag, he announced to Luke that he was going to visit the outhouse and that he might be in there a while.

"Too much information there, buddy," Luke teased.

Locating a flashlight, he walked outside and followed the beaten path to the small structure in the rear. Once inside he unzipped the bag and pulled the semi-automatic weapon from the shoe compartment. He opened the box of bullets and looked at the gun. *So George,* he thought to himself, *how do you get them inside?* He slid the upper carriage back and looked down through the top. There he could barely see where the bullet was supposed to enter the chamber. He turned it upside down and found a ridged button. He gently pushed on it releasing a black metal mechanism, sliding it out of the bottom through the handgrips. *This must be it.* Taking a bullet from the box, he held it up against the magazine. It was the correct length, but the only place it seemed to fit was where it had been designed to come out.

It may not be right, he thought, wishing he had asked Moose to provide some basic instruction, *I'm just going to shove them in here.* He stacked as many bullets into the magazine as it would hold and slid it back into the gun until he heard it click into place.

That's all there is to it? he wondered, while stuffing it into his bag.

"Dinner's ready," Luke shouted. He had finished grilling a couple of burgers and had warmed a can of beans.

Startled, George jumped causing the flashlight to fall into the hole. It sunk out of sight in only a couple seconds, leaving him in total darkness. There was no way he would attempt to retrieve it. Kicking the door open he headed back to the cabin.

"Hungry?" Luke asked.

"You know it." George replied. He decided that he'd make his move once they had eaten. After all, it would be discourteous to Luke since he had done all the cooking.

George slowly worked on the hamburger. It was the slowest he could ever remember eating one, or at least it seemed that way. Time had slowed down to the point where he felt he could count his own heartbeat. One beat at a time, developing a rhythm that left him both anxious and calm at the same time.

Luke had been talking away about how nice the lake was and the area around it, at least what he could see of it at night. The moonlight bounced off of the landscape providing a faint image of the entire valley. Their faces flickered in the campfire light. George stared into the hot coals at the base of the fire, appearing to be in a trance.

"George!" Luke shouted. "I'm talking to you."

He snapped out of it, "Huh, what?"

"I said that I should bring Holly out here," Luke replied, "I think she'd like it."

That was it. Enough talk about Holly. George walked into the cabin and pulled the gun from his bag. He stepped outside holding it out of sight, behind his back. He needed to get Luke into the cabin so he could block the doorway to prevent him from running away.

"Hey, Luke," George said, "How about a game of cards before we hit the sack?"

"Great idea," Luke replied, "I stuffed them into my luggage so they wouldn't get lost."

Luke entered the cabin and walked over to his bunk. His bag was on the floor. He knelt down and rummaged through it to locate the cards.

George stood in the doorway and brought the 9mm into view, now pointing directly at Luke.

"Found them," Luke announced, turning as he held them into the air. He saw George standing in the doorway, but it was the barrel of the gun that got his attention. It looked much larger than anything else in the room.

Now holding both of his hands up, he calmly said, "Now George, be careful with that thing, someone could get hurt."

"That's the idea," George replied, his eyes as cold as stone, "someone has to get hurt. Unfortunately, it has to be you."

"Why, George?" Luke asked, while both shocked and perplexed, "I've never done anything to hurt you. I've never even spoken as much as a single negative word *about* you."

"I know, Luke," he continued, "it's not even about you. You're just a victim in all of this. *This* is about me." He raised the gun.

"Wait," Luke pleaded, "don't do anything rash. Think this through. If it's not about me, it can't be justified. You're a scientist, you know that's true."

"Well, I guess it is *sort of* about you," George paused, "I may as well tell you. It's fair to say that you won't be leaving this cabin alive tonight. I've spent a lot of time thinking this through. I've thought until my head ached. I really don't think there's any other way. You see it *is* about me... about Holly and me."

"Holly?" Luke was stunned. "What does this have to do with Holly?"

"Yes, Holly," George continued, "Holly and I are in love, and we plan to be married in just a few weeks."

Luke knew that couldn't be true. Holly didn't even care for George all that much, "She doesn't love you George, where did you hear that from?"

"She told me herself... she tells me every day."

"How could she tell you these things," Luke asked, "She's with me almost *all* of the time. If she got together with you, don't you think I'd know about it?"

"You don't understand, my friend," George replied, "our relationship is rock solid. We are together every day, all day long, all night too. She is my soul mate, and I am hers."

"You're confused George. How can she be in both places at the same time?"

"That, my friend, *is* the million dollar question, and only I know the answer."

"It's just not possible!"

"Oh, but it is. There's another world out there that no one knows about. One they can't even comprehend. I know because I've been there. I've done the research, and the facts prove that Holly loves me.... and *only* me. This is the final step that has to be taken to ensure that she stays with me forever."

"Let me prove it to you," Luke said, while holding up his phone. "I'll call her, she's at home, right now."

"You people, with your small minds, would probably think that. It proves nothing! I could take you to my apartment right now and prove to you that she's there. She's always there. She could tell you herself that she loves only me. Face it, she doesn't want you around anymore. Get real, Luke, I'm doing you a big favor here. Trust me, this will keep you from doing it to yourself later."

Luke was running out of ideas. How could he convince George that he was wrong? He was adamant that he was right. "George, listen to reason. If you kill me, you'll spend the rest of your life in prison, you'll *never* see Holly again."

"No one will ever know," he replied. "Do you think that this cabin was chosen by accident? Check your phone again, you'll see that there's no phone service way out here. We are remote enough that anyone hearing gunshots, would need to drive into town to report them.

By then, I'll be long gone, and so is the evidence. Do you actually think that I haven't considered all of this?"

George extended his arm, zeroing the sight of the gun on Luke's chest. He no longer feared if he'd be able to pull the trigger. He felt calm, as calm as if he were relaxing on a beach far away from the hustle and bustle of civilization.

Luke was trapped with nowhere to run or to hide. The only option left, was to attack. He knew that he was at a major disadvantage, but was determined that if he were going out, he'd go out fighting. Luke transitioned into a mode that provided him with an ultra-crisp focus using a technique he called a *forced reaction*. In this mode he was able to eliminate the distractions surrounding him and focus all of his attention on the resolution of the problem at hand. All he saw in that cabin was George, the gun, his duffle bag, and the door. Reaching into his bag, he grabbed an alarm clock and with all his might hurled it toward George. At the same time he made a dash toward the door. This was it, he had no more time. He would either be shot dead right here, or he'd throw George off balance enough that he'd be able to escape.

George ducked when he saw the flying alarm clock, which narrowly missed his head. This provided Luke the distraction he needed to make his move. George saw Luke racing toward him, but still managed to position the gun between them and squeeze the trigger. The gun failed to fire.

Luke powered into George at full force, knocking him completely out of the cabin. He fell backwards and into the dirt outside. Luke never stopped running and disappeared into the forest.

"Why didn't this damn gun fire?" George complained. He pulled the slide mechanism back so he could once again look inside. This time he saw a bullet rise into the barrel of the gun. *Damn it, I didn't cock it.* He knew that it was now ready to fire and followed Luke into the woods.

Luke was out of breath and panting, yet trying to be as quiet as possible. He was being stalked by a deranged hunter, treating him as if he were wild prey. *Come on Luke*, he thought to himself, *you have to stay quiet, but you can't stay here... keep moving.*

He carefully stepped another forty feet before a twig snapped under his foot. That was the signal George was waiting for. He ran in the direction of the sound, quickly zeroing in on the location. He saw movement in the shadows. It didn't matter, George blindly fired a shot in that direction. This time the gun did fire. A large chunk of bark splintered off of the tree directly behind Luke, missing his head by only a few inches.

He bolted into a full sprint, running down the mountainside, until he met up with a huge boulder. The boulder was at the boundary of a twenty-five foot cliff. He only had two choices; run along the ridge, or go over the cliff. With no time to deliberate, he chose to run the edge of the ridge.

George caught sight of him yet again and fired another shot that glanced off the rocks beside Luke's leg. His theory was to keep shooting and just maybe one bullet would eventually meet its target. It would only take one. Several more shots were fired.

Luke continued to fight his way through the brush and rough terrain. His foot became lodged between two jagged rocks that were each about the size of an engine block. He struggled briefly, but knew there was no time to waste. Jerking as hard as he could, he pulled his foot free, but there was no longer a shoe on it. Luke heard another gunshot. The bullet ricocheted from the rock after piercing the shoe that had been left behind. Startled, he fell over the edge. He tumbled down the steep slope, bouncing from tree to tree ending at the water's edge.

George heard a splash as Luke hit the water. Wondering if he had hit his mark, he peered over the side. He saw Luke pick himself back up, climb out of the cold lake and scurry into the bushes.

Stepping out of the water, Luke was temporarily mired in the thick mud along the shoreline causing him to lose his other shoe. He knew that George wasn't about to back off. He needed to get away from here, far, far away. He scanned the area for other campsites or boats in the water that could be used, at a minimum to get out of range of George's semi-automatic. Nothing!

He decided that the only logical choice that remained, would be to circle back to the cabin, where he'd use his own car to escape. Ironically, losing his shoes actually worked to his advantage. He could now feel with his bare feet twigs, rocks or other debris with each and every step. If he remained careful, and concentrate, he should be able to move about in virtual silence. As he worked his way up the hill, he heard another gunshot. He turned. George was positioned along the shoreline and had just blindly fired a shot into the water. Luke was almost two hundred yards above him and knew there would be no more obstacles between him and his car. He decided to make a run for it. Even if George heard him now, Luke believed, he'd have enough time to get to his car before being caught.

Shooting up the hill like a jackrabbit, it seemed to be a lot steeper going up than it had been coming down. Luke's legs were burning. His feet were now bleeding from pounding over the sharp sticks and rocks.

George heard the movement on the hillside above him. He fired a shot into the woods. Not knowing exactly where Luke was, he was firing aimlessly, unlikely to hit anything. He began to climb the hill in pursuit.

Several minutes later, Luke found himself at the Cayenne. He jumped in, started it and dropped it into gear. Spinning the tires, he slid it around a full one hundred and eighty degrees. Flooring it, he barreled down the narrow road. Rummaging through the center console, he produced a gun of his own. It was a .38 caliber Rossi revolver. He just assumed that he'd never need anything bigger than that. After travelling less than three hundred yards, George emerged from the trees and stood in the center of the small mountain road. He saw Luke speeding directly toward him, raised his gun, and fired a shot at the oncoming vehicle. The windshield shattered into a cobweb impeding Luke's ability to see clearly. Unable to get the Rossi into a proper firing position, Luke aimed the car directly at George and hit the gas.

A few seconds later, George vaulted to the side, falling to the ground, barely missing impact with the front bumper by only a few inches. The vehicle scraped along a tree near the edge of the road tearing the driver's side mirror off. As Luke drove away, George fired one last shot, blowing out the entire rear window.

Luke held the accelerator down as he sped away from the danger zone.

It looks like I'm safe, he thought, a*t least for now!*

CHAPTER 33

Luke didn't slow down for the next thirty miles. Once he'd reached the small historical mining town of Silverton, he pulled into the San Juan County Sheriff's Department. It was just past midnight. The building had been vacated for the day, but there was a telephone number posted in bold letters on the front door for calls after nine pm. He dialed the number.

"Sheriff Lomax," a sleepy voice answered. Luke explained in detail about the attempt made on his life, and that the assailant was still on the loose. "Okay," he said, "I'll check it out. You stay put, and I'll stop by the office to get a statement from you."

"Sorry, Sheriff," Luke replied, "I'm worried that my fiancé may be in danger. I need to head back to Denver right away. Could you call ahead and let the local police know what's happened here?" He gave the Sheriff his address and other pertinent contact information. After providing a description of George Graf, and the details surrounding the altercation, the call ended. Luke pulled into a twenty-four hour mini mart and fueled up for the return trip.

Back on the road, his phone rang. "Sheriff Lomax here. I've been in contact with the Evergreen Police. They'll have someone patrol the area around your house 'til morning, then you *must* appear at their office no later than 8:00 am to file a report. Until we collect all of the details from you, we're working partially in the blind."

"You won't need to worry about that, Sheriff," Luke said, "I'll have pictures and everything."

"I'm heading to the cabin site now" the Sheriff replied, "I'll call you with an update."

"Thank you sir, you are more than kind." Anxious to get back, Luke had been pushing the speed limit boundaries.

He dialed the phone. "Hello," said the groggy voice on the other end.

"Holly, is that you?"

"Luke?" She immediately sensed the tension in his voice. "What's wrong? It's almost 12:30. Are you okay?"

He didn't want to give her a reason to be afraid, but he felt the need to ensure her safety. "Listen," he said, "I need you to gather your things and sleep in the safe room tonight." When the Evergreen mansion was originally built, a high tech *safe room* had been installed. It was specifically designed to be locked down from the inside to protect the owner from an intruder. Built much like a bank vault, neither Holly nor Luke thought that they would ever have a need to use it.

"What's happening Luke?" she said, knowing that he was in some kind of trouble.

He didn't dare say too much, he knew that she'd worry more about him than she would for herself. She'd been staying in that ten thousand square foot house all by herself. Raj hadn't returned from Pennsylvania with the race car yet. He wouldn't be home until sometime the next day. "Just do as I ask sweetheart. As long as you stay put, you'll be safe. I'll tell you all about it in the morning."

"Oh, Luke," she said, "I don't know what's happening, but I am worried. I wish you were here."

"I wish I were there too," he replied. "Just get some sleep and I'll be home soon."

Another hour passed, and Luke continued to remain focused on the road, as well as he could while looking through the damaged windshield. He tried to make sense of what had happened back at the cabin. The things George talked about just didn't add up. What did he mean Holly loves *him*? Luke knew Holly so well, it was as if her thoughts were an extension of his. Furthermore, it was impossible for her to be at George's apartment every day. She'd been at home with him most of the time. He said that she had been at his apartment every day, all day, and all night. It's just not true. What could have caused him to become so confused, that he would even think that?

Luke reached into his pocket and removed his wallet. Opening it, he slid out a small piece of paper with George's contact information written down, along with his address. *Maybe I'll find some answers there,* he thought.

The phone rang again, "Sheriff Lomax here. It seems to me that you were telling the truth. When I pulled up, no one was around. It looked like everyone had left in a big hurry. The bags, groceries, and fishing gear were still inside. No sign of this Graf fellow."

"Where do you think he went?" Luke asked.

"Hard to say exactly, if he wandered out into the wilderness, it would be like trying to find a needle in a haystack. It would be a lot of ground to cover with only a few men to do it. Besides no one's actually been killed, or even hurt at this point. We couldn't justify a full-fledged manhunt, but we will continue to keep our eyes open. I surveyed the area and found several spent 9mm casings that match your story." He abruptly lowered his voice to just a whisper. "I'll call you back Monroe, someone's coming."

From off in the distance, down the long lane leading to the cabin, the Sheriff saw a flashlight bouncing methodically in an up and down motion. He took cover behind his patrol car, drew his gun from its holster and waited. As the light drew closer, he could hear the footsteps crunching through the freshly laid gravel. He waited. This person didn't appear to be moving fast at all. Certainly not like a man on the run. Well within range, the Sheriff stood with both of his hands now on the gun and aimed at the intruder.

"Hands in the air," Sheriff Lomax ordered.

The flashlight fell to the ground as the startled man followed his instruction.

"Identify yourself," he barked.

"Ross Simpson," the man replied. "I am here looking for the Sheriff. I lost my car."

Realizing that this was not the man he had been looking for, Lomax lowered his gun and stepped from behind his car motioning Ross toward the light. Ross picked up his flashlight and walked to the Sheriff's car.

"I'm renting a cabin," Ross began, "about a mile up the road. I saw your car drive by and figured there couldn't be too many cabins up this way, so I thought I'd come looking for you."

"Okay.... how exactly did you *lose* your car?"

"Well, you see," he continued, "I try to get the family together at least once a year for vacation. It's harder for them each year. I got three kids, Vicky, Joan and Jon. Each of them got married a year ago. Can you believe that? All three of them, the same year? Oh, and can you believe this, all three of them are pregnant. Yep, going to have a baby. Well not Jon I guess, but his wife sure is. I 'spose that makes me a grandpa huh, three times over. I ask you, do I look old enough to be a grandpa?"

"The car?" Lomax reminded him.

"Oh, yeah," Ross replied, "the car. We drove it out here all the way from St. Louis. That's where we're from. St. Louis Missouri. Lived there my whole life. That's where I met Edna. She's my wife. Been together for what seems like forever. She's a great cook too. She's famous for all the baking she does, wins a ribbon at the county fair every year, but she can hold her own on the barbeque grill, as good as the best of 'em."

Now becoming impatient, Lomax raised his voice, "Mr. Simpson, how exactly did you lose your car?"

"The car, right," he said while trying to remain focused. "I think it was stolen. I heard a noise outside the cabin. When I poked my head out, there it was, driving away. I stepped out and yelled at him, but nothing, he didn't stop. There was no reason for him not to. That car could stop. I just had the brakes done on it last week. They worked so well in fact, that......"

"*He?*" Lomax interrupted.

"I guess I didn't actually see the driver. I just assumed it was a man. On all the TV cop shows, it's always a man. Shoot we were watching a show just the other night and that's exactly who it was, the man. Guess if you're a woman, you could get away with a lot more, no one would ever think for a minute that you did it."

"That's not always the case Mr. Simpson."

After several more minutes of continuous chatter, Sheriff Lomax returned the call to Luke.

"Monroe," he announced, "unfortunately, that was not our guy. It was just someone staying at a cabin down the road. Still no sign of Graf."

While speaking with the Sheriff, Luke could hear a lively conversation in the background.

"It sounds like you've got a lot going on there Sheriff," Luke said. "Do you need to take care of it?"

"No," he replied. "Believe it or not, that's just *one* guy. I'll get to him in a few minutes. I'll work on the warrant for George Graf's arrest, and put the word out state-wide. In the meantime you need to be careful, I just received information on a stolen car about a mile from here. That is most likely our man."

"Thank you Sheriff," Luke said. "I'll be extra careful."

Now pushing 2:45 am, Luke was satisfied that Holly was safe. The safe room was deemed to be impenetrable by the manufacturer, who claimed it had been tested against an armed military special task force who, after eight hours, failed to gain access.

Luke once again focused on George, trying desperately to come up with some kind of explanation for his bizarre behavior. They had been friends since college. Nothing from their past could have been the catalyst for any of this. He wouldn't have even known Holly back then.

Approaching the exit to Evergreen, Luke chose to drive on by. He was heading into Denver, to the address written on the tiny piece of paper. He was headed to George's apartment.

At 3:30 am, Luke found himself trolling through a severely depressed neighborhood. Buildings were dilapidated with steel bars mounted over many of the windows. Graffiti had been sprayed on several of the homes and most of the businesses in the area. He slowed as he came closer to the number written on the paper. There it was.

Good grief! Luke thought, *George lives here?*

He saw the abandoned storefront. Bars had been mounted over the windows, but that hadn't stopped the punks in the area from breaking the glass. A rusted metal frame hung over the top of the busted window, which had once supported an awning of some type. Luke looked around to make sure he was alone, then stepped out of his car while shoving the Rossi into his belt.

There was a screen door on the primary entrance, hanging by only one hinge. It remained three quarters of the way open and the residents appeared to just leave it that way. Another door leading to the inside obviously hadn't been lubricated in years. It creaked as Luke pushed it open. Loud music was playing upstairs, but there seemed to be no sign of life. He guessed they just fell asleep that way. He walked up the stairs, each one creaking loudly as he climbed. Then he saw the door on the second floor, apartment 2A. This was the apartment located directly above the abandoned storefront. It was the only thing in the entire building that looked secure. It was equipped with a locking doorknob, plus two additional deadbolt locks.

If I lived in this neighborhood, Luke thought. *I suppose I'd add extra locks too.*

After studying the situation for less than a minute, he came to a conclusion, *Screw it, that son of a bitch just tried to kill me.* Backing up to the opposite side of the hallway, he ran, with all of his might, slamming the entire weight of his body against the door. The noise created by this action had been muffled by the loud music blasting from apartment 2B. The jamb splintered into hundreds of pieces and the door swung wide open.

Luke stepped inside and turned on the light. Cockroaches scattered everywhere to find shelter. There was very little in the way of furniture, a table, bed, and computer desk. The only thing on the walls were pictures of.... "Holly?" Luke said aloud. They were indeed pictures of Holly, and they filled the entire studio apartment, floor to ceiling. He was aghast. There were pictures of her at his home in Evergreen, in her garden, at the pool. And yes, there were even several nude shots as well.

He rubbed his eyes. They certainly looked authentic, but he knew that Holly wouldn't cheat on him like that. Studying a few of the photos, he ruled out that they might be of Hannah. She had shorter hair and more freckles than Holly. He quickly walked around the room removing all of them from the wall. Then he set his sight on the computer. There was what appeared to be a primary computer with a black box of some type attached to it. Connecting to the black box were several external hard drives, all larger than a terabit in size. The front of the box was labeled *ANT Receiver*.

Why does that seem so familiar? he wondered.

The computer had been left in the *on* position. Luke wiggled the mouse and it came to life. It displayed nothing but a blank screen except for a menu at the top, which read Ackerman Nano Transmitter – Device 3. Then at the far right he saw a familiar logo with the name printed alongside of it, *SIA Medical Technologies*. That's where he'd heard about the ANT device. It had been developed by Sam and George at SIA. As best as Luke could remember, the ANT program was highly secretive and under tight controls.

He dialed the phone.

After several rings it was finally answered, "Sam I am," he said slurring his speech, barely able to get it out.

"Sam, wake up, it's Luke."

Sensing that it was urgent, Sam sat up in bed. It was unlike Luke to call so early in the morning. "What time is it? He asked.

"Listen Sam," Luke said. "I've got a lot to tell you. George tried to kill me last night."

"He what?" Sam shouted in disbelief. "George Graf?"

"I'll tell you more about that later," Luke continued, "but right now I'm in his apartment and I'm looking at something that I think belongs to you." He described the ANT system to him and asked what, if anything he should do.

"You did the right thing by calling me," Sam replied, "What you see there, is stolen property. It rightfully belongs to SIA. I need you to retrieve it, if you can."

"You bet I will, Sam. I just don't have much time. He'll likely be here before long."

They quickly disconnected so Luke could do what he needed to on behalf of SIA. Curious, before disconnecting anything, Luke selected *playback* on the menu bar. A video appeared of Holly swimming in the pool at Luke's house. He heard what sounded like George's voice, "Do you still love me?" It appeared that George had been holding the camera. "You know I do silly, I love you more than any man alive!"

Luke fell back into the chair. He couldn't believe what he was seeing. It appeared that George was telling the truth. But how was that even possible? When would they have had the time for an affair? Luke knew he was running out of time himself and needed to get the ANT disconnected and loaded into his car before George returned. He decided to collect up the hard drives, numerous flash drives, and a couple of notebooks he saw lying around as well. He took the pictures of Holly and loaded everything into his car. Starting it, he pulled away from the curb feeling betrayed, but at the same time failing to believe that Holly could have done what the evidence had clearly shown that she had. He felt confused.

Less than ten minutes after Luke had pulled away, George arrived in the stolen car. He was angry that Luke had gotten away, and that he now knew of his intent. The proverbial cat was now out of the bag. There would be no more waiting, he needed to finish the job, pronto. He also needed to ditch the car before he'd be spotted in it, and round up some additional help. He would, without a doubt, see that Luke would never escape again.

Walking up to the second floor, he immediately noticed that the door had been kicked in. He ran through the opening and looked around. Everything was gone, the pictures and the ANT receiver. That was his only link to Holly. Luke had taken his bride to be. Up until now, he could reach out to her anytime he wished, and she was always there for him. Not anymore, Luke had ruined all of it. He was determined to end this once and for all.

With his heart breaking, George stood in the doorway of his tattered apartment, trembling with both fear and unbridled rage, reflecting on what once was his life, the one Luke had completely torn apart. His face turned red as his veins bulged from his neck.

He screamed at the top of his lungs, "LUC-AAASSSS!"

CHAPTER 34

It was 5:00 am and still dark outside. Luke finished unloading the equipment from his car and carried it into the *white room*. He carefully reconnected all of the components, just as they'd been configured when in George's apartment, and powered it up. The fans inside the device whirred as they wound up, providing extra cooling while it slowly walked through its initial startup procedure. Once rebooted and online, Luke saw a password screen. Playing on a sickening hunch, he typed the word *HOLLY* into the keyboard, which immediately gave him full access to the system. The blank screen appeared just as before, with only the SIA menu displayed at the top.

In a desperate attempt to understand exactly what was happening between George and Holly, Luke accessed more of the recordings. One by one, he clicked through the list. There had to be thousands of hours of Holly and George together. As George had stated back at the cabin, it was both day and night, and it appeared to be happening virtually all of the time. After twenty minutes, he had clicked through about fifty recorded files. They were in different settings, at different times of the year. This had obviously been going on for some time, but it still didn't make sense.

He spotted the college ruled notebooks and picked one up. What he saw inside, were the meticulous notes that explained virtually everything from the beginning, when George stole the equipment from SIA, to the daily updates that had been captured while he experimented. *The answer has to be in here somewhere,* he thought. He decide to fix a cup of coffee. Exhausted, he was worried that he might overlook something.

With a fresh cup in one hand, and the notebook in the other, he walked into the living room and started to untangle the facts leading to his current predicament. Desperately trying to sort this all out, he began to pace. There had to be some sort of explanation. Up to this point he had been drawing a blank, but the details that were unfolding from George's journal were beginning to provide some desperately needed clarity.

At the entrance to Luke's driveway, an old Chevy van pulled up to the gate with its lights turned off. Inside, George sat in the passenger seat. Moose was driving. Marco was uncomfortably sandwiched between the other two members of the gang, on the bench seat in the rear.

"Just so we're straight on this," Moose said, "We do this, and you give us *ten grand*, right?" He typically didn't trust anyone, and rarely ever met people who had that kind of cash to throw around. Dealing with George somehow felt different. He'd already witnessed how fast he could produce a thousand dollars. It was done in just a few hours. If he said ten thousand, why should Moose doubt him? He just wanted the other guys to hear it first-hand.

"Yes," George confirmed, "Ten thousand dollars. You'll have it this afternoon."

"We're in," Moose said as the spokesman for the entire group. "So you want to take this guy out because he kidnapped your fiancé, that about right?"

"That's it," George said. In his mind, he was convinced that's exactly what had happened. Now he just wanted Holly. He no longer cared, which one. At this moment, he didn't have either.

They idled part-way up the drive, but being an older van, it was much louder than George was comfortable with. He made the decision to shut it down, leave it behind and walk up to the house on foot. As they got closer, George saw Luke's shadow pacing back and forth in the living room. The mere sight of him made his blood curdle, but it also inspired a brilliant idea. He patted his front pockets to locate the keys to his Firebird, which was still parked alongside the SkyKar hangar. He explained to the others that he would drive the car through the front window, and simply run Luke over. If that didn't work, the guys could rush in behind him, and take care of Luke before he had an opportunity to get away. It was certainly plausible. George, proud of himself, considered this to be the best plan he'd had so far.

Everyone checked their weapons. Moose flashed his .38 special, and Marco had finally retrieved his derringer from his Grandmother's house. The other two thugs, completing the foursome, brought whatever they could round up on such short notice. Tyrone held a wooden bat, and a guy they disrespectfully nicknamed *Spit,* had strapped a six inch bowie knife to his side. George still had the 9mm semi-automatic, but since he was to be the designated driver, he handed it to Tyrone. "This will work better than that bat."

With the plan in place, George looked again to see if Luke was still pacing. Remaining in a consistent, steady rhythm, he could actually count his steps. One, two, three, four, and turn; one, two, three, four, and turn. George would be able to gauge exactly when he'd be dead center. "*Dead* center," he chuckled.

George quietly climbed into the Firebird knowing full well that he'd be creating some noise as soon as he turned the key. It had to be done quickly, in a single flowing motion, with zero hesitation.

A nod to Moose indicated that he was ready. The reliable, trustworthy, wreck of a Pontiac started without hesitation. Using his right hand, he slid it into gear and hit the gas. It was a little more than a hundred and fifty feet across the courtyard to the front of the house. As he drew nearer, he saw the rest of the gang running on foot.

He held his breath and squinted just before impact. At the same time he visualized himself blasting through the front window and running Luke down. That wasn't exactly what happened. Instead, upon impact, the six hundred dollar Pontiac Firebird, folded up like a two hundred dollar accordion. Much like most everything else on the car that *didn't* work, the airbags failed to deploy. George was jammed into the steering wheel and against the windshield. It was far more violent than he could have ever imagined. He suffered a cut across the bridge of his nose and felt a severe stabbing pain indicative of a possible broken a rib.

Stunned, he slowly dragged himself from the car and only then did he realize that he had driven it straight into a concrete wall.

Unknown to George, Luke had become fascinated with the transparent concrete that he'd seen at the Building Museum in Washington, D.C. Nor did he know, that he'd contacted the manufacturer to have the front window in his house replaced with it. Hell, George didn't even know, until that very moment, that such a thing even existed. What a time to find that out!

The problem now, was that Luke was inside and they were all still outside. Surely he would have heard them by now. There was no time to waste, they needed to somehow gain access to the massive house that appeared to be built more like a fortress than a home. With the intent to finish this once and for all, George snatched the 9mm away from Tyrone, leaving him without a weapon, then stated the obvious, "We need to find a way inside."

Luke, startled by the bang against the front of the house and the commotion outside, darted upstairs to check on Holly. The bedroom was empty, which was a good indicator that she had taken his suggestion and locked herself away in the safe room.

Inside the safe room, Holly was awakened by the abrupt crash against the front of the house. Her first thought was to check it out, but then remembered what Luke had said, "As long as you stay put, you'll be safe." With her military background and extensive combat training, this was counter intuitive for her, but she knew that he was probably right and resisted the urge to investigate.

The room had been wired into the home security system giving her access to all of the cameras placed throughout the estate. Twelve cameras monitored the external areas beyond the main house. Inside, there were only four, one facing each door leading to the outside.

She toggled through the various camera views looking for something that could provide a clue that might explain the loud crashing sound. *It's got to be something big,* she thought. *It shook the entire house.*

Locking into the view from the camera mounted on the front of the house, she saw the Pontiac wedged against the wall and a group of men huddled behind it. Taking control of the camera with a small joystick, she centered on them and zoomed in. From this angle she couldn't see any of their faces, but she did see something she recognized. It was the boldly tattooed head of another acquaintance.

"Mr. Moose," she said to herself, "what are *you* doing here?"

The huddle split up and they ran in opposite directions. It was then she recognized the others as being members of Moose's gang, plus one. *George?* She knew that George had been with Luke on a fishing trip, *why would he be here now?*

George, followed by Marco, ran to the rear of the house just outside of the dining room. Peering through the windows of the stylish French doors, he raised his gun and fired. One of the small glass panes disintegrated as the bullet sped through and lodged into the wall on the opposite end of the room.

Reaching through the broken pane, George unlocked the door and shoved it open. He was now in a room that he'd virtually spent hours in, trying to figure out how to interact with the ANT device. It was decorated just as he'd remembered, the buffet table along the wall, the mirror running the length of it, and the mantle clock sitting near the center. His eyes locked onto it. Everything else in the house was eerily quiet, except for the constant tick tock of that stupid clock. It was annoying. It was as if it were trying to pull him back to a time before he had discovered that Holly's world ever existed, as if it were telling him that he'd gone too far, and that perhaps he was approaching this all wrong. He thought for only a second, then aimed the 9mm semi-automatic and pulled the trigger. The clock exploded, scattering debris in all directions, followed by the mirror mounted on the wall behind it.

Luke carefully crept down the stairs undetected, but when he bolted across the foyer toward the hall, George spotted him and fired a shot, missing him by only inches.

Holly could hear the gunfire, but couldn't see what was happening. She couldn't just sit still and do nothing, but knew she needed to stay put. She called the Evergreen police and reported the intruders. With her back against the wall, she slid to the floor and waited.

The others arrived only seconds later. "He went that way," George said. "Follow me." Holding his gun firmly with both hands, he moved down the hall, his back sliding against the wall. He tucked his elbow tightly against his side to help ease the pain from his broken rib. Tyrone spotted a set of fireplace tools sitting in a rack on the hearth in the living room. He selected the poker so he'd at least have a weapon, even if it was crude and archaic. Everyone followed George who cautiously stepped past the first open doorway which led to Luke's office. Confirming that no one was inside, he continued his trek down the hall. Reaching the second doorway, he paused.

Marco stepped into Luke's office searching it thoroughly. He stuck his head outside and motioned everyone over. They ignored him at first. "Psst! Psst," he whispered, while wildly waving his arms in a desperate attempt to get their attention. They slid back down the hall toward the office.

"What is it?" Moose asked impatiently.

"Do you know whose house this is?" Marco asked.

"How would I know whose house this is," Moose snipped. "Why would I even care?"

Marco motioned for him to step inside the office, he obliged. "That's whose house we're in." He pointed toward a photo sitting on the credenza. It was a picture of Holly.

"Oh hell no!" Moose said. "Screw this! We're out of here."

All four men started toward the door. George grabbed Tyrone's arm, "Where the hell are you going? You get back here."

"Nothin' doin'," Marco said. "Not if we gotta deal with that.... that, devil woman." He pointed toward Holly's picture.

"Holly?" George asked. "Are you serious? That's my fiancé!"

"Sorry man, that's your problem," Tyrone said, while handing George the poker, "this ain't our fight." He joined the rest as they all rushed out the front door leaving George to fend for himself.

"Freaking idiots," George said, as they disappeared from sight.

Luke, hiding in the *white room*, heard voices in the hall, but couldn't quite make out what was being said. Knowing he was outnumbered, he set up the *white room* in an attempt to gain a tactical advantage. He used a virtual controller triggering multiple obstacles to rise up from the floor. Sam had built the room to accommodate a vast array of simulations. To be able to include them all, the floor was programmable with what seemed to be an unlimited number of configurations. Luke believed that this might just give him a fighting chance. He was no stranger to bad guys, and frequently fought them in this room. He and Raj regularly programmed the system with four dimensional simulations of the old Wild West, or settings staged in the 1930's, where they would chase gangsters as they wreaked havoc along the south side of Chicago. This situation was much different. This guy's gun was real, *not* a simulation. Even though Luke felt this was his best bet, he also knew that he had become better skilled in self-defense. By spending some of his free time at the local shooting range, he was better than average with a gun. Holly had also been training him in hand-to-hand combat techniques. It was comforting to know that he at least had *some* training.

At that moment, the ANT receiver linked up with the transmitter in George's brain. He was now within range and images began to appear on the walls in the *white room*. A view of a gun was seen from the perspective of the camera. Aimed toward an image of Luke, it fired, shooting him in the center of his chest. Luke witnessed himself falling over, writhing in pain. He watched as his leg twitched just before he died. The scene repeated over and over.

Impatiently, Holly returned to the security monitor and browsed through the various camera views. She selected one that overlooked the gate and entrance to the driveway. From there she saw the police arrive. Just as the first officer reached the entrance in his patrol car, a speeding van backed out of the drive and struck it broadside. A second officer, following close behind, wedged his car against the front of the van pinning it between the vehicles. A third officer arrived only seconds later. The three police officers surrounded the Chevy van with their weapons drawn. Holly could see the ragtag band of losers exit the van one by one. She saw them as they were ordered to the ground and handcuffed, but she only counted four. *Someone's missing,* she thought. Then it hit her; *George!*

George entered the *white room*. It was large, spanning twenty feet in one direction and forty feet in the other. There were several white boxes covered with a shiny plastic material scattered throughout the space. Luke could be hiding behind any of these.

"Where are you, Luc-ass?" George asked. He spotted Luke as he scurried between boxes. Squeezing off a round from his gun, a box splintered near the top. Luke peeked around the side of it and fired his Rossi. George, taken by surprise, hadn't considered that he might actually be armed. "So you want to play rough?" George asked, as he ducked behind one of the boxes.

Hearing the gunshot, Holly realized that George was still in the house. *But what is he shooting at?* She wondered. Her heart stopped as the gravity of the situation hit her like a ton of bricks... *Luke!*

The displays on all four walls in the *white room* began to change from a single repeated image of Luke being shot, to multiple images of Holly repeating random statements that appeared to be out of context with one another. They seemed to be a distant, yet stark departure from what Luke knew her true personality to be.

"Know where your target is," she said, as if to provide instruction to George.

Another image appeared, "Hide the body."

"Luc-ass?" George taunted him.

"You know George," Luke said, "I've always hated that stupid nickname. You called me that when we were just kids. Don't you think it's a bit juvenile to continue to use it today?"

"But it suits you so well," George quipped, as he rose up and fired another round, landing it into the wall directly behind Luke. It penetrated the polymer on the display, leaving a dark spot on the screen.

Another image of Holly appeared, "I do George! I really do love you."

On the opposite end of the room another began, "I love you more than the sun and the moon."

Luke concluded that it couldn't be Holly. This looked like her, but sounded more like a teenage girl with a crush. Holly was a true lady, and carried herself with more dignity than that. He spotted George and took a shot, blasting one of the many hard drives off the table.

"Hi-Hi-Hi, Hide the body." The image stuttered.

"Dammit, Luke, knock it off." Unknowingly, by taking out that hard drive, he erased an entire month from George and Holly's past.

"I do George! I really do love you."

"This is inevitable Luke. For God's sake, take it like a man." He stood and fired three rounds in rapid succession.

Luke immediately returned fire. The bullet successfully penetrated George's forearm, causing him to lose his grip on the gun which promptly fell to the floor. With blood on his sleeve, he quickly ducked behind another box.

"Know where your target is."

George scrambled along the floor losing track of where the gun had fallen. Noticing he was moving in the opposite direction, away from the gun, Luke stood and slowly made his way across the room.

"I love you more than the sun and the moon."

Cautiously, Luke made his way over to George and found him cowering in the corner, tightly gripping his bleeding arm.

"Hide the body."

"Alright.... alright, don't shoot," George said while holding his hand in front of his face.

"You're pathetic," Luke said, shaking his head in disgust. "I won't shoot, but you're staying right there until the police arrive." With his free hand, he dialed 9-1-1 and provided the dispatcher with the pertinent information.

"We've already received a call from your residence," the man replied, "and officers have been dispatched."

Way to go Holly, he thought.

Instructions were provided to make sure the guns were secured and moved as far away from the perpetrator as possible.

Seeing that George was still cowered in the corner, Luke walked over to retrieve the 9mm that had been dropped on the floor about twelve feet away.

When he turned, George surprised him with a body slam shoving him face first into the wall, causing his Rossi revolver to drop to the floor. Tightly wrapping his arm around Luke's neck, he pulled with all of his might.

Luke drove his elbow hard into George's ribs, causing him to release his grip and double over in pain. Before he could recover, Luke punched him in the face which caused him to lose balance and fall over one of the boxes protruding out of the floor.

While attempting to stand, Luke hit him again, this time in the throat. He fell to his knees grasping his neck, struggling for air. Luke returned to retrieve the Rossi.

Once he was able to breathe, George stood, and with a blank, yet determined stare, headed toward Luke. Struggling to understand why George wanted to kill him, Luke raised his revolver and ordered him to stop. That's all he really wanted. He had no desire to hurt George, but he couldn't let any harm come to Holly or himself.

George had enough. The sight of the gun in Luke's hand didn't seem to concern him anymore. He was not thinking that he could actually get hurt, he was simply thinking that there was only one option available to him, and that option was to *kill* Luke. He was so focused on that task, the revolver looked like nothing more than just a prop. It could have been a water pistol for all he cared. He was convinced that he *would* complete his task and Holly would once and for all, belong to him. No one would *ever* get between them again.

George was like a raging bull and just kept charging. Luke fired. The bullet made contact, barely missing his collar bone.

"Stop, I said." Luke ordered a second time, but he wouldn't stop. He kept coming. Luke squeezed the trigger again, this time striking George in the upper thigh. He stumbled. It slowed him down slightly, but he still wouldn't stop.

Luke saw the crazed look in his eyes. He knew that George had no intention to back off. Left with no choice, Luke fired again. This time George fell back and toppled over a box, dropping out of sight.

Cautiously, Luke walked over to him and saw him lying still. He lifted George's leg with the tip of his shoe. Once released, it fell back to the floor, motionless. It appeared that George was gone.

Feeling both anxiety and relief, Luke slowly walked over to the 9mm pistol. As he knelt to pick it up, he was struck directly in the back of the head by a solid steel object. Luke fell to the floor knocked completely unconscious.

George stood, looking down at him, grinning, with the steel poker held upright over his shoulder like he was waiting for the next pitch of the World Series.

"Know where your target is."

Luke was lying on his side, out cold. George kicked him in the shoulder, causing him to roll flat onto his back. He tossed the poker down. It made a muffled clang as it hit the polymer coated floor.

Taking two steps, he knelt down and picked up the 9mm. While pulling the slide back to cock the gun for one last time he rambled, "Mr. Luc-ass Mon-freakin-roe. You have been a royal pain in my ass. I promised you, that this would be your last day on earth. Now I'm going to make good on that promise." He positioned the gun with the barrel pointed directly at Luke's head. His index finger tensed against the trigger just as the steel poker landed against the side of *his* head. Stunned, everything around him began to move in slow motion. He saw a flash appear from the barrel of the gun, followed by a wisp of white smoke. There was no sound. All he could hear was his own heartbeat. The impact from the poker came with such force, that the cast iron tip broke completely off the end, leaving only the steel shaft.

"I do George! I really do love you."

Dazed, in a stupor, George fell to the floor. A gash appeared that extended from his cheekbone to just above his ear. He was bleeding profusely. The gun, lying on the floor near his side, was still smoking. A foot appeared and kicked the gun out of reach.

The last thing George saw, the last thing he would *ever* see, was Holly, the love of his life, his one and only soulmate, straddled across him, thrusting the steel shaft of the poker deep into his chest. The displays in the *white room*, went blank.

Losing himself in her large, beautiful, tear filled eyes, he could only recognize her as the angel he'd always known her to be. Reaching out, he softly stroked her cheek one last time, smiling. Unable to speak, his mouth moved

STEVE ALLEN

slowly to form his final thought: *I love you,* as both of his world's faded away forever.

INTO THE MINDFIELD

CHAPTER 35

"We have chosen to put even tighter restrictions on our research," Dr. Ackerman explained. "When the experiments are properly administered and controlled in a safe, stable environment, we'll be able to make great leaps forward in our continuing understanding of how the brain works. Through that understanding, we will be able to create a state where the brain has better control over the healing process, not only for itself, but the body as a whole. We believe that it's possible to expand our knowledge through the use of nano-technology to perhaps someday communicate to one another telepathically. Furthermore, we could possibly, in the not too distant future, link our brains together to form a network so vast, it would make the internet pale in comparison. Think of the magnitude of what I am suggesting. Imagine these steps, from where we are today, as representing one single letter within a novel containing the knowledge of all of mankind."

Dr. Ackerman paused to take a sip of water. From the crowd, a hand rose. It was one of the students at the college, a man appearing to be in his early twenties. Dr. Ackerman gestured for him to proceed.

"What about the creator of the device?" He asked. "There are rumors that Dr. Graf had stolen the ANT equipment and experimented on himself. I read that he claimed to have opened the door to another dimension."

"A very sad story indeed," the doctor replied. "I'm afraid that this type of experimentation, outside of a controlled environment, proved to be costly. In George Graf's case, deadly. You see, his brain had unfortunately created a synaptic bridge to the dorsolateral prefrontal association, located here." He used his laser pointer to pinpoint the area on the diagram still displayed on the wall behind him.

"What does that area of the brain control?" the young man asked.

Dr. Ackerman looked to the floor saddened by the tragic loss of such a brilliant scientist. He raised his head, and with a heavy sigh, answered with one single word...

"Imagination."

EPILOGUE

General John McBride was known as one of the toughest generals in the Marines. He stood over six foot, six inches tall, and had a reputation for not taking guff from anyone. He was one of only three generals designated with a four star ranking and the only one living who had received the Medal of Honor. He stood quietly in an office facing a mirror. He was in full dress uniform, adorned with scores of bars and medals, all of which stood out prominently covering his broad chest. Over the years, he'd officiated countless military events, some had been mere pageantry, while others had not been as easy. He'd made those dreadful visits to inform families that their son, husband, or father was never coming home. But today would be the most difficult of them all, because today he was doing it out of love for his daughter.

A knock came from the door. "Yes," General McBride replied.

The door opened a crack large enough for a man to poke his head inside, "They're ready for you, General."

He nodded as the man gently closed the door and disappeared.

Standing tall in front of the mirror, he gave himself one final inspection, checking his hair and uniform. He cleared his throat, picked up his cap and tucked it under his left arm, then opened the door and stepped out of the room. He walked down a dimly lit corridor. Its walls were covered with oak panels from floor to ceiling. The ceiling was arched with backlighting, causing it to glow the entire length. With glassy eyes, twitching ever so slightly, he began the walk down the long corridor.

He stopped in front of a large set of oak paneled double doors, rising to no less than twelve feet above. They had a unique design that was both elegant and ornate. Turning to face the doors, he cleared his throat a second time. A small group of people began to form in the corridor. A door opened from behind and a woman stepped out taking the general's arm. He was a full foot taller than she was. Looking down, he gave her a nervous smile. It was his daughter, Holly.

The huge doors opened and the sound of an organ played the familiar wedding march. Everyone stood and turned to face the bride. Step by step, the general escorted his daughter down the aisle. He was as proud as any father could be. Like Holly, he was never given the opportunity to see his little girl have her big day. She looked so lovely and was happier than he'd seen her since Eric had been killed so many years earlier. He could hardly contain himself as everyone's eyes were locked on Holly as they walked.

Upon arriving at the altar, a tear formed and ran down his cheek. He shook Luke's hand and then placed Holly's into it. He stepped back one full step and raised his right hand offering a salute to Luke. Luke was a civilian. He'd always been one. The general was under no obligation to offer him anything. He did so only because of the level of respect that he felt for him, and Luke was the only man he deemed worthy enough for his daughter. Realizing this, Luke began to get choked up himself.

The wedding was beautiful. Holly felt as if she had finally made it to the ball, and that now, the handsome prince would be hers for all of eternity.

Even though the crowd was large, the wedding party remained small. They decided to have *two* best men, Sam and Raj, as well as *two* maids of honor, Marilyn and Hannah.

Holly delivered the vows that she had meticulously prepared. As expected, Luke, hearing them for the first time, thought that just like Holly…. they were perfect! When it came time for Luke to deliver his, the minister handed him the microphone. Luke reached into his pocket and produced a five inch tall crystal cube. He held the microphone under it and pressed the button. A four inch tall image of Luke appeared inside. It wore the same tuxedo that Luke now wore. The image dropped to one knee, while professing his love to her forever. Sam, standing next to Luke as his best man, teared up with pride, as he witnessed the look on Holly's face, smiling, while affixed to the miniature version of Luke. As the inventor he was satisfied that it had achieved its desired result.

As part of the ritual, they presented each other with the rings and were promptly announced, husband and wife. They kissed.

As they turned and stepped down from the altar, they both saw the general, now sitting next to Miriam.

This was the man everyone knew for being tough as nails. The man Luke respectfully called *Big Mac*.

The man Holly still referred to as *Daddy*.

The same man, now full of emotion, was crying like a newborn.

Made in the USA
Middletown, DE
25 March 2016